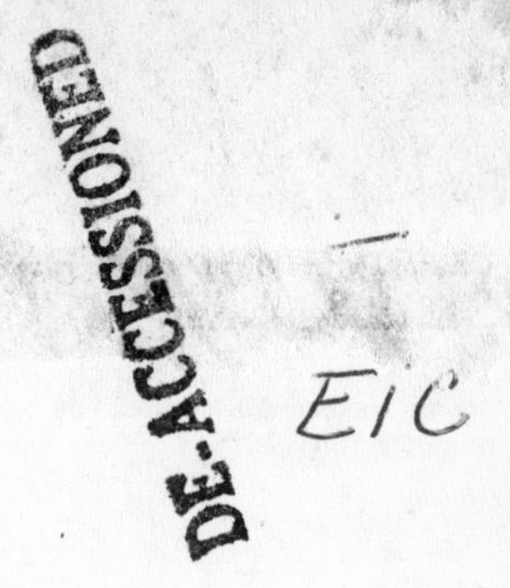

Rebecca's PROMISE

JERRY S. EICHER

HARVEST HOUSE PUBLISHERS
EUGENE, OREGON

Cover by Dugan Design Group, Bloomington, Minnesota

Author photo by Brian Ritchie

This is a work of fiction. Names, characters, places, and incidents are products of the author's imagination or are used fictitiously. Any resemblance to actual persons, living or dead, or to events or locales, is entirely coincidental.

REBECCA'S PROMISE

Published by Harvest House Publishers
Eugene, Oregon 97402
www.harvesthousepublishers.com

Library of Congress Cataloging-in-Publication Data

Eicher, Jerry S.
Rebecca's promise / Jerry Eicher.
p. cm.—(The Adams County trilogy ; bk. 1)
ISBN 978-0-7369-2635-5 (pbk.)
1. Amish—Indiana—Fiction. 2. Fiancées—Fiction. 3. First loves—Fiction. I. Title.
PS3605.I34R425 2009
813.'6—dc22

2008041577

Printed in the United States of America

09 10 11 12 13 14 15 16 17 / RDM-NI / 10 9 8 7 6 5 4 3

Chapter One

The buggy slowed as it approached the Duffy side road, then turned right toward the old covered bridge. The horse, a sleek black gelding John Miller purchased last fall at a farm auction, was tired from the fast downhill drive. Its nostrils flared, specks of foam lathered its chest strap as it obeyed John's gentle tug at the reins.

Rebecca, seated beside John, had tossed the top of her shawl on the shelf above the backseat of the buggy. The lower part of the shawl hung over her shoulder on John's side. She left it there, not certain how to remove it in the tight buggy without touching John. Not that she would have minded, but she knew he stood strong when church rules were concerned, and never had he voluntarily touched her yet.

Out of the corner of his eye, John saw Rebecca tuck a strand of her dark hair under her *kapp* and look off to her left—east to the community of Harshville. To the west, just around the sharp bends of the road and across a smaller creek, was her home. Lester and Mattie would surely be expecting Rebecca soon, but John was in no hurry to take her there. Instead an idea, long in the back of his mind, now took sudden, solid form. He knew this was the time and the place. At the realization of what he wanted to do, his hands tensed on the reins.

To calm himself, he breathed in deeply the late November air, winter on its edge. Wispy clouds, driven by the eternal Ohio wind, scurried across the sky. He tried to hide his nervousness by glancing at the sky and opening the front of his black suit coat, loosening the hooks and eyes with one hand to let in the warmth of the sun.

"Weather's nice. Especially for this time of the year," John offered, stealing a glance in Rebecca's direction. Not that he was shy around her. They had been dating now for two years, but today he was taken anew by her freshness and form.

Rebecca had captured his attention when he first saw her after her family had moved to Wheat Ridge from Milroy, Indiana.

A right smart move for the family, the general consensus had been, because it validated their own choices to settle in the pleasant community. And so the Keim family had been accepted readily, as had anyone else who left where they were to move to the smaller Amish community here along Wheat Ridge.

Lest someone else beat him to it, John had wasted no time in making known his interest in the Keim daughter. Rebecca wasn't the oldest, although it had appeared so when the new family arrived because the two oldest children were already married with families of their own.

"Yes, it *is* nice," she allowed, turning to look at him, "although a few weeks ago, it was better. The trees had their full color."

He had turned toward her when she started to speak. That was when he knew he could look into her face without any embarrassment. Not that she seemed to object at other times, but he always tried to keep from showing too much emotion, lest she think him forward.

He glanced away quickly when she was finished speaking, keeping the reins taut on the gelding. Yet the softness of her face stayed with him. It was as if she was thinking extra gentle thoughts today. He felt a desire to reach out to her, to brush her face with his fingers, but he held himself in check. It would not be right, he reminded himself sternly, or in line with his faith. Such actions led to downward paths and away from the *Da Hah's* will.

"Let's stop at the bridge," John said. Yes, today was surely the day he could do something about his feelings for Rebecca. As he slowed the horse, he hoped his nerves would not betray him too much.

Bouncing slightly alongside the ditch, John drove the buggy half on and half off the road, stopping the gelding near a fence post. "This should work," he commented to fill the awkward space around his own heart.

Rebecca's silence made John want to look her way all the more. But he dared not risk it again. His face might reveal his thoughts, and that must not happen.

Then from the other side of the bridge, a red sports car came slowly down the hill. The bright color of the car caught John's attention as he descended from the buggy. With his hand poised to reach for the tie rope, he studied the car as it approached. The occupants were a young boy and girl. The girl had her head on the boy's shoulder. *The English,* John thought. *They sure mess things up good with their way. In love and out of love each new day of the year. No fear of God in their eyes.*

Then John remembered his own feelings for Rebecca. *May God help us,* he silently prayed as he glanced toward the sky. Opening the small snaps on the back buggy door, his fingers found the tie strap.

Forcibly relaxing his face, he walked to the other side of the buggy where Rebecca was already coming down, nimbly balancing on the round buggy step with her one foot while using the momentum of the leaning buggy to descend to the ground.

"The weather has turned really nice." He turned again to the weather to cover his nervousness. Why she affected him this way, he wished he knew. *Was it what the English called "being in love"? Is this what the two in the red car felt too?* He doubted it, finding the comparison between the two worlds too improbable.

Rebecca lifted her eyes to his. "It's nice," she said again, holding his gaze. "This morning Dad thought it might turn warm, but you never know this time of the year."

"Well, it's beautiful now," John said, letting his eyes fall away from her and then back up toward the bridge. "Have you been here before?"

"I come here sometimes," she said quietly.

"Really?" he asked, immediately interested. "By yourself?"

"Mostly," she allowed. "Sometimes Katie comes with me. Mostly though, I come by myself. My sister Margaret used to like coming here too when she was home."

"What do you do here?" he asked.

"Well," she replied, casting her eyes to the ground, "woman things I suppose. Look at the river. Watch the squirrels. Think about life. Nothing like skipping rocks on the water."

He glanced sharply at her and was rewarded with a slight chuckle. "Isn't that what boys do?"

His usual confidence vanished when her eyes turned on him. And yet he couldn't let this moment be lost. He mustn't say the wrong thing, but his response hung up in his throat. And then he decided to take the chance. Let the ripples go where they wished.

"You shouldn't judge us all the same," he said. "Some boys do more than skip rocks on the water. We all grow up sooner or later..." He hesitated, not knowing quite what else to say. She was still looking at him.

He had better get a firm grip on his emotions, he told himself, if he was to say what he intended to say.

"Let's go see the bridge," he muttered quietly, turning in that direction. He couldn't help notice that she was following quite willingly, her step right by his side, her form so near.

"Where do you go when you come down here?" he asked, stopping at the edge of the road, the clear sound of running water beneath them.

"Sometimes," Rebecca said, "I go down to the water over there." Her hand rose to point to the other side. "But the path is a little rough, and we are in our Sunday clothing."

He nodded. "Let's try it though."

As they walked across the bridge, he was again taken by the sense of her presence. She was so close to him that her arm almost brushed against his, and the sound of their steps echoed in the enclosed area.

The possibility that this might be the girl he would spend the rest of his life with overwhelmed him. He so wanted to take her hand, swinging there beside him, so near and yet so far. They were separated by a chasm, as deep as it was wide, of church rules and personal commitment. John was not about to bridge it, except under extraordinary circumstances. Those had not arrived yet.

He kept his eyes straight ahead, not looking at her until he could think of something other than her closeness. Awkwardness was almost overwhelming him, but he could not become clumsy now. She was too fine a girl to be proposed to by some bumbling boy.

As if breaking a spell, the sound of an automobile came from the road behind them. Slowly the same red sports car approached.

"They went by us when we first stopped," John said.

"I thought so," she agreed. "Lovebirds out for a Sunday afternoon ride."

He chuckled at the thought, again struck by the contrast between the two worlds. *Could they be feeling what I am feeling? A boy and a girl in a flashy car? Could it be different than a boy and a girl in a simple buggy? It must be.* Nothing else made sense to him. Turning, his eyes found her face. He accepted the love he saw, allowing it a place in his heart and feeling at home.

"You think they are like us?" she asked him.

"They can't be," he responded.

"You'd be surprised," she said. "A car doesn't change people that much."

"Oh yes, it does," he insisted, moving easily into a discussion of church beliefs. "It has to. It makes you a whole different person. If it doesn't, then why's it so important that we don't have one?"

She shrugged. "In that way, yes, it makes us different, but in this way," she looked at him with her eyes now sparkling, "we are all the same."

Her answer both startled him and reassured him.

"Let's go see where you watch the river," he said, pulling his eyes away from her.

"It's over there." She raised her hand to point, all fingers extended in the gesture. To him the arch of her arm pointed not just toward the spot she intended but into the future itself. Almost wrapping itself in powers beyond flesh and bone, her hand pointed toward his hopes and dreams, toward a tomorrow he would gladly enter with her. Beneath him the bridge and the murmur of the water added to the voice of his emotions.

Above him a few leaves still hung on the trees in their last attempt to stay the turning of the seasons. Like his single life, he thought, but he was not going to hang on to anything. He would let it go. Let it go for her and for their life together.

Silently he let her take the lead. She stopped at a small ledge overlooking the river.

"So this is where you come?" he asked without looking at her.

She said nothing, but gave a slight nod. She pointed a little further down the road. "That's where the path goes down."

"You think we should?" he asked.

"Yes, let's do."

As they reached the bank of the river, they stood silently watching. Then Rebecca raised her eyes to meet his, and John knew with a certainty that she understood what was coming. This was what she wanted too. This was what love was, and he welcomed it.

Unable to stop himself, he reached out and gently took her hands. The sensation of her fingers in his shocked him, moving him into what felt like a frightful, forbidden realm. Yet it was right, he told himself. Did not this feeling confirm and validate the feelings he had earlier, which he was certain were from God? This love he felt for her and her love for him, it must be right.

She never flinched or pulled back as he held her hands and formed the words, "Rebecca, I want to marry you. Will you marry me?"

"Yes," she said, without breaking eye contact. "I would like that very much."

He slowly let her hands drop from his. The last brush of his fingers thrilled her, creating as strong a feeling as when he had first taken her hands only moments before. This was a boy she could truly love for all the right reasons. He was strong, not just in body but in moral convictions and fortitude.

"When do you want to?" she asked him, hoping he would embrace her and hoping he would not.

"In the spring," he said with certainty.

"This coming spring?" she exclaimed in surprise. "That quickly?"

He turned back toward her, a twinkle in his eye. "No, a year from next spring, after the winter's gone," he said softly. "That will give us plenty of time to plan. I can get more of the farm paid off."

She knew what he meant by the farm, having been to see it when he first purchased it two months ago—a simple white framed building for a house and a red barn on eighty acres on the ridge. In the back, a creek meandered through the land, feeding the pond on the property before flowing into the river.

"Yes," he said, looking out over the rippling water again, seemingly lost in his own thoughts, "the farm. When the winter is past."

Thinking it must be okay now that John had gone there, she tenderly slid her hand back into his. She knew it was all right when he tightened his fingers gently. After another long look into each other's eyes, they turned their gaze outward across the water. Deep in thought, they planned what life would be like, content that they would be forever—he and she.

They stood for a few minutes holding hands—the soothing sound of water and nature around them—until the noise of another approaching vehicle reached them, disturbing their world. Rebecca felt his hold weaken, and she slipped her hand out of his.

If it was an English car, it would not matter if they were seen holding hands, but even then, it was better that they didn't. One never knew what rumors might come back to haunt one. A dropped word here or there, even from innocent English parties, could stir up trouble.

John stepped away from her in preparation for the car's passing, but she moved with him, nearly touching his shoulder. To his own surprise, he did not pull back.

The vehicle on the road was a van, and as it passed, John recalled that he had seen it that morning at church. The black hats and bonnets of the people riding inside confirmed the memory.

"Those people were in church this morning?" he both asked and stated.

She glanced only briefly at the passing van. "Yes, I saw them," she said without dropping her eyes from his face.

"Visiting from somewhere," he said, searching his memory for the clue. Usually names of even strangers stayed with him, but not this time.

"Yes, visiting," she said quietly, lowering her gaze that held an unexpected sense of recognition.

What was it he had seen in that moment? Fear? Her reaction faintly registered, but it was enough for him to ask, "You know them, don't you?"

"They come from Milroy. In Indiana where we used to live," she said, with what seemed like hesitation.

"So?" he asked, still remembering the brief glint of fear in her eyes.

In his mind a quick flash of the visitors appeared, at least those whom he could remember, and revealed nothing. He cleared his throat to say something and then recalled the face of the black-haired boy. The one with the stubble of a little beard on his chin that ached from its attempts at growth and slicked-down hair that curled up in the back. The sound that came out of his mouth was, "Ah," in a knowing sort of way, as if he had discovered the great secret before him. "An old boyfriend from Milroy?"

This brought her eyes up from the ground in a jerk. "Silly. That was Luke Byler. He wasn't my boyfriend. Never would be."

"So how did you know which one I was thinking about?" he asked.

"That tone in your voice and because Luke was the only boy there this morning. The only visiting boy," she added as explanation. "I never had anything to do with him."

"So what is it then?" he asked, tilting his head toward the bridge side. "You seem...nervous. Is it about people from your old community? Secrets, have we?"

He surprised himself with the force and tone of his voice, as if he had a right to ask her these questions, even demand to know. Taking a deep breath, he tried to calm the emotions stirring so suddenly in his chest. Why had there been fear?

She made a valiant attempt to smile. "Not really. Just memories, I guess. Childhood things...growing up...you know. We all lived in the same community. You do things as children. Silly things. Luke lived in our old district. Still does. He could probably tell you dumb stuff I did growing up."

"Really," he said with uncertainty, remembering the fear in her eyes. "Is that what you're afraid of?"

"Oh," she gave a little gasp, "I'm not afraid. Why would you think that?"

He shrugged his shoulders, not sure if he wanted to go down this road or not. This was their afternoon. How could either of them spoil it? Surely it was nothing. She must just be jumpy from seeing someone from her own community.

"No reason, I guess. Probably just my imagination. Do you know anything more about these people...the Bylers?"

"Yes." She tilted her head and leaned slightly toward him. "They might be moving here. I think it's still supposed to be a secret."

"Are you the only one to know?" he asked.

"My mother knows. She's sort of in on it since we come from there. I have an aunt still living there. An uncle too. On mom's side of the family."

"I see," he said. And then the thought crossed his mind that one never knew what went on among wild Amish young people during their *rummshpringa* days, but surely Rebecca wasn't like that.

Still he had to ask. "You do anything in your wild days? Something I should know about?" Certain the answer would be negative, he continued, "I never did, of course. We don't take the time to sow our wild oats. Something about not liking the crop it produces."

"Of course not," she retorted, genuinely indignant. "I never was wild. We were raised better than that."

"I didn't think so," he told her, lifting his one hand in contrition. "Just asking."

"Shouldn't you have asked a little earlier? Before you asked something else? We just got engaged, if I remember correctly."

He met her gaze firmly. "Okay," he said, "just forget it. It never occurred to me to ask before. You don't seem like that kind of a girl. Not at all, really. I mean it. It was just that van going by and this Byler fellow that brought it to my mind."

"You don't have to worry. He never was my boyfriend."

"Agreed," he allowed. "Now where were we?"

"A spring wedding," she said. "Not this coming spring but the next spring. Just you and me."

"Yes," he said.

It was getting late, and Rebecca remembered her duty at home. "John, I have to chore tonight. We better go." Then she added, "Do you want to stay to help?"

He wrinkled his face as if in deep thought, although he already knew the answer. "No singing tonight in our district, right?"

"No, not tonight. So why not stay for choring?"

"I can't resist," he said. "Let's go then. Your parents probably think we've gotten lost."

She led the way back across the bridge to their buggy, pulling him gently by the hand before letting go to walk a little ahead of him.

"Hey, a wife should walk behind her husband," he said in mock severity. "You're starting things off on the wrong foot."

"You think so?" she asked playfully, looking back at him but not slowing down.

"Yes, and I also think you're beautiful," he said, glad to say it out loud.

"John! You shouldn't say things like that."

"We're engaged now," he said. "Remember?"

"I haven't forgotten," she answered as they arrived at the buggy.

John stowed the tie rope, walked to his side, and climbed in as had Rebecca. As he let out the reins, the gelding pulled the buggy out onto the road and the covered bridge. Its hooves made echoing sounds in the enclosed area, and Rebecca let her shoulder lean against John's.

John let the sensation flow all the way through him as she looked at him—her presence, her smile, her eyes, all rolled into one. "I'm glad you said yes," he told her playfully.

"I am too," she said, as they headed out of the covered bridge.

Around the curves going west and then up the hill, John drove the buggy to her place. Keeping his face forward, he allowed the corner of his eye to fill with the side of her face. Breathing in deeply, he thanked God for having made the world so good.

Chapter Two

Where's Rebecca?" Mattie Keim asked her husband, Lester, as she rose from the couch to walk to the front window. "Wasn't she coming home with John?"

"I suppose so," Lester faintly replied, his mouth full of Sunday afternoon popcorn. The bowl sat on his lap, the white kernels stark against the dark gray color of the container. His hand stopped halfway to his mouth, giving him time to reply, "They probably stopped somewhere."

"There's no place to stop," Mattie said.

"Young people *always* find places to stop," he said before his hand completed its trip to his mouth. "*We* did."

"Maybe they stopped at the bridge?" she mused. "You think it's warm enough?"

"I don't know," he said. "Depends, I guess, on what you want to do."

"The bridge," she stood looking out the window in the direction of her thoughts. "I hope…"

"John's a pretty upstanding boy," Lester said. "I'm sure they're fine. Wherever they stopped."

"Well, there's no place else to stop," she told him."You don't just pull over on the side of the road. They certainly wouldn't have gone all the way into town."

"They'll be here," he said, absorbed in his popcorn. "It's about time for the chores, isn't it? Rebecca helps tonight. She's always good about being here at choring time."

"Yes, that she is," Mattie sighed. "That's why I'm worried. She doesn't just turn up late for no reason."

"They'll be here," he repeated, seeking to reassure her. "Rebecca is almost twenty-one. Remember? Sit down and have some popcorn before I eat it all."

Flustered, she reached for a handful and picked at the kernels one at a time.

"Get a bowl and relax," he said. "You and I can have a date."

"Us?" She glanced sharply at him. "Are you going English?"

"Me? English? Surely not."

She shrugged, still keeping an eye on him. "Then where is this romantic stuff coming from?"

He stared at her and replied, "Now how do you, a good Amish woman like yourself, even know the word 'romance'? That's English, if you ask me—using words like that."

She bounced up for another look out the window. "There's still no sign of them. Don't you think you should go look for them?"

"No," he said, still concentrating on his popcorn. "Tell me where you learned of romance."

"Oh," she replied and waved her hand weakly in a half circle, "you know...books. They are all over the place nowadays. Every young woman has a loved one...and all the troubles that follow the English."

"You shouldn't be reading those books," he said mildly. "They don't settle the constitution well. We don't need romance...we're in love. After all these years."

She continued to look out the window, her face concerned.

"We are, aren't we?" he asked in her direction.

"Are what?" she replied absentmindedly.

"In love."

"Of course," she replied without hesitation. She turned toward him suddenly and asked, "Why are you asking all these strange questions? We have been married for nearly thirty years."

"And in love too," he said, a twinkle in his voice.

"You're certainly acting strange." She turned away from the window, the missing couple forgotten for the moment. "Is something wrong with you?" She crossed the room and gently laid her hand on her husband's forehead.

He allowed it, saying nothing.

"No." She shook her head. "Feels fine. You're not picking up that flu are you?"

"Of course not," he said. "I feel as fit as a fiddle."

"Then what's wrong with you?"

"Maybe it's all this love in the air," he said, reaching for the last of the popcorn.

Mattie was silent for a moment, then said, "Oh, you mean Rebecca and John? Surely not." She resumed her vigil at the window. "Where are they anyway?"

"Yes," he said quietly, "them."

Sure that she had not heard him, he was about ready to rise from the couch to look out the window himself when she turned back toward him. "You have already married off two children. None of them affected you this way. What's wrong with you?"

He settled back down and replied, "Nothing's wrong, really. It's just different, these two are."

"They seem the same to me. Maybe it's because it's Rebecca. You were always closest to her. But you can't hold on, you know."

"I'm not holding on," he said. "Just remembering."

"If they're not here in five minutes, you're going after them," she told him firmly, turning away from the window.

Lester leaned back and closed his eyes. Yes, he did remember. Rebecca, his third child, still so young and yet mature for her age. The seriousness in her eyes after church still bothered him. Had something happened that he was not aware of? Why would she seem troubled today? She'd be twenty-one in just days. A grown woman. Lester could almost see it, but he couldn't put his finger on it.

"Oh, here they come!" Mattie announced. "Where could they have been so long? They so worry me sometimes."

"They'll be fine," Lester reassured her as he pulled himself up from his chair. "They'll be just fine," he repeated since Mattie wasn't listening anyway. He needed to hear himself say it and found comfort in the words.

Chapter Three

John checked for oncoming traffic before letting the gelding slow to cross the little creek and head up the Keim driveway.

"You think your parents are worried?" John asked.

"Mom might be," Rebecca said, "but she'll get over it. Dad's fine as long as I'm home to help chore."

"Are you going to tell them?" John asked, without looking at Rebecca.

"You mean right now?"

"Yes."

"We'll have to see," she said. "I doubt it. Not in front of everyone."

"It's not everyone," he protested. "Just your mom and dad."

"Maybe not since it's Sunday afternoon. The younger ones could be around."

"You afraid of what they'll say?" he asked.

"No, of course not," she said, mildly offended. "My parents like you. Why should I be afraid?"

"I guess you're right. Your parents have always been nice to me."

"Okay, then stop worrying about it," she said. "Let's not say anything for a while though."

John pulled the buggy to a stop in front of the house. The Keim place lay on a knoll just off the riverbank—a white two-story house with a prominent front porch and two smaller, white pole barns in the background. Lester Keim farmed a hundred and twenty acres, a large part of which was river bottom. The Keim farm was neat, the buildings in good shape, the barns clean. To John it spoke of a well-ordered life. That was what he wanted in a wife. And he found it in Rebecca Keim, of that he was sure.

"You worried?" she asked over her shoulder.

"I'm okay," he said quickly. "Just a little nervous."

"It will be fine." Rebecca's eyes were lit up now, her smile certain.

They stepped into the living room, and John took off his hat and immediately began fiddling with it. Both Mattie and Lester were seated on the couch, the empty popcorn bowl between them.

"Ah," he started to say, not sure where to go from there.

Lester, seeing his confusion, came to his rescue. "Mother's been just a little worried. She didn't know where you were. I told her you probably stopped at the bridge."

"Ah," John stated again, "that's where we were. I'm so sorry," he said in Mattie's direction.

"It's nothing to be sorry about," Lester told him, reaching for the empty popcorn bowl and rattling it. "Why don't you get more, Mother? John might want some. I could use more myself."

Rebecca spoke up. "John's staying for chores. To help me. For supper too since there's no singing in our district tonight. You shouldn't have worried, Mother. We were perfectly safe and sound."

"Well, you know how I am," Mattie said, a little sheepishly. "You know how it goes with children. Nowadays you never know what can happen. I guess I worry too much."

"Yes, Mother, you do," Rebecca told her. "I'll make some more popcorn while you visit."

"That's fine." Mattie's face broke into a smile. "John, it's good to see you looking so well. Has anyone ever told you that you have a kind face? Did it come from your father or mother's side?"

John felt himself relax. He even allowed a slight grin to play on his face. "I didn't know I was that good looking," he told her, finding a chair across the room to sit on.

"Oh, it's not just that, although you are good looking, I must say. But it's deeper than that. You must have inherited it, I think. You're not old enough to have it on your own. There's wholesomeness in your face. It must come from your family line somewhere."

John felt a little touch of red gather at his collar. "I'm not sure," he managed. "We try to live right. As all of us do, I'm sure."

Lester chuckled, remembering his own awkwardness as a young man in the presence of Mattie's parents. "She's trying to say she likes you," he explained. Truth was he liked this boy too, and there was no need to have him feeling ill at ease in his living room. "She just takes the long way around saying it sometimes," he continued, while smiling in Mattie's direction.

"The boy's just fine," she said facing Lester. "He needs to get used to us one way or the other. That's if he wants to be around Rebecca, don't you think? I was just trying to make a point."

John cleared his throat, wondering if he should say what happened this afternoon. But no, they had decided not to. Besides, it would be Rebecca's place to tell them, and also his Amish instincts were kicking in. You simply didn't really go around announcing such things.

"I'm glad you think I come from a good family," he said instead. "You have a nice family yourselves. Your place looks good too."

"We like to think so," Lester said, receiving the compliment with ease. "Not as big as some folks have, but comfortable. We are blessed of the Lord."

John nodded. "All of us are here on Wheat Ridge. We are really blessed."

"So," Lester declared, changing the subject, "you're staying for the chores. I have some old clothing you can wear."

"Don't be making the boy work," Mattie protested. "He doesn't have to. Rebecca can handle it by herself."

"I thought he might be *wanting* to," Lester said, a mischievous note in his voice. "After all, he is here to be with Rebecca. Choring is where Rebecca will be."

"Well, he still doesn't have to." Mattie made sure John was looking at her when she said it.

"Oh, I do want to," he assured her. "Just show me where I can change. I'll be ready to go."

"There's time for that later," Lester interrupted him. "The popcorn is coming. First the popcorn, then the chores."

True to the prediction, the popcorn was ready. Appearing at the kitchen door, Rebecca carried in the big bowl heaped high with white kernels. Smaller bowls were passed around, and each took a turn filling their bowls to the brim. Rebecca then pulled another chair beside John, sat down, and gave him a quick glance.

I'm okay he told her with his eyes and saw her body visibly relax into the chair.

Mattie then brought up the subject of the visitors in church that morning—the Bylers—and from the flow of the conversation, John gathered that the Byler family was well-known to the Keims because they lived close by each other in Milroy, Indiana. In no way did he detect in Rebecca any of the tension or fear from earlier at the bridge. He must have imagined it, he decided, because Rebecca seemed perfectly at ease now.

Chapter Four

The hired van, its driver a retired trucker who drove for the Amish people in Rush County, Indiana, was well on the west side of Cincinnati on Interstate 74. Much of the buzz of conversation had died down, as the hours whiled away. Luke Byler, along with two younger children, sat in the backseat of the twelve-passenger van. His mother and father sat in front of them.

In front of them were unrelated members of the Milroy Amish church community who were returning from their weekend at Wheat Ridge. Reuben Byler, a stout man, a farmer, and a deacon at his home district, had made this trip with clear intentions of seeking to move to Wheat Ridge.

His wife, Rachel, was a former Miller, related by some cousin connection to the Millers who owned the businesses along Wheat Ridge. She was in full agreement with both the trip and the planned move. This came partly out of the Miller family connection and partly out of the hope that her husband might do better financially with a move.

Not that the family was going hungry in Milroy, but they were not prospering either. During her childhood, Rachel was used to a much higher standard of living. Her father, old Millett Miller or M-Jay as he had been called, now gone for fifteen years, had been known among the Millers in the Amish circles for his industrious business acumen. In Rachel's childhood, money had always been available—so much so that her father had invested in two other cattle farms in addition to the one on which Rachel and her siblings had been raised.

It had been a shock that upon his death, Rachel's father, by now a widower, had left his entire holdings to his youngest sister, Emma. This strange turn of events had left his children—particularly Rachel—feeling betrayed by their father.

It was true that old M-Jay had objected to Reuben dating Rachel, but this had not stopped her from eventually marrying Reuben. Reuben had come with good credentials, both from keeping the church standard and from being the local bishop's favorite young man. Reuben, though a charming fellow in some ways, was never quite able to turn that charm into solid cash. That was to become Rachel's first disappointment in life, and it caused her all the more to turn her hopes to an inheritance at her father's passing.

Her father was an eccentric man, even by Amish standards. He confirmed that opinion in his will. All written out and overseen by a lawyer from town, he had left not a green dollar more than a token thousand to each of his six surviving children.

The will had said nothing as to why he had chosen as he had. Just the black letters on paper, read to all six of them in the lawyer's big office in town. They had all felt so out of place, nervous, and distressed in their black hats and shawls that winter day. To this very day, Rachel still shudders to think of it.

M-Jay's sister Emma, the last surviving member of the family of eleven and as eccentric as her brother, defied even Bishop Mose to do anything about the will. Instead, immediately after the funeral, she moved in to her brother's home, nearly causing a scandal in the Amish community among those in the know who all felt M-Jay had done badly by his children.

Things settled down only when the majority of the children agreed to make no fuss, as it was apparent that Emma was in her full right. Even Bishop Mose eventually let the word go out that Emma was to be left alone. On her part Emma wrapped herself tighter in her shawl, made sure her dresses were well below the *ordnung* standard, and survived the storm.

The storm had never quite settled in Rachel's heart though. It was softened only by the certain knowledge that Emma, now with a history of heart trouble and getting on in years herself, would surely do the right thing and leave the money to her nieces and nephews at her passing. So certain was Rachel of this that she was already making plans for the money.

Lately, however, she had been given to doubts. Could it be possible Emma might *not* do the right thing? What if the money went somewhere else? What if the tragedy was only to be repeated?

She had heard, only last week and through a trusted source, that Emma had seen the doctor and a fancy car had been spotted at Emma's. The man who drove the vehicle was reported to be dressed in an English suit, right smart, Rachel had been told. What he was doing there, the rumors did not say, but eyebrows were raised and the unspoken word "lawyer" was on the minds of those most concerned.

If Emma was in poor health and talking to a lawyer, then nothing good could be coming out of it. Was the money slipping away again? It was enough to keep Rachel awake at night.

In the meantime, Reuben had gotten it into his head that the family needed to move to Wheat Ridge. Rachel had cousins there, and maybe Reuben would succeed in Wheat Ridge where he had failed in Milroy.

With the sound of the tires of the van humming on the interstate and the conversation with the others having died down, Rachel wanted to press Reuben about their prospects.

Turning to him, she wondered again why she ever thought of him as good looking. His face was rounded now, his cheeks filled out where formerly there had been firmness. The roundness extended down his body, starting to spill over his pants. What the man needed was some hard work. But he already worked on the farm, and that did not seem to keep him from putting on weight in places other than his checking account.

This move to Wheat Ridge might allow for something other than manual labor—and it might surely pay more. Perhaps working as a salesman in the Miller's retail stores would do the trick. On Saturday she had seen the layout of all the furniture, grandfather clocks, and merchandise catering to the wealthy from Cincinnati. The tourists came looking for a slice of the old Amish life so different from their own.

Leaning toward him in the van, she half whispered, "So you liked Wheat Ridge?"

Reuben nodded, not really wanting to engage in this conversation. He was tired and would rather have joined several of the others in the seats in front of him in a nap.

"What do you think then?" she persisted.

"Should be a nice place," he answered.

"I mean about moving?"

He shrugged.

"Well." She was not going to settle for this. "You were the one who wanted to move. It was your idea for this trip. These drivers aren't cheap. Surely we didn't just waste our time?"

"I liked it." He was fast becoming annoyed.

"Are we moving then?" She wanted to know.

"How do I know that?" he mumbled. "I haven't decided yet. I have to go home and think. It would mean a lot of hard work. The moving and all. Selling the farm. I'm not sure about prices right now. We can't sell at a loss and expect to make it in Wheat Ridge. Those people have lots of money."

She glared at him. "You're not changing your mind, are you, Reuben? You wouldn't get my hopes up like this, then let them fall to the ground. I don't expect miracles, but this could be our only chance for a fresh start. You're not scared of their money are you?"

Now he glared, whispering back, "Why would I be? Sure I've never had much of it. You knew that when you married me. You didn't come into this blindfolded. And it's not my fault you were cut out of your father's will. It's just that I am what I am."

"You could at least *try,*" she said, keeping her eyes focused on the changing landscape visible thorough the van windshield.

He scooted himself up on the seat until his head was raised as high as it would go. "I am a deacon," he said, falling back on his one winning hand. "Have you forgotten that? The lot sure thought I was good enough. That's driven by the hand of the Lord. Have you forgotten that?"

She said nothing as the tires sang their rhythmic song, weighted down with its cargo of twelve humans.

Reuben leaned toward her again and said, "Then there's this to think of too: I am under the church's authority. I'll have to talk to the bishop before we could move anyway. I would need a good word from him to be accepted in Wheat Ridge."

"So why have you not thought of this before? There are other important things too," she said, her voice now strained.

"What, like money?" he whispered, knowing her well enough. "You should be ashamed of yourself. I'm a servant of God in service of His church. That's more important than worldly goods. Those stay here once we are gone. Nothing in this world can go with us when we go. You know that. Our spiritual values are what are of great price to God. I'm a minister of those things."

His tongue is loosened at last, she thought. *He always was good with words. Too bad it can't talk some cash loose once in awhile.*

"I'm grateful for what the Lord has given us," she said.

"Including me?" he asked bluntly.

"Including you." She turned toward him, forcing a smile.

He nodded. Satisfied, he proceeded to slide down in his seat and lean his head back to get some sleep. "We'll see about moving," he said before nodding off.

Yes, she told herself, *we will see. That means we're not going. After all this buildup, he will do nothing.*

"We're not going," Luke whispered into his mother's ear from the backseat.

She nodded, glad someone understood even if she could do nothing about it.

Luke said nothing more for a few seconds, then asked, "Who was that we saw by the bridge today?"

She shook her head and answered, "I'm not sure. I wasn't really looking."

"It looked like Rebecca Keim," he said. "They moved from Milroy a few years ago. I didn't know the boy."

"Oh," Rachel said, turning around to face him, "was she someone you liked?"

"No." He grinned a little. "She's a little out of my shooting range. Always was. Even in Milroy. She was a grade behind me in school."

"Then they have nothing to do with us," his mother told him, turning back around in her seat.

"I was just curious." He shrugged his shoulders, but she was not listening.

Chapter Five

Walking toward the barn that afternoon at four thirty with Rebecca leading the way, John glanced down at his chore clothing. They fit, sort of, he supposed. Not that the bagginess in the legs really mattered, but he just liked things to be right.

Seeing his glance downward, Rebecca chuckled. "Dad's clothes are a little too big for you."

"Yeah," he allowed, "wrinkled too."

"Don't let it bother you."

"I guess I'm not used to farming." He glanced at her. "Probably never will be. You ever want to marry a farmer?"

She looked at him sharply and answered, "No. I never thought about marriage in those terms."

"Some girls do," he offered as explanation, suddenly feeling like his question needed one.

"Some girls do? So you have a lot of experience asking girls about marriage?" she asked, only half joking.

"No, of course not," he said. "I've never been engaged before."

She allowed a smile to spread slowly across her face. "Ever asked?"

He allowed the air to come slowly out of his lungs. "Look, before you I never even dated a girl. You were the first."

"Oh," she said, as she faced forward, but not before John thought he saw that look of fear flash again briefly in her eyes. Then he thought to ask, "You ever been engaged before?"

"No," she said, continuing to walk and not looking at him.

"Seriously dated?"

"A little. In Milroy. Not seriously…no."

"How much is a little?"

"Don't you think you should have asked these questions first?"

"They didn't seem important," he said, because they hadn't. Why they were important now, he couldn't figure out, but they were. Was it the fear he had seen in her eyes?

"How much is a little?" he asked again.

"Once," she said.

"How many dates would that be?"

"Two."

"So," he asked, "did he drop you?"

"No," she said. "I said no after the second time."

"Was there trouble?"

"You sure are something," she stated, the fire gone from her eyes. "No. I just said I wasn't interested."

Rebecca seemed to want the discussion to end. She reached out and took his hand. "Let's get to the chores."

"All right," he said, "but we need to be careful." He pulled his hand away from hers. "Your parents will see us."

"I don't care," she said.

"Well, I do. We have to keep our relationship right." He noticed a hurt look on her face and added, "Rebecca, it's going to be hard enough."

"It's just those rules, isn't it?" she asked.

He thought for a moment. "Yes, it's the rules. I want to keep them because I think they're for our good. But it's more than that."

"And?" She kept her eyes on his face.

"It's…" He found himself stumbling to say it. "It's just that I don't trust myself." His eyes softened as he stood looking into hers.

She was still for a moment and then said, "I trust you." Pausing a moment more, Rebecca broke away saying, "We have some chores to do."

He let his breath out slowly, mixed emotions running through him...but best to drop them now.

"How many cows do you milk?" he finally asked awkwardly.

"Thirty," she replied. "Dad says that we're among the last dairy farmers in the county."

"Yeah," he agreed, "there aren't too many around. Has your father ever thought of doing something else?"

"He likes farming," she said. "We raise most of our own feed. Saves money...and milk prices are up a little. Besides what else would he do?" she asked with a chuckle. "Compete with the Miller's operations on the hill?"

"Your uncle already does that," he said dryly. "Keim Family Market, but we get along."

"There you go," she told him. "A dairy farm is safer. But Dad does work at Keim's sometimes. Brings in extra cash." Arriving at the barn, she held the door open for him, waiting as he entered.

Stepping inside, the sounds and smells of a dairy barn hit him—the faint smell of cow manure hung in the air, the lowing of cattle just outside the sliding wooden doors.

"We just whitewashed," she said, seeing that he noticed. "The inspector passed us on his first trip out. He said Dad does a good job of things."

John nodded while thinking how much he preferred work tools that didn't splatter the ground with smelly droppings from their backsides. "When does the milking start?" he asked.

"Fifteen minutes. Let some feed out of the shoot over there. Give each cow a shovelful. Keeps them occupied till we get the milkers on."

He responded by finding the feed shovel and lifting the sliding board that controlled the feed flow. The pressure surprised him as the spray of brown feed, smelling of molasses and squashed grain, shot down to the floor by his feet.

"Not too much," she said calmly. "Save the extra for next time.

They can't reach it from there anyway, so it will keep. I'm going for the milkers now."

He picked up the shovel, scooped up a portion he figured was equivalent to the prescribed amount and deposited it in front of the first open station. When all sixteen spots were done, he retreated to the back and waited.

She pushed open the swinging door behind him, coming out with a milker in each hand, their hoses hanging just shy of the floor.

"I'll take them," he offered, reaching out his hand.

She gave him one and lifted the other up to snap in place on the wire suspended from the ceiling. Obviously she wanted him to follow suit, so he did, feeling the weight of the effort quickly tire his arm. He wondered what she was doing carrying two of these at the same time.

As if in answer, she said, "I wouldn't have brought out two if you hadn't been here. They can't touch the ground outside the milk house. Cleanliness issue."

He nodded. "What time did you say the milking starts?"

"Five sharp," she said. "The cows should be coming in any minute now."

The sound of the approaching cows confirmed her words. As Lester came into the barn, he smiled at the sight of John in his oversized chore clothing and asked the two, "Ready to start?"

Rebecca grinned, noticing the reason for her father's smile, and nodded her head. Lester opened the door to the outside barnyard. The first cow stuck her head in, looked around as if deciding what to do, then proceeded forward, nervously glancing about.

Standing motionless and staring intently at the advancing cow, John missed the exchange between daughter and father. The cow overcame whatever contrary thoughts it had as soon as it caught sight of the feed John had shoveled out. Lifting its head, the cow headed for the closest station. Rebecca was ready and pushed the two side rods together as the cow stuck its head through the stanchion. The metal snapping closed around its neck caused no reaction, its nose deep into the shovel of feed. The cow munched contentedly, its eyes looking at nothing and glazed over in contentment.

The other cows lost no time following suit. Lester counted under his breath until sixteen had entered, then he slapped the next cow in line on its nose to keep it from entering. "There now, Bess," he said, "next time's for you."

"Cows never listen," Rebecca said, standing at John's elbow. "You have to give direction."

She turned to reach for the milker on the overhead line and then stepped back, moving away from the cow. The switch of its tail almost caught her in the face.

"Missed," she muttered under her breath. "Try harder next time."

John had to chuckle. "It's not on purpose, is it?"

"Maniacal things. Cow brains," she retorted. "You never know sometimes."

He laughed, the sound vibrating in the enclosed milking parlor. She turned toward it. There weren't too many times she'd heard him laugh out loud, and each time her reaction had been the same. It was as a man's laugh should be—delightful, serious, and yet merry to the soul.

Her smile warmed his heart when he saw it.

"Ah," he cleared his throat, "how long does it take to milk?"

Her smile deepened. He was trying to change the subject, and she now knew why. It was because he cared for her, deeply cared for her. She let the thought linger as he was looking the other way, seeming to be watching the milkers doing their jobs.

"We should be done by a quarter after six," she told him, with her smile still lingering. "Supper's right after that. Mother makes a wonderful supper."

"I suppose she does," he allowed. "Passed the training on to you?"

She grinned. "Of course."

Chapter Six

Under the hiss of a gas lantern, the family gathered in the dining room for the evening meal. Another lantern hung in the kitchen and one more was glowing in the living room. Except for the rooms here and there with kerosene lamps burning, the house was dark.

"Thanks for helping us tonight," Lester told John from across the table.

"It was nothing," John assured him, both because that was the proper thing to say and because of his interest in Rebecca. "I just shoveled a little feed," he added. "Not enough to work up much of a sweat."

"Well, it's Sunday," Lester allowed. "Where's Mother? I'm hungry."

"Coming," Rebecca told him.

Mattie appeared in the kitchen doorway carrying a bowl of steaming gravy. She set the bowl carefully on the table and warned, "Don't touch it just yet. It's hot. Let me dip it out."

"The best gravy cools slowly," Lester said with a wink. "Come sit down, Mother. We can have prayer. The younger ones just have to be careful."

"We already know that," eleven-year-old Matthew offered, feeling like he was being included in the instructions. "Mother usually serves things hot."

"We weren't talking about you," Lester assured him. "Supper food tastes best when it's hot. Now can we have prayer?"

"The Amish way," Mattie pronounced, "fresh out of the oven."

Getting a word in yet before taking her seat beside Lester, she folded her hands and waited.

Lester took the signal, let his eyes move over all of them, and without saying anything, he bowed his head. They followed. Leading out in a prayer he knew by memory, he prayed in High German and concluded, "*Im Namen des Vaters, des Sohns, und des Heiligen Geistes.* Amen."

Not a head rose until Lester finished, and even then a brief hush hung over the room. Silence seemed to be in order.

None of the younger children understood the High German, but they knew it was used for spiritual occasions. It was God's language. The words carried a weight all their own. It was the sound used on important occasions—for church services, weddings, for Sunday morning songs, and for funerals. Whether the High German words were pronounced slowly by an elderly minister or rapidly by a younger speaker, it meant for them that the work of God was near.

Matthew first broke the reverent silence. "I saw Phillip Mast today and talked with him in the barn after church." His young face alight with pleasure. "He's big now."

"You're big too," Lester said teasingly. "Remember, you're too old for children's instructions."

"Well, I guess," Matthew muttered in response, suddenly not sure whether he wanted to be big or not.

"He means the Mast family who was visiting today," Rebecca said, as she leaned in John's direction, bringing him into the loop. "He and Phillip were good friends in school."

John said nothing, noting only that there was no fear in her eyes when she mentioned the load of visitors who had accompanied the Byler family. *That look of fear in her eye couldn't have been from them,* he thought.

"So how is business up at the Miller hill?" Lester asked in John's direction.

"Same as always," John said. "Tourists still are tourists. I suppose it will be like that for awhile at least. Most of the business comes out of Cincinnati. That's not affected much, no matter what the economy does."

"I suppose so," Lester allowed. "Too bad cows don't attract tourists."

"You think that would pay better than milk?" John chuckled.

"Without a doubt," Lester said, making a wry face. "What would Amish people do without tourists?"

"There does seem to be plenty of interest," John agreed. "We would find something else to do, no doubt. Amish people didn't always have tourists. There was many a day not so long ago when things were a lot harder."

"Well, the Lord gives and the Lord takes. It's all in His will and plan. Perhaps it's our time to give His message to the world. This might be God's way of doing it."

"You think so?" John raised his eyebrows. "I never thought of it from that angle before."

"Sure," Lester told him. "A little honey always works the best. Works for child, man, or beast."

"I thought our concern was first for our own people," John said.

"Sure," Lester replied, "that's the way it should be. Preserve the message securely first. Then it can be spread around. Loses less of its potency that way."

"Are you talking about mission mindedness?" John asked, not sure he wanted to go there with his future father-in-law.

Lester quickly put his mind at ease. "No, I'm not missions-minded. Not in the least. The Lord knows where we are. I suppose if He wants to use us, He can do what He wants."

"Sure," John agreed. "The Lord can do what He wants. It's just that a lot of people think of themselves as spiritual, then believe they should do the Lord's work."

Lester chuckled. "I think the Almighty is quite able to do what He wants to do. Obedience is what is required of us. The rest is in His hands."

"Agreed." John let the air slowly out of his lungs. So Lester was not one of those secret liberals who might well leave the faith to save the world.

"You were afraid Dad would be liberal," Rebecca whispered, leaning near and eyeing him carefully, having noticed his discomfort.

"Not really," John said softly, not wishing to admit his fears and most certainly not wanting his voice to carry to Lester's ears.

"Well, he's not," Rebecca whispered. "You don't have to worry."

"You two have secrets?" Mattie asked, hearing their whispers above the hum of the younger children's conversation.

"No, Mom…no secrets." Rebecca turned to smile at John.

"Well, then." Mattie scraped her chair on the hardwood floor as she stood up and asked, "Everyone still have room for pies?"

"What kind?" Matthew and one of his younger sisters asked at the same time.

"Cherry and pecan. One of each."

"Only two?" Lester asked. "What about next week?"

"I'll bake some more on Monday," Mattie assured him and went to get the pies.

"We usually bake enough pies on Saturday to last all week," Rebecca offered for John's information. "Yesterday we were too busy. These are still left over from last week…but they aren't stale," Rebecca said in her mother's defense.

Mattie came bustling in, a pie balanced on each palm. "Now just small pieces," she told the children. "We want some left for the visitor."

Finding several eyes turned in his direction, John chuckled. "You're going to make them wish I wasn't here."

"It's good for them," Mattie assured him. "Teaches them to share."

"I guess so," John agreed.

In moments the pies were passed around and properly divided. John was glad to see that the children's pieces were not too small. It made his own slice of cherry pie taste better.

"So," Lester asked him, his forkful of pecan pie halfway to his mouth, "are the English going to be right about the snow tomorrow?"

"It sounds like a high chance from what I heard."

"They're probably right," Lester agreed. "Little early, but the Lord runs those things too."

To this John nodded his agreement.

A few moments later, John, having finished his dessert, thanked Mattie, excused himself, and got up to leave. Rebecca followed him to the door but did not step outside.

"I'll see you Wednesday night," she whispered, her eyes soft in the light of the gas lanterns.

"At the Mullets," he said quietly. "Goodnight then."

"Goodnight," she said, as he stepped out into the darkness.

Returning to the dining room, Mattie was already clearing the table, and Rebecca joined in. After that Rebecca went to her room. She stood by the window looking out into the night. The stars were bright, and little clouds dotted the sky. A brisk wind was picking up as if winter was making a serious effort at settling in.

"So I'm engaged," she said softly. "Who would have thought it?" A flush crossed her face in the darkness. Then the uneasiness she had felt earlier with John returned. The fear. What was wrong with her? After all, *what happened all those years ago isn't important now,* she told herself. Rebecca tried to shove the thoughts away, but it was useless. Her twenty-first birthday was quickly approaching and with it, the promise she had made so long ago.

Finally she walked over to her dresser, slowly opened the third drawer, and dug deep into the stack of dresses. Her fingers searched for a moment, then wrapped around the object. She paused, wishing her hand had found nothing.

"Oh, *Gott,*" she breathed softly, half prayer, half groan. "I still have it."

Pulling her hand from the dresser, she lifted it toward the window. By the dim starlight, the ring's gem flashed between her fingers. She heard Atlee's voice, as clear as on that sunny summer day by the river when he had given it to her. His voice just in its first stages of changing, husky with emotion.

"But we were so young," she whispered. "It didn't mean anything."

Chapter Seven

Rachel Byler, restless and fretting, had been tossing in bed all night. Unable to drop off for more than an hour at a time, her mind was frigid with fear. The money. It was going away—slipping through her hands. She could feel it, and the terror filled her.

"Would you calm down," Reuben had muttered at midnight. "*Hayb shtill.*"

She made no reply. He wouldn't hear it anyway. *Small help he is.* She tried to keep from moving, which worked for a few minutes, but then things just got worse.

Visions of poverty flashed in her mind, a continued life of living on the money supplied by Reuben Byler, deacon though he was. The image did not translate into comfortable living. Even now they could use a few more cattle on the back pasture, if only there was money to buy the young calves. Such potential all going to waste because her father had denied her her rightful inheritance.

Cantankerous he had been, she told herself. While her father was alive, she had thought highly enough of him. She had in fact admired him, seeing that they were wrapped in money as they were.

Why did he do it? The question almost brought her bolt upright in the bed. Halfway up, the movement caused Reuben to stir and moan, so she flopped back down.

Small help he is, hopelessly lost in his own world. What does he care about our troubles? Huh! With food on the table and a little money in the bank, he says any woman ought to be happy. So he thinks. Deacon's wife, he says, it's a great honor and responsibility. Honor and the old ways are more important than money. That's what he thinks, but that doesn't put cattle in the back pasture.

So why did Daddy do it? Her eyelids snapped open again. *Why did he do it? Maybe if I could find that out, the money would get loosed. No, I suppose not. It is too late. Emma has the money. And when she passes? Will she give it away to others...or will she do the right thing?*

She caught herself as a moan escaped her lips. Reuben turned over on his side of the bed. She stiffened, but his snoring resumed.

Lying there, she imagined the figure of her father. His tall walk, his firmness as the family's head, his voice when he spoke. *Why had he done it? Where in the recesses of his mind had the thought or inclination come from to give so much to his sister?*

Rachel remembered that when she was a little girl, her father had not had much. Faintly she could feel those times—the worried look on her mother's face and the talk of what to do when a single cow died on the farm. She had been small then, but even now the memories were strong. Memories of want.

Memories too of Emma, the single aunt who had always seemed old to Rachel. It was strange, remembering Emma in that way. Why had she not married? Rachel couldn't remember ever hearing of Emma dating or being escorted home from one of the singings.

Why did Emma never have a young man? Emma wasn't bad looking. In fact while growing up, Rachel had always thought of her as beautiful. *Maybe that was just because I was young,* she decided.

No matter how hard she searched her memories, no reason surfaced for Emma's single status. It had always just been so. Her mind went over her teenage years, years colored with a golden hue of comfort and unhurried ease as she made choices in life. Always she was assured that her father's money would be there to tide things over.

Would she have married Reuben if she had known? That question caused a blush of shame to creep over her face, even in the darkness of the night. What if someone found out she was even asking such a thing?

Marriage was sacred to the Amish and not to be questioned or second-guessed. To even wonder was to tempt the Most High God to move His hand to awful things. She quickly pushed the thought away. Whatever would have happened with her choice of Reuben, it would have been nice to know ahead of time that life with him would be entirely different from what she was used to. That little things in life could no longer be taken for granted. That simple things, like potatoes and peaches, could not be purchased just because one wanted them. That the bank account would have to be consulted for the most mundane of household projects.

This lack hung over the Byler home like a limb from the old oak in her father's yard, where Emma now lived. Growing up, she had always wondered when it would fall. Yet it never had. The last time she saw it, the limb seemed to be hanging by the slimmest of threads, but still hanging. That was her life now. The dread of poverty was hanging over her, threatening to fall at the blowing of the slightest wind.

Numbly, she turned over to see if sleep would come if she lay on the other side of her body. Yes, it seemed to feel better, and she pulled the covers around her. The Big Ben clock downstairs struck twice. Two a.m.

That was the last she could remember until the little windup alarm clock by the bed woke her up three hours later.

Her hand shot out from under the covers and fumbled for the little round globe. Bumping it, the vibrating little creature crashed to the floor. It missed the rug, where its racket would have been muted. Instead, its dance continued on the bare hardwood, amplifying the noise even more.

"Can't you shut it off?" Reuben muttered from his side of the bed.

She swung her feet to the floor, her head aching from the lack of sleep, and stood up. The world swam in the darkness as she leaned over toward the noise, her hands reaching out for it. The rug under her feet, though, slipped slightly.

In an effort to keep from falling, she overcompensated, and the rug slipped even more. With dizzying awareness she went toward the noise on the floor at much too high a speed. Despite her efforts to break the fall, she hit the vibrating clock with her left shoulder and groaned from the sting of the pain.

The noisy clock went skidding across the floor, hitting the wall with a *thunk.* It bounced back violently, coming to rest only inches from her face.

By now the little creature had almost used up its wound up energy and was slowing down. The clanking was decreasing in volume, like the slowing of a spinning top. It went quieter and quieter until it stopped with a final loud clank, right under her nose, as if the little thing was disgusted because there was no more noise to make.

"Was all that necessary?" Reuben asked, still under the covers, his eyes still closed, his awareness still dulled from sleep.

She said nothing, her arms straight in front of her and her body aching.

Reuben swung his feet out and onto the hardwood floor. Finding a match, he lit the kerosene lamp, carefully replacing the chimney, and then looked across the bed. "Why are you on the floor?" he asked.

She still said nothing, lying motionless and in pain.

"Are you hurt?" he asked, coming around the bed. He rubbed his sleepy eyes, trying to bring her into focus in the dancing light of the kerosene lamp.

She waited until he was close, then rolled onto her side to get up. "No," she said, "the rug slipped."

"You should be more careful," he said, his deacon voice vibrating low in the morning stillness.

She rubbed her head. "I was trying to shut off that terrible racket."

"It's a little noisy," he allowed, "but if we got something quieter, then how would we wake up?"

"You don't shut it off anyway," she said.

He turned around to look at her, then changed his mind, shaking his head and reaching for his clothing on the floor. "I'll be a little early for breakfast. I did some of the chores last night."

"Okay," she said quietly, "I'll get Luke up."

After Reuben dressed and left the room, Rachel began her own preparations for the day. As the lamplight played softly on the wall, she remembered why she felt so tired. The grandfather clock. She had heard it chime at two o'clock.

Oh yes. The money. Now it was coming back. The money problem and the lawyer coming out to Emma's place. Or was it a lawyer? That was the rumor, but was it true? Someone would have to find out and find out soon. Maybe it was the doctor visiting about her health.

Clearly Reuben would be no good. If she raised the subject with him, he would just lecture her about interfering with other people's lives and the fleetingness of money, its corrupting power, and how no one could take it with them. Well, that might all be true, but one could use it while one was here. Surely that was not a sin, especially if the money was rightfully yours.

And it was hers, was it not? *Yes,* she assured herself, *it was.* Then it was also up to her to see that the wrong was made right. Walking downstairs, she lit the other gas lantern and hung it on the hook in the kitchen ceiling.

Soon the lantern's hiss was joined by the sound of sizzling bacon in the large skillet. Glancing out the window into the darkness, Rachel saw snowflakes bouncing off the glass.

Turning to her task at hand, she made her plans regarding Emma. She and Luke would have to do this, and that was all there was to it. All the hard work, all the hard thinking that would be involved—it would all lie on their shoulders.

Luke would help, of this she was certain. He was willing. He would listen to her and be sympathetic. He would also keep his mouth shut. He might even have a helpful idea or two.

Yes, she would speak to Luke as soon as the opportunity presented itself. Together, tragedy might well be turned around, lest her father's error keep on bearing its bitter fruit. After the night spent thinking of what needed to be done, she was certain now.

Chapter Eight

Rebecca needed no alarm clock to awaken by—the soft creak of the floorboards in the kitchen directly under her room was usually sufficient. Her mother would be up, stirring batter for biscuits and laying the bacon pan out on the stove. The sound of wood clunking against the sides of the cooking stove's metal box added to the morning's sounds. The final sound to pull her from bed would be her mother softly calling her name up the stairs lest the younger children be awakened.

It was Rebecca's responsibility to help milk in the morning. Matthew was almost old enough to help, but his trial attempts had consisted of evening chores so far. Slowly she slid out from under the covers, conscious of the rush of cold in her room.

The temperature had surely dropped overnight. Her feet touched the floor and quickly found her slippers. Reaching one foot out, she found the damper to the register directly above the kitchen stove and slid it open. Warm air rose around her, its comfort welcome now that she was awake. Sleeping was meant to be done in the cold, but getting up was another matter.

She stepped to the window, her attention drawn to the snowflakes drifting by. The English had been right—it was snowing. Great flakes drifted by, swirling when the wind moved them sideways by the pane. Conscious that she needed to be downstairs soon, she moved over to the register to dress.

The morning chill caused a shiver even when she was fully dressed. A heavy homemade coat hanging in the downstairs closet and boots from Wal-Mart would complete the attire and hopefully supply the needed warmth. This morning's chill seemed more than just due to the weather. Memories of last night and the ring came back with a rush.

Why have I kept the thing? She asked herself, dimly thinking she knew the answer but still unsure. *A promise is a promise,* a voice sounded in her head, its voice as solemn and fatal as Bishop Martin when he pronounced prayers over the communion bread and wine cup.

You promised Atlee.

She shivered again.

Why didn't I just throw it away when we moved here?

To that question, she didn't have an answer.

We were young, she told herself again. *We have moved away now, and that was a long time ago. Why is this bothering me?*

Rebecca pulled her dress around her tightly, longing for the heavy coat downstairs. Opening the door to her bedroom, she stepped out into the hall and found the steps in the dark. By memory, she went down without stumbling.

Knowing her mother would be busy in the kitchen, Rebecca simply walked past her, heading for the utility closet by the front door. Mother, of course, would hear her footsteps and realize that she was up and on her way to the barn.

The living room had no light in it, but the kerosene lamps from the kitchen cast a faint glow halfway to the closet. It was sufficient for Rebecca's purposes, guided by habit and memory.

Expecting a blast of cold when she opened the front door to step out, she was surprised instead by the softness of the snow. A nip was in the air, but blunted by the glory all around her. Each flake that she could see lit by that hushed light from the gas lantern in the kitchen, swirled past her.

She paused for a moment, her own troubles with the ring forgotten in the effect of the moment. Snow instantly began to gather on her scarf and coat sleeves. Standing without moving, she watched with wonder as the snowflakes balanced one on top of the other.

Then she thought of the ring again...and the fear, the uncertainty. Yes, something wonderful had happened yesterday in John's proposal, but with his promise of love, the memories of an earlier promise to Atlee came to her mind...and the ring...and her approaching birthday.

Surely I wouldn't want to go back? What reason would I have? I love John. Why am I afraid? I should have left the ring in Milroy, she told herself. *Maybe then I would have forgotten all about Atlee.*

No, that wouldn't have solved the problem, the voice in her head told her. *You still promised him. You loved Atlee. You promised him you would meet him at the bridge in Milroy.* A chill spread deep throughout her body. Startled, she came out of her thoughts so quickly that every snowflake slid off of her sleeves as she started abruptly toward the barn.

Dad will be wondering where I am, she told herself. Her heart leaped in her chest as the knowledge of last night came back with force. John had walked this very ground with his eyes on her. She had walked in front of him, enjoying every sensation. *What happened with Atlee in Milroy is nothing,* she told herself.

Then horror filled her. *Do I have to tell John? Surely not, I haven't done anything wrong. But if I tell him, surely he'll understand.* That thought brought a little comfort until the voice inside her head reminded her, *John's a man of strict moral values. You know what kind of wife he wants. Are you sure he'll understand?*

The obvious answer chilled her. She pulled the coat around her to ward it off but without success. *Atlee told you to keep it,* the voice inside said, *and you said you would. You promised.*

Her thoughts became a snowstorm of their own, falling too quickly to keep track of. Instead of cold snow, they fell like white fire, piercing her heart. Tears formed and fell, getting themselves lost in the ground around her. The rosy day of yesterday had descended into depths she would never have thought possible. The innocence of yesterday had returned not as sweetness and light but as a memory that threatened.

It's not really serious, she told herself firmly. *I can tell John about the ring and Atlee, and he will understand.*

Reaching out through the snowflakes, she found the doorknob to the milking parlor. Around her, the morning's dull glow had increased slightly, but she hardly noticed, shutting the door firmly behind her.

The heat of the milking parlor hit her—its warmth coming from the cows as much as the heater burning in the corner. Two gas lanterns hung from the ceiling, one on each end. The cows closest to the door, their necks in the stanchions, turned in her direction with only mild interest. The rest ignored her, their minds and mouths on the feed in front of their noses.

Her father already had a milker going and was ready to step away from the cow. Rebecca reached for the other milker that was hanging by its straps from the ceiling. She shook the snow off her coat before bringing the milker down.

"Good morning," her father said, keeping his eyes on the milker he had just attached, which was making strange noises under the cow's udder.

"Good morning," she replied, without much enthusiasm.

"There's something wrong with this milker," he commented. "You notice anything last night?"

"No," she said, "it was working fine then."

"That's how things go," he muttered. "A snowy morning. Just the time for equipment to act up. Harder to get into town. Harder for everything."

Rebecca made no reply, the comment making perfect sense to her. It did seem like that was the way things went. *Like me and John,* she thought.

She suddenly became conscious of her father's eyes upon her. He was standing beside the cow, the milker now ceasing from its strange noises.

"How are you and John getting along?" he asked. "Takes an interested young man to help a girl with choring."

"Okay," Rebecca told him, not looking up.

"Sure?" he asked her. "You seem troubled this morning. Last night too."

"I'm okay," Rebecca insisted, still not raising her eyes from the floor as she headed toward a cow with the milker in both hands.

"You're not misbehaving?" Lester asked, with concern in his voice. "You know the church rules."

"Of course we do." Rebecca smiled at the thought, raising her eyes to meet his, a picture of proper John flashing in her mind. "He's a stickler for the rules."

"That's good," her father allowed, "but sometimes that's not enough. We need convictions of our own."

"John's got convictions. Don't worry. We're not doing anything wrong."

"Have *you*?" he asked, his voice serious. "Convictions, I mean."

"I try to," she said, raising her eyes to look at him. "I really do."

"Yes, I imagine you do," he replied, sounding satisfied. "I'm glad to hear you're doing well. John's a nice boy."

Rebecca nodded her head in thanks. "I like him too."

"All right then," her father said, moving along to the next cow.

The snowfall had increased as Rebecca headed in from the barn. The dawn was now an early morning glow, making each flake visible right up to the front door. Stopping on the porch, she shook her coat backward from her shoulders to throw off some of the snow.

After stepping inside, she kept the front door open long enough to remove her coat and give it one last shake outside. She hung it in the utility closet, away from the other coats to give it time to dry.

"It's really coming down," her mother called from the kitchen.

"Yes," Rebecca said, "the English sure were right this time."

"They usually are in those matters."

Rebecca poked her head into the kitchen. "Pancakes?" she asked, seeing her mother mixing batter.

"Yes." Mattie smiled. "When I saw it was snowing, I decided this was the morning for pancakes. Lester will take the time to eat properly because he can't get outside work done."

"You want me to get the children up?" Rebecca asked.

"Sure," her mother replied, as she piled golden pancakes on a plate. "Matthew should have been up already. School and all."

"Who's teaching this year? I can't seem to remember," Rebecca asked.

"Yost Byler's Margaret, with her cousin Naomi," her mother said dryly. "A little young, both of them, if you ask me. Inexperienced too. I guess we have to take what they give us."

Rebecca nodded. She supposed by the time she had her own children, it would all have changed. For now she largely ignored the yearly search for parochial schoolteachers to staff the little schoolhouse in the valley just north of the town of Unity.

"We always had Emma," she commented, nostalgia in her voice.

"Of that you can be thankful," her mother replied. "A solid person Emma was. It did you school children good. Smart too. A little strange in some ways. Never being married like she was. Still good. Year after year, the same teacher. That's the way it should be."

"We all liked her," Rebecca said, the inflection still in her voice.

"With good reason," her mother agreed. "Not that everyone liked her, but most did. She really knew how to run a schoolhouse. Did twice the work as these youngsters do nowadays. She never asked for or needed another teacher—ran the whole twenty of you by herself."

"Eight grades," Rebecca added, vague numbers running through her head. "Now there are close to forty students here, aren't there?"

"Something like that," her mother said. "I suppose even Emma couldn't have taken care of that many. She was good, though."

"She always liked me," Rebecca said quietly.

Mattie huffed. "A little bit of a teacher's pet you were. I never saw that it did you harm."

"Of course not," Rebecca assured her. "Emma never showed favorites. I just knew."

"Well, that was then. No sense going on about it now. Set the table and stop thinking about your school days," her mother told her. "Being special can give you the *grohs kobb.* The past is the past."

"Now, Mom. You're making a big deal out of this." Rebecca placed the first plate on the table.

Her mother sighed. "I just never wanted my children to be teacher's pets. We are called to be ordinary people. That's our faith. Secure in God's love for all of us. Then in our love for each other. Being special makes for trouble I say."

"She didn't like everyone in school," Rebecca said, thinking that was a good defense for Emma.

"That's what I mean," her mother said. "See where this leads?"

"She had a good reason," Rebecca insisted, coming to the end of the table and the last place setting.

"That's what they *all* think," Mattie said. "Now start the eggs. Dad will be in any minute."

Setting the heat on low, Mattie opened the oven door and carefully placed the platter of round golden pancakes inside to keep warm.

Rebecca wanted to continue the conversation and tell her mother that Emma *did* have reasons. Good reasons they were, she was certain, but that would require saying his name. Atlee. Then, with the name and her mother's eyes upon her, might come questions.

Even if she tried to answer with her best explanations, there might come more questions after that, each more difficult to answer. So she simply set the egg pan on the stove and turned the gas burner to a medium flame lest the eggs burn when she dropped them in the pan. Reaching for the butter, she dabbed a large slab into the just warming pan. It slowly melted, sliding across the surface toward the lower left-hand corner, in the direction the kitchen floor slanted in this area.

Splitting the eggs expertly, she dropped them in, just in time to have them sizzle as they hit, their outer edges turning white in seconds.

"So, who were the children Emma didn't like?" her mother asked from across the kitchen.

Rebecca's face, flushed with the heat from the pan, kept its color, although she felt her strength draining away. *I can't lie,* flew like a dagger through her mind. *I'll just have to confess it later if I do, so I can't. Better to stick with the truth.* "One of the boys," she muttered, without turning around. She stabbed her spatula at one of the eggs, nearly splitting the yolk.

Her mother laughed. "That makes sense. Old Emma probably had it in for the male species. Never being married. Want and desire. It works that way sometimes."

Rebecca would have spoken up in Emma's defense even risking her own hurt, but she couldn't.

Her mother laughed again. "Nobody could ever explain why Emma never married. She was good looking enough. Came from a good family. There really was no reason anyone could see. I suppose she had offers. At least you would think so."

Rebecca paid total attention to the eggs in the pan, flipping the first one out and onto the waiting plate. It made a soft slapping sound on landing, its yolk gently vibrating as a properly done Amish fried egg should.

"There were rumors once," her mother continued, "that she might have been seeing a Mennonite boy. Must have been when she was around eighteen. My! It's been so long ago, I can't remember exactly. No one could ever prove it. She was already a church member. Her dating a Mennonite would have caused terrible problems, which of course it should have. Maybe her heart was broken," Mattie mused.

Rebecca found her voice. "You're just imagining things, Mother. That's just gossip."

"Probably," her mother allowed. "A person just thinks about it at times."

"Emma was a good person," Rebecca replied, bringing the last egg out of the pan.

The front door swung open, the noise and blast of cold air startling her. Her hand jerked and made the egg slip off the spatula and slide across the floor.

"Now you've made dog food out of a good egg," her mother lamented. "We're not like the English. They feed their pets out of cans."

Rebecca drew in her breath sharply and knelt down on the floor to gather up the ruined egg. Getting to her feet again, she dumped it into the slop bucket. "I'm sorry," she said.

"Well, if you ever have a mind to marry that John, be more careful," her mother said. "Young couples have a hard enough time. Starting up and all. Wasting even an egg can be hard."

"I know," Rebecca muttered, not because it was true, but because she wished she could tell her mother that a greater danger than broken eggs lay between her and a marriage to John.

She suddenly wanted to reach out, as if for air, to tell her mother real good and loud that she was engaged since yesterday to John, that the wedding was planned for next spring. To tell her about the wonderful time at the bridge yesterday. To tell her how John looked at her, how he had held her hand...but she could not.

Rebecca came out of her thoughts to find her mother staring at her. "Now, now, it wasn't that bad. It's an egg. I didn't mean to be that hard on you," her mother said. "I'm sure John will understand a broken egg now and then. He probably has enough money to cover that, but you certainly shouldn't be thinking about that as a reason to be marrying him."

"I wasn't," Rebecca said, returning to her troubled thoughts.

"Pancakes!" Lester's voice boomed with good cheer at the kitchen door. Having put his chore coat and boots away in the basement, he had come up silently on them. "What a treat. Now if we just had maple syrup, things would be perfect."

"We *have* maple syrup," Mattie said, making a face at him. "You don't think I would forget. I always keep some around for you."

"Well, times are hard," he grinned. "You never know." Catching sight of Rebecca's face, he paused. "What's wrong with her?"

"You startled her when you came in. She just lost an egg to the dogs. I made things worse. Told her that John couldn't afford a wife who lost too many eggs. What an awful thing to say to a young girl in love. I should have my mouth taped shut at times. Now come, Rebecca. It's really nothing at all. It's just an egg."

Rebecca nodded numbly, as if it was the egg that troubled her.

"Ya," Lester allowed, "one egg more or less. It won't matter."

"Why aren't the children here?" Mattie asked. "Breakfast is ready."

"I forgot to call them," Rebecca said, sorry to have made yet another mistake.

"Well, that's easy enough," Lester said, moving toward the stair door quickly. He hollered up the stairs, a full bellow, full of hunger for pancakes, "Breakfast, children. Now!"

There was an instant response. The sound of covers being pulled from creaky beds and feet hitting the floor was followed a little later by a patter on the stairs. Each child slid into his or her seat, and the table was quickly lined with five sleepy-eyed children, hungry for the pancakes set before them.

"Let's pray now before we all starve. Shall we?" Lester said, as the children bowed their heads in silence. Then after the "Amen," there were no sounds except those made by a hungry family at the breakfast table.

Mattie brought up the first conversation, after pulling the last pancake onto her plate. She announced quite suddenly, "Aunt Leona is having her baby, probably next week. She's asked for Rebecca to help out. What do you think, Lester?"

"When would she need to go?" Lester asked, turning options over in his mind.

"There's a load coming through on the way to Milroy. Saturday, I think," Mattie said. "That might be a good time to catch a ride."

"Who's going to Milroy?" Lester asked. "On Sunday, people were just here from there."

"No, this is a load from Holmes County," Mattie said. "They want to be here by Wednesday, then travel out on Saturday morning. Older people. They have relatives here and in Milroy."

Lester nodded in understanding.

Rebecca finally found her voice, grasping the implications of her mother's words. "But what about the chores around here? And I'd have to tell John. Why didn't you say something sooner?"

"That's because I didn't know. I only made my mind up this morning," Mattie replied. "Leona has been after me about this, but I figured there would always be local help. Then I just got a letter from her on Saturday, saying that there have been two other births in the area, and two more are expected right soon. There does seem to be a real need. I'll mail a letter this morning, telling her that you are coming, if that's okay with you, Lester. I think it would be good for you to go, Rebecca. Matthew can take care of your chores. If not, I can fill in."

"Fine with me," Lester said, shrugging his shoulders. This was women's business, and he would only get so involved, and this was his limit.

"Good, then it's decided," Mattie said. "You can tell John at a youth gathering this week, and I'm sure he'll understand."

"But..." Rebecca started to say something, but her mother interrupted.

"You'll find a way. John will understand. It's only for a week or so."

Rebecca nodded, knowing John probably *would* understand, but what she really wished he would understand had nothing to do with Leona's baby.

Chapter Nine

Rachel Byler stood by the kitchen window, washing the dishes. The suds rose on the water, stirred by her vigorous hand movements. And in her mind, thoughts were rising to the surface too, not yet forming a solid plan of action.

She needed to speak with Luke. She had thought that after breakfast there would be a chance, but with the snowstorm, Reuben had wanted Luke to scrape the driveway.

They were out in the driveway now, Reuben driving the steel-rimmed tractor with a drag attached by a chain. Luke followed, shoveling the trail of snow left on either side of the drag farther off to the side of the driveway. His shoulders were humped over, as his arms rose and fell with the swing of the shovel. Snowflakes, big, round, and heavy, swirled around the tractor and the shoulders of the two men.

Anger rose up in Rachel as she watched them make the circuit—up to the barn, turn around, and back down the driveway. Visions of what some of the other local Amish farmers were no doubt using this morning flashed in her mind. Bishop Mose himself, his oldest son-in-law in charge of his farm, had a well-used, though still smart-looking, New Holland front-end loader on the place. Seated in such a contraption, a man could clean out a driveway in mere minutes. Such a machine would leave straight lines behind him in the snow and eliminate the need for hand shoveling. But that took money, which they did not have.

Rachel sighed, forcing her eyes away. It would just have to be the way it was for now, but by God's help and her own willingness to help Him, that would all change.

Luke would be going to work as Emma's hired hand later in the morning. Rachel knew she shouldn't dislike Emma so much—after all, they certainly could use the money Emma paid Luke, which was more than the usual going rate for hired help on farms. Yet even so, Rachel couldn't get past the fact that Emma was living on the farm that should have been hers. Even the money Luke was paid might have been from her father's wealth.

They, not Emma, should be living on that farm. Reuben and Luke should be running it. She belonged inside, cooking and taking care of the house. That beautiful house, with its fireplace in the bedroom, was really hers. And Luke ought to be looking forward to owning the place some day instead of working as a hired hand.

She looked back at Reuben and Luke, now making their last round with the tractor, then disappearing into the barn with snow swirling around them. Moments later, Luke reappeared by himself, heading for the house. Reuben was nowhere in sight.

Good, she thought, *he's coming in to get ready to go to Emma's. Reuben won't be in right away.*

When Luke opened the utility room door and stamped the snow off his boots, Rachel stuck her head and asked, "You going to Emma's?"

"Yes," he replied, not looking up.

"I want to talk to you first."

"How long will it take?" he asked, opening his coat, half taking it off. "With this snow, Emma will be expecting me to check on the cattle right away."

"This won't take long," she said.

He finished taking his coat off, dropping it on the utility room floor. "So what do you want?" he asked, stepping inside and onto the rug.

"Sit down," she said.

"Then I have to take my boots off," he protested. "I don't have time."

"Look," she said sternly, "you have time for this. It involves your future."

Luke pulled his boots off and crossed the kitchen floor to take a chair. He waited there impatiently.

"You know the story of how my father left his estate to Emma? All of it," she began.

"Of course," he said. "Everyone knows that."

"I think she's getting ready to do the same thing," she told him flatly.

"To us?" His face brightened.

"No! To someone else."

"Has she told you?" he asked.

"No! Of course not!" she snapped. "I wouldn't be talking to you if she had. I think she's doing the same thing my father did. She will cut us out…again."

He raised his eyebrows.

"Do you remember telling me that a strange car was at Emma's house the other day?"

He nodded. "I couldn't see much from the back field, but the gray car was parked in front of the house for at least an hour."

"I think she's talking to a lawyer," she said solemnly.

"Emma wouldn't need a lawyer," Luke said. "Surely she's leaving the money to us. Who else would she leave it to?"

"I don't know," Rachel said. "But before Dad died, he talked to a lawyer too. We found that out afterward. We didn't know what to look for then. Maybe we would have noticed. Now," she paused to look at him and then continued, "we know what to look for. There's no reason to miss the signs."

"So what am I supposed to do about it?" Luke muttered, not convinced. "Ask her who it was? I don't think she likes me all that well."

"Don't say that," she told him. "Don't even think it. Of course she likes you. You're family. She pays you well. For now, just keep your eyes open. If something comes up in a conversation, try to ask questions without sounding suspicious. Find out what you can about who's visiting her."

"I can try," he said, unpersuaded.

"You have to," she told him. "It's our only chance for good information. There's no use in me asking her anything. She's not going to tell me. If Emma *is* contacting a lawyer, it can only mean one thing."

"So what are you going to do about it?"

"I don't know." She turned to look out the kitchen window, catching sight of Reuben heading toward the house. "Depending what her plans are, maybe we can go to Bishop Mose."

"Like he's going to meddle in a family matter," Luke said.

"If it's bad enough, he will." She glanced out the kitchen window again. "Your dad is coming in. You'd better go."

"How much money is involved?" Luke asked, as he walked toward the utility room in his stocking feet, stopping at the rug for his boots.

"An awful lot," she said.

His face gleamed as he reached for his boots. "That and some farms?"

"Yes," she said. "Now you see why I'm worried?"

He just grunted without looking at her, pulling on his boots. When his father opened the door, his coat was already on.

"Leaving for Emma's?" Reuben asked.

"Yeah," he muttered, without looking up. "I'm a little late."

"Well, our driveway needed to be done," his father said. "The work at Emma's could wait."

"I suppose so," he allowed. "It's just that there's feed to put out. Then I need to make sure the cattle can get under shelter and out of the weather."

"Has she got enough room for all the cattle inside?" Reuben asked, not remembering Emma's layout exactly.

Of course she does, Rachel thought bitterly, *with all that money.*

"With the shelters in the fields, there's enough," Luke said.

"How many cattle are on the home farm?" his father wanted to know.

"Over two hundred head," Luke replied. "The other farms—I don't know."

"She's got a lot of money," Reuben chuckled. "No wonder your mother wanted some of it. Seems like there should have been enough to go around. Include all the family. Ever wonder why old M-Jay didn't leave your mother her share?"

"Maybe he didn't like us," Luke said.

"I doubt if that's the reason," Reuben said. "M-Jay was a strange fellow. Good church member though. Never gave us a bit of trouble. At least during the time I was deacon."

Rachel cleared her throat, suddenly desperate to steer this conversation in another direction. "You shouldn't be calling your father-in-law strange," she said. "You married his daughter. Remember?"

"That I did," he acknowledged. "It was a good choice. Still a good choice."

Luke opened the door to leave. "I'll be back at the regular time," he said over his shoulder.

Moments later his buggy went out the semi-plowed driveway, his horse shaking its head against the flurry of snowflakes.

Reuben settled down at the kitchen table and said, "Rachel, there's something I need to talk to you about."

Pulling a chair up to the opposite side of the table, she nervously sat down. "Yes," she said meekly.

"We have a problem in the barn," he said, without looking up from the kitchen table. "The black driving horse is down."

"Is it serious?" she asked.

"I don't know," he replied. "I should go down and call the vet. It can't get up in the stall."

"We just drove it yesterday," she said. "There was nothing wrong then."

"I know," he acknowledged. "Maybe it's nothing serious."

"So when are you calling the vet?" she asked him.

He sighed, his eyes still focused on the kitchen tabletop. "That's the problem."

"What?" she asked.

"Money. The checking account is empty," he said flatly.

"When is more coming in?" she asked.

"I took some cattle in to the sale barn last week. It'll be another week before we have the check."

"It's that bad then," she stated, more than asked, bitter feelings rising as they had so many other times when money was short. It brought her conversation with Luke to mind. "Maybe you should have been more concerned when my father left me with no money. If you had tried harder, the bishop might have been willing to do something with Emma."

He sighed deeply. "You know how I feel about that. Money isn't the answer to everything. Just something to cause family feuds over. We must leave money matters in God's hands."

Anger flooded through her. She bit her tongue. It would be no good to tell him what she thought—it would only complicate things.

"God will surely supply," Reuben concluded.

"It would be nice if He supplied us with something now, when we need it," she said, keeping her voice even.

"I'm sure He will," he replied. "We'll make it somehow."

She said nothing more as he put his coat and boots back on and headed out the door. But one thing was clear to her: Something would have to be done.

Chapter Ten

Luke kept his hat low on his head, even though the snow couldn't reach him inside the single-seated buggy. Although the roads were nearly impassable for automobiles, one did pass him, going slowly down the road near where he turned toward Emma's on South Base Road.

Ahead of him and on the left, he made out the entrance to the home farm—now Emma's farm—where he had gone as a child with his mother many times and where he now worked. The graveled driveway curled upward from the main road, cresting on a slight knoll three hundred yards in.

A large red bank barn flanked the white two-story house. Behind the house were two more barns and metal structures that were built while his grandfather was still living. Fences came up to within a hundred feet of the front yard, leaving its dozen or so large oak trees standing free. Like solitary sentinels in a clump, they stood beside each other. They had been there since Luke could remember.

He drove his buggy straight to the bank barn and parked under the overhang on the lower level before climbing out. Unhitching, he took the horse into the barn, tied it up, and ran over the list in his mind of what needed to be done that day. Emma would be expecting him to head straight to his duties. He supposed his mother's concerns would simply have to wait for whenever there was time for them.

After his horse was fed, he headed for the year-old New Holland front-end loader. He turned the key for the warm-up in preparation for starting, the display showing it needed nineteen seconds. While he waited, he got out and opened the sliding door in the direction of the driveway.

Behind him, his horse kicked vigorously on the side of the stanchion he had placed him into. "Quit it," Luke shouted. The horse was now well-fed, so there was no reason for unhappiness.

Sticking his head into the New Holland, the display told him the warm-up was done. He climbed in and turned the key. Almost new. Emma had told him last year to trade in the old New Holland at the equipment dealer in Rushville. He never mentioned such transactions at home, knowing how his mother would react. If he reported Emma's expenditures, the news always caused a severe pained look to cross his mother's face.

He doubted whether Emma wanted the driveway cleared before he looked at the cattle, so he headed toward the pastures, pushing snow out of his way as he went. Cattle met him at the gate behind the house, their heads dusted with snow. He shooed them away before opening the gate. After driving through, he hopped back out to shut the gate behind him. Heading to the nearest shelter where the hay was stored, he chased more cattle away.

Emma kept beef cattle on each of her three farms, preferring that to milking, which was the preference of most of the Amish farmers in the area. Luke's father was no exception, of which he was glad. Milking held no attraction for him.

"Less work," Emma had once told him, "yet it still brings in a nice income."

That it did, he supposed, if you had three farms. She paid him well enough though, and he was not about to complain. At Emma's other two farms, she maintained renters who took care of the cattle for a reduced rent.

Luke was aware that requests were periodically made to Emma to sell her farms, because she had told him. He also knew that she always refused, but she had never told him the reason for her refusals.

Opening the gates surrounding a long row of round hay bales, he then cut another notch back on their plastic coverings, picking up a bale with the forks and driving outside. The cattle paid scant attention to him as he dropped it beside the partly eaten bale that was already there. They were well-fed, these cattle, at Emma's insistence. This came as much from her principles as from a desire for fat cattle, he supposed. Too much hay allowed the cattle to trample it under their feet, but that bothered Emma less than cattle without hay at their beck and call.

An hour later, after checking two more pastures, he headed back toward the house and parked the New Holland in the front yard. Knocking on the back door, he waited.

"Come on in," Emma called, his signal to enter.

Emma was in the living room, seated at her little roll-top desk, a legal tablet open in front of her. This was how she appeared to him when he thought of her because she was often here when he came into the house, businesslike, perched at her desk. A gas lantern was lit and hung from a hook just behind the desk, even at this time of the day. The usual Amish frugality required that lights be turned off as soon as the sun came up, but Emma was different.

This morning he was struck again by her commanding figure. Her hair, done up in the usual Amish head covering, did little to dilute the effect of her presence.

She turned to him, her eyes characteristically serious, and said, "Good morning, Luke."

"Good morning," he replied, waiting just under the arched opening between the dining room and kitchen. Built by the English in the early 1930s, the house had features not normally seen in Amish homes, including the elaborate stone fireplaces in both the living room and the master bedroom. Not that Luke had been in the bedroom recently, but he remembered it from his childhood visits.

"Cattle looking okay?" she asked him, nodding her head toward the falling snowflakes drifting past the window.

"Okay," he answered, staying by the opening. "They don't seem to mind."

"Shelter and hay should keep them," she said, "unless the weather turns worse. Let me know if anything looks unusual. I'll want to go out myself and look."

He nodded.

She swung her chair around to face him, strands of gray hair from beneath the head covering hanging loose on her forehead. "I need this envelope dropped off at the post office today. Do you think you can run it into town on your way home? There's not much to do around here with the snow still coming down."

"Does it take special postage?" he asked.

"Yes," she said, "but that's not the reason I want you to drop it off. It needs to be mailed today. With the snow I doubt the mailman will make his rounds. I have extra stamps here and could take a guess at it, but if you're in town anyway, you could get the exact postage."

"Sure," he agreed, extending his hand to take the large brown envelope.

She gave it to him, along with five dollars. "That should cover postage. Have it sent first class."

He nodded again, closing his fingers around the envelope.

"Before you leave, I want you to clear the driveway," she said. "If it needs it again this afternoon, I'll do it myself."

That she was capable of it, he well knew and turned to leave. Then he remembered his mother's concerns and cleared his throat. "Was there trouble with the cattle prices the other day?"

She looked at him sharply. "Why do you ask that?"

"Oh," he said offhandedly, as if it were of no great matter, "it's just that I noticed a big car in front of the house last week."

"No," she said, "it had nothing to do with the cattle. The markets are good right now. We hope they stay so. Your father probably knows that too." She looked questioningly at him before continuing. "It was just someone I asked to come out."

"I see," he said.

"You'll see that the envelope gets right in," she reminded him, turning her chair back toward the desk again.

Knowing he was dismissed, he turned to leave. Walking out to his buggy, he placed the envelope on the front seat, shaking off the snow from the brown paper before setting it down.

It was then that the address caught his eye. Carefully he gave the envelope a half turn to get a better look. Reading out loud, he sounded out the words, "Bridgeway & Broadmount, Attorneys at Law, 1058 Bridge Street, Suite A, Anderson, Indiana."

For the first time, a twinge of fear ran up his spine. *Maybe Mom was right. But what could it mean? It was a lawyer's office alright, and Emma must have real business with them. Yes,* he told himself, the snow swirling around his head through the buggy door, *she no doubt did. Surely it was nothing serious.*

Then why go to Anderson for an attorney? There were good lawyers in Ridgeway and even one in Milroy. It would have to be left for his mother to figure out, he supposed. His job was to deliver the letter for Emma safely to the post office. That was what she paid him to do.

Then the thought occurred to him, *Open the envelope. See what's in it.*

I can't, he told himself, *it's not honest. Emma trusts me, and I won't break that.*

But what about what your mother wants? There might be money involved in it for you too, the voice whispered.

I don't know that, he told himself. The word "money" kept going through his head, an image of green bills slowly growing with each passing second. In moments he saw pockets full of it, then buildings full of it, money hanging out of the windows and doors.

He shook his head to make the vision go away. The falling snowflakes came back into focus, and he took a deep breath. "I have to clean the driveway," he told himself out loud, pushing the sight of the envelope from his mind and turning to move his eyes away from it.

He climbed down from the buggy and walked over to the New Holland, turned the key, waited for the warm-up to complete, and then finished turning the key. The machine roared to life, shutting out any thoughts of money and the envelope.

Chapter Eleven

After the breakfast dishes were cleaned up and the house was put in order for the day, Rebecca knew what she had to do. She headed upstairs to her room, shut the door, and turned the lock. There was no one home, but she wanted her privacy. She had to think this thing through. There simply had to be some way of coming to terms with the fear that had come upon her yesterday before John proposed.

Walking to the window, she drew the blind. For some reason the darkness of the room made her feel safer. Then she lay gently on the bed and began to think—and remember.

It had been no more than a schoolgirl crush. That's what she had decided it was. *Why then couldn't I just let it go? Surely Atlee wouldn't really expect me to keep my promise.* She had John now. She *loved* John.

Then it came to her. *It was the love for John that had brought back feelings I had thought I had forgotten—a schoolgirl's desires, first hopes, longings that Atlee had satisfied. Perhaps Atlee had been only a simple schoolgirl's first love, but those feelings had run deep. And now they were being replaced. My heart has become my enemy. Those feelings for Atlee must not remain while I love John.*

Looking at the ceiling, she remembered Atlee's face, the freckles on his chin, his utter joy in living. With him she too had found utter joy.

With John was she leaving that behind? Did she want to forsake Atlee's memory? No, she did not. And yet, for John she had to.

On impulse, Rebecca let her feet slide down the side of the bed until her knees hit the floor. It was then that the tears began. And the prayer.

Oh, God, she groaned, *You have to help me. I know I am an evil person, just like Your book says, but I wasn't trying to do anything wrong. I was just a child when I liked Atlee, but we were not meant for each other. Help me, please.*

She looked at the ceiling, imploring the heavens, but there was only silence. Outside a gust of wind hit the window, moving the drapes she had drawn. What if someone saw them drawn at this time of the day, knowing she was usually not in her room?

A fresh wave of fear swept over her. *Oh, please, God. You have to help me. I don't know what to do. Is loving a sin? I know I promised Atlee...but he's surely not coming back, and I can't destroy what I have with John for someone who is gone forever. Yet my heart doesn't want to let go.*

Swaying silently from side to side on her knees, she reached for her pillow to bury her face in. She continued praying, *I love John. I never have met anyone I liked more. It's different, though, than with Atlee. Is my promise to Atlee going to destroy that?*

Lifting her head and opening her eyes, she saw nothing but the white painted wall in front of her. Staring at it, her eyes lost their focus, and the wall became a door, a door that opened into her memories. She saw Atlee running in front of her, waving, his face lifted skyward in his joy at Rebecca's promise.

And there...over by the schoolhouse...another image...Emma standing by the door watching, shaking her head.

Then she saw herself, as if from a distance, follow Atlee. There was grass beneath her feet, its leathery softness between her toes. The trees along the road stood out, green branches bending down, reaching as if to hold her back, but she kept going.

Her body trembled at the memory. And then the wall became normal again. She let go of the pillow and clutched the sides of the bed. Beads of sweat misted her face.

"What can I do?" she asked aloud. *Why not just go and tell Mother first, and then tell John what happened? Tell them how I had felt about Atlee.*

Surely they would understand. Understand that it had been long ago and that feelings change. Yet deep down, she wondered if her feelings really *had* changed. And that made her afraid. The whole jumble of memories ran together in her head—Atlee, the school, Emma, the ring, and the bridge. And the promise.

Getting to her feet, Rebecca walked to the dresser and opened the third drawer. This might be a good place to start. With a glance first toward the door, she dug into the clothing. From underneath she pulled out the ring and held it up to the little light available in the room. She would have to tell John about the ring of course.

Even in the darkened room, the ring's one stone, set atop the gold circle, gave off deep colored light, as if it were alive and communicating Atlee's love down through the years.

She ran her finger gently over the stone, the smooth surface slid effortlessly beneath her touch. The wonder of it moved her deeply, just as it had the first time she saw it.

Was this what she was afraid of, to have this taken away from her? It was forbidden, she knew, at least to wear it. Turning the ring, its colors changed. She searched her mind for the answer and decided that no, it wasn't the ring. It wasn't the source of her fear.

Yes, it was beautiful and lovely, but even in Milroy, she hadn't thought of it much, other than to keep it hidden and in a safe place. It simply did not mean enough to be causing her this fear.

Was it what she had done then? Rebecca searched her memory, letting her mind run where it wanted to. The river came into focus. She saw more flashes of Emma in the schoolhouse and of Atlee, his face delighted at the sight of her.

Holding out his hand to motion for her to come, she saw herself walking beside him. School had been dismissed. The other kids had gone. Walking together was not unusual; after all, they lived in the same direction. He lived a little further down the road than she did.

Most of the time, both their brothers and sisters walked home with them, but at other times, they got to walk alone.

Then there were the Saturday afternoons they played together in the woods, at times wandering as far across the fields as the Moscow covered bridge that spanned the Flatrock River. Those times were rare, she remembered. Mother objected if she was gone too long, even on lazy Saturday afternoons after the work was done.

What was it she had with Atlee? Yes, it was a love they shared. Yet would love cause the way she felt now? There seemed no reason why it would, and yet it was there, springing up with renewed force.

"I can never love him anymore," she whispered. "He's gone. Keeping the promise won't do any good. It will just destroy what I have now."

Dear God, she prayed silently, *I don't know how to let go of something so beautiful that I felt back then. I don't know how to make myself want to. If loving him was something terrible to do, please forgive me. Just please make this fear go away. I love John and don't want anything to destroy our love. Please help me.*

Tears were in her eyes, and she reached up to wipe them away. The ring sparkled as it moved with her fingers. Walking to the window, she watched the snowflakes swirl by the glass.

Glancing at the ring again, she considered simply throwing it away. She could do it now. This very minute. If someone saw her, no one would think her strange to be walking in the snow. It would be most common and ordinary for her to be enjoying the weather fully. With the ring stuck firmly in her pocket, she could walk down to the little bridge and get rid of the thing forever.

Then she remembered that she was going to Milroy on Saturday. Maybe *that* was the answer. The Lord might already have His plan in place, working through her mother. Aunt Leona's place was right beside the Flatrock Amish School. Perhaps she could find peace and let go of the past at the very place where she had loved him. The idea burned in her. It was surely God's answer to her prayer.

It would be good to go back. To see the school. To see where she had made so many good memories. Perhaps in seeing the old again, the glow would lessen, and she could be where she ought to be, by John's side. Emma, no doubt, would no longer be teaching. She couldn't be by now. She would be too old. But the memories would be there.

To forever let go, a voice told her, *that is what you need to do, and there is where it can be done.*

Yes, she decided, *this might be the answer.*

In Milroy, among the roads and woods of her childhood, she could let go of a love that no longer fit her heart. A love that would shame and defile her if her dear ones were to ever find out. They must never find out, she resolved. It would hurt them too much, all for nothing and to no gain.

Taking the ring, she carefully placed it back under the pile of dresses in the third drawer.

"I promised," she whispered at it, "to keep you. So I will, but you must go away soon, and I will no longer be afraid of my heart."

She smiled to herself, pulling the stack of dresses over the ring, completing the task with one final dress, and spreading it as a thin layer over the top.

As she closed the drawer, everything just missed the top frame, sliding in smoothly. If her mother, by some chance opened this drawer, everything would seem to be like it was supposed to be. *Like my life,* she thought ruefully, opening the door to go downstairs.

Chapter Twelve

Luke pulled the New Holland out of Emma's driveway as snowflakes whirled around his head. The last thing he wanted to think about was that large, brown envelope lying on the seat of his buggy, yet, it was the very thought he couldn't get away from.

What am I supposed to do with it? he thought to himself, slowing as he came to the main road. Carefully he turned left, then right with his bucket lowered to push all the snow into the ditches. Emma would want things looking neat even in a snowstorm.

Behind him, the flakes were already landing again, quickly piling on top of each other. Luke, in backing away from the road, crunched his tire into the white snowdrift.

"What am I supposed to do?" he asked again, this time out loud.

Just mail it, was the thought that came to mind most readily. He wondered why he didn't just do that. He liked Emma. Liked her a lot, in fact. She had always been good to him. Paid him on time, even a little extra on the side sometimes. "Don't tell anyone," she would say, handing him a twenty or even two of them at a time. Her smile was communication enough, as if she were his fellow conspirator. Both of them knew that until he was twenty-one, all the money he was paid was supposed to go home.

He had felt a little guilty about not mentioning the extra money, but Emma surely knew what was right. The extra she gave him was all stored away in his savings bank—in a tin can in the haymow under the last bale on the side away from the house.

The money was wrapped in plastic, although the tin can had

seemed protection enough. What he really was concerned about was his mother finding out. He doubted very much if she would approve of Emma giving him money to keep on his own. Only if it added to the general household fund, would it be okay. This way it most certainly was not and would likely meet with her disapproval.

A savings account at the bank was out of the question, though Luke vowed he would have one as soon as he turned twenty-one. The money in the tin can would be the opening deposit. Neither his mother nor his father ever need know how much he placed in the first deposit. *Anyone knew,* he had told himself many times, *that savings accounts could be opened with one dollar, if one wished.* It would then remain his secret whether he opened his account with just a few dollars or with many.

So the tin can's contents came from Emma, secret money stashed away like a pirate stashes his gold in a cave. The thought reminded him of the book on pirates in the school library he had once read. That particular book had lasted only part of one school year. From what he remembered, Emma had brought it in, and most of the boys had passed it around to each other with rave reviews.

Maybe that was why the head of the school board, Herb Mullet, made a surprise visit one afternoon on the pretense of seeing how things were going. Where he spent most of his time, though, was in the library. The long and short of it was that when Herb left that afternoon just before school closed, with several books under his arm, the pirate book must have been among them because it was never seen again.

So now his heart was really for Emma in this matter of the envelope. She always seemed to know what she was doing, and if it really was true that Emma might be giving away all of this to someone other than family, might there be reason for it?

Turning the New Holland around to head back toward the house, he pulled back on the twin levers to bring it to a halt. He sat looking at what lay before him—the old homestead, its white two-story house muted in the falling snow, and the red barn, its colors deepened from the same effect. This was what was at stake or at least part of what was at stake.

Did he really want to lose this? Not that he had ever really thought of it like this before, his thoughts on money usually rose no higher than the contents of his tin can. That seemed like gobs of money already. He was not totally certain, but at the last count, there had been over five hundred dollars. Even that amount made him stagger.

But this, he shook the snowflakes from his eyes, was really another matter. His mind raced to fit it into a thought he could handle. The farms Emma owned could hardly fit into tin cans. Yet if they could? His mind spun. There must be thousands and thousands of dollars involved. Maybe he ought to reconsider his feelings for Emma if he was about to lose something this big.

Would Emma actually give the farms away to some unknown person and not to him and the rest of the family? He found it hard to imagine. From what his mother said, the money should by all rights go to the family. Would not the Emma he knew, who snuck him money on the side, money she felt he deserved, do the right thing?

Yes, she would. He would stick with Emma for now. This lawyer stuff his mother was worrying about could or could not be true. He would deal with all that later. He would inform his mother about the envelope, but for now he would not open anything belonging to Emma.

If he were to open the envelope, and it should ever come back to Emma, the amount in the little tin can in the haymow might not continue growing, and that would simply be too great a tragedy to chance. The decision then was firmly set.

Roaring the New Holland to full throttle, he headed back up the driveway. Coming to the barn, he parked inside and walked back out to the fence for one last look at the cattle.

If Emma was watching from the house window, she would be impressed with his concern. If she was not, then these were really his cattle, one way or the other, he figured. He smiled to himself. They really were his, either by the way of his tin can or somehow through the family. Once transferred to the Byler family at Emma's passing, his mother would see to it that they came to him, he felt certain.

A feeling of contentment and warmth flowed through him, even with the snow falling. Life seemed certain and spelled out now. Poverty was something he would never have to face. Others may fear it, but it would never touch him. He was the relative of a rich Amish woman who was already making him richer than most boys his age, and now his mother was sure to see to it that things got even better. Life was looking real good.

Amish life was the life he wanted—to be, to live, to marry, to have children, and to grow old in the faith.

He stopped as the thought crossed his mind. *Wasn't it about time to think about marrying? Yes, to marry.* His pulse quickened. *But to whom? Certainly not someone like that Rebecca Keim,* he thought. *How could Mother even have mentioned such a thing? No, I want someone quite unlike that, someone comfortable, lowly, able to live where I live, without the flash of such a high-class life that Rebecca gives off.*

She always had been like that, even in school, always too good for some people. *Emma had liked her though.* He frowned at the thought, then allowed that even Emma had her faults. At least Emma had been right about someone else Rebecca always hung around with. He searched his mind for a name, but came up with none. Anyway, Emma hadn't liked the fellow who had often been seen with Rebecca, probably sweet on her. Rumor was he went Mennonite eventually, or at least his parents did.

Still, Luke had never liked him. There was just something about him. Maybe it was the good grades both he and Rebecca were always getting. They had the gall to actually frown when they *only* achieved a ninety-five percent on a test, something that would have made his own face nearly split with a grin.

Yes, it was surely time that he think about girls and marriage.

Girls. He laughed into the snowflakes, blowing one off his nose. Then it suddenly occurred to him what he should do. He was seeing it clearly now.

He was beginning to feel what he had been seeing in Susie Burkholder's eyes. He even blushed out there in the snow, as he let the thoughts of her drift through his mind. Now that they started, it was hard to stop them, even if he had wanted to. The way her hair stuck out from under her head covering. Her hands, her nails cut short, but never showing signs of being chewed. He liked that in a girl. It showed signs of stability instead of a nervous temperament.

Now, with some money stashed away and a farm coming his way, it was high time to make his move. Surprised at how much he already knew about what he wanted, he let his mind take another good look at Susie. Always before, he had ignored the look in her eyes, but now that he allowed himself to consider it, he saw it all. She wanted him, wanted him badly. That she was a little plain didn't present much of a problem to him. Her eyes more than made up for it, the way they dropped just after he would finally look at her in the singings or at church.

No doubt she had long wanted me to ask her out. The thought warmed him. Why, yes, he would do it—he would indeed. He would ask her this very week, and by Sunday those eyes would be for him alone. Susie would be beside him in his buggy as he drove her home after the singing.

Shaking the snow from his coat with a shrug of his shoulders, Luke took one last glance at the cattle gathered in front of him and turned to leave.

"You don't know anything about love or money," he told them, as if they could understand. "Just chew your cuds and be quiet. I am now ready to take a girl home."

Chapter Thirteen

"Time to start the pies," Mattie's voice echoed up the stairs, startling Rebecca as she had just closed the drawer in her room, the ring now well-hidden.

Knowing that she needed to respond and concerned that her face might betray her, Rebecca opened the door but didn't show herself. "I'm coming right away," she said.

A measure of peace was in her heart now. The answers seemed to be coming, and the fear was fading away. "The Lord is helping me," she whispered.

"We need to start before lunch," her mother added, softer now that she could see that Rebecca's bedroom door was open. "Your dad wants some for supper, I'm sure."

There was silence at the bottom of the stairs after her mother's soft footsteps faded away on the hardwood floors. Rebecca knew she had only moments more before questions would start, if she did not come down the stairs.

Taking a deep breath, she prayed one last quick prayer. *Let this be the right thing, Lord. I don't want to be making more mistakes than I have already made. And please don't let me lose John.*

A calm came over her, and she thought again that the upcoming trip to Milroy must be God working things out through her mother and her aunt. In Milroy, she could walk the roads and the woods where she had been with Atlee and perhaps discover how to finally let this all go. Perhaps there her memories of first love would find their proper resting place, and she would bring her heart home, whole and new again.

Then she could finally throw the ring away. She could now only remember faintly where he had given it to her. Flashes of summer's woods went through her mind...sounds of water running...and of a bridge. *The Moscow covered bridge,* she thought.

Yes, that was it. The Moscow bridge. And then she remembered Atlee's hand holding it out to her. The ring. The first thing she had noticed about it was how it sparkled. Then she could hear him asking, "You will keep it, won't you? For me, please? I will come back for it and you..." She suddenly refused to finish the memory. She must get downstairs.

But her mind wouldn't let it go just yet. She remembered slowly taking the ring from his hand and saying, "Yes."

Taking another deep breath, she walked out the door and down the stairs to the kitchen. *I'll be okay,* she told herself. *John loves me, and I love him. Is that not enough?*

Her mother already had bowls spread out on the table. Two small ones and a larger one in front of them.

"Can you get the flour?" her mother asked, with a glance at her.

Rebecca nodded, letting what she hoped was a smile play on her face. Walking to the pantry just off of the kitchen, she opened the large bag of flour. A smaller dipping bowl was already in the bag, and so she grasped the edge closest to her and sent the other end plunging deep into the soft flour.

Shaking the now heaping bowl over the bag, she lightly brushed the edges with her hand. A good Amish girl did not spill flour. Her mind still distracted and hoping she wouldn't spill any flour, Rebecca walked toward the kitchen table, where she would measure it into cup size measurements as it was needed.

"Don't fill it so full," her mother said, glancing at the amount she carried in the bowl. "It spills too much on the table."

Rebecca nodded.

"It's better to make two trips. With smaller amounts you don't have to spend so much time being careful," her mother said. She then added gently with an unspoken question in her voice, "You learned that years ago."

"I know," Rebecca said.

"Is something wrong?" her mother asked, catching a full look at Rebecca's face and placing both hands on her hips. "Is it something between you and John?"

Much as Rebecca had been dreading questions, the start of them was almost a relief. "No," she responded, feeling herself actually relaxing.

Her mother was silent for awhile, then said, "You and John have been together a lot. Has he talked marriage yet?"

"Yes," Rebecca told her, not wanting to go further than that. "It has come up."

"Oh," her mother smiled and continued, "that's good. John's such a nice boy. A good Amish church member. Family seems solid and all. How long have you two been dating? Time goes by so fast with us old people. It's probably much longer than I think."

"Some two years," Rebecca said. She walked over to the icebox to get the eggs.

"Well, that's plenty of time! You ought to have figured out by now what you think of him. Maybe even whether you'd want to marry him." Mattie glanced in Rebecca's direction. "I know that's such a big decision. Yet done in the Lord, it is always good." Mattie reached for the cup to measure the flour, glancing again at Rebecca's face. "Oh!" she exclaimed with a smile. "Maybe he has asked already."

Rebecca felt the redness spread across her face.

Her mother needed no words to confirm her suspicions. "That was what the visit to the bridge was all about yesterday. A right romantic fellow, John is. Asking the question the real English way, now did he?"

Rebecca still said nothing. There was no need to. Her mother might as well know, and figuring it out herself was just fine with Rebecca.

Mattie dipped the measuring cup into the flour and then looked at Rebecca. "Your daddy was that way too." She paused as if in astonishment herself. "I know you would never guess it. He lets on terrible like..." Mattie explained, waving her loose hand, "like there's nothing to it. But he was. Yes, he was. Stopped the buggy one night right soon after we left the singing. We had been seeing each other for about three years."

The second cup en route, Mattie paused. "All the other buggies had already broken off. Down other roads. Never thought of it like that, but your daddy had to have it all figured out. We were all by ourselves on one of those open bridges. You could hear the water running underneath us. Right there with his horse barely wanting to stand still, he asked me. Yes, he did," Mattie pronounced.

"Dad?" Rebecca said, totally surprised. "You say Dad did this?"

"Yes, that's how it went. He took my hand when I said 'yes' and squeezed it real hard, he did." Mattie quickly glanced up at Rebecca. "Now don't you be getting any ideas. That's *all* he did, mind you. A right proper young man he was. The Lord knows. I wished sometimes, especially in that buggy while riding beside him, that he wasn't. Yet, in the end I always knew what a good man he was."

"Yes, I can see that he is," was all Rebecca could think to say, thoughts of John flashing through her mind.

"John's right proper too, I suppose. You two are behaving yourselves?" Mattie questioned, looking her full in the face.

"Yes, Mother!" Rebecca answered, a little exasperated. "Dad already asked me that this morning. What do you think I am?"

"You are a *good* girl," Mattie allowed. "It's just that we're all weak in the flesh. That's a fact, now. We need to have someone watching over us at times. I thank God we did as well as we did. Our parents were concerned. I wondered sometimes why Mother didn't ask more questions than she did. It's such a hard time in life. I suppose that's why I'm asking now."

"Yes, it is a hard time," Rebecca said with emotion, content in knowing her mother wouldn't fully understand exactly why she thought so.

"It will all come to an end," Mattie intoned. "Soon enough you are married. Then there's nothing in the way. It is a right good time, it is. Even after all these years. It was well worth waiting for. Made even sweeter, I think, by the waiting. God must be honored in all His ways. Especially on this thing. It's too powerful to get wrong."

"I know," Rebecca said, cracking a third egg into one of the smaller bowls. "We will do our best. We want to walk in a way that is right and holy."

"That's good to hear," Mattie said. "We must always be on watch. One never knows when the devil might throw something in our way. Trips us right up."

"That's for sure," Rebecca replied, wrinkling her forehead.

"Ah! It's already hard then," Mattie replied, sighing at her daughter's reaction. "You will make it though. God will help you." Then after a moment's pause, she admitted, "You had me so worried." And Mattie poured the last cup of flour into the large bowl.

"I already told you. We are behaving ourselves," Rebecca responded, irritation in her voice. "Are you ready to have the eggs beaten?"

"Yes," Mattie said. "It's not that though. I was talking about something else. It's when you were going to school in Milroy."

"To school?" Rebecca managed in what she hoped was a normal voice. A chill was creeping up her spine.

"Ya. That Atlee fellow you used to spend so much time with," her mother said.

The chill increased. *What did she know about Atlee? Did Mother know how much she had liked him? She must have.*

"What about Atlee?" Rebecca asked, as casually as possible.

Her mother gave her a strange look and said, "You should know. You were the one always walking home with him from school. It seemed innocent enough, you know. The schoolgirl crush we all have had. You were young though," she quickly added.

"So why were you worried?" Rebecca asked. She was ready to start beating the eggs but stopped to hear her mother's response.

"It was always you and Atlee this—you and Atlee that. You were even with him sometimes on Saturdays." A look of worry crossed Mattie's face, but she said nothing more except, "Beat those eggs. I need them right away. I'll start melting the butter."

Rebecca nodded, laying her shoulder into whipping the eggs. As the racket of metal hitting metal filled the room, the yellow and white mixture quickly blended, and there was no more distinguishing between the two. Her mother, in the meantime, turned on the gas burner on the stove and dropped a bar of butter into the pan. It turned golden brown and slowly spread across the bottom.

With the eggs whipped, Rebecca left the bowl on the kitchen table and switched places with her mother. Mattie dumped the eggs into the flour, stirred them gently, cleared her throat, and jumped back to the unfinished conversation. "I never did worry about that, you know."

"What did you worry about then?" Rebecca asked.

"After his parents went Mennonite. He didn't stay on at the school for the rest of the year. I sure hoped you didn't have your heart too set on him. He was a nice boy and all. But *Mennonite.* That's another matter, I would say! I'm just so glad that you are getting a good Amish boy in John Miller."

"I am too," Rebecca said truthfully. Not just because he was Amish, but because she knew she loved him.

Chapter Fourteen

With a last look at Emma's house from the end of the driveway, Luke slapped the reins and headed down the road. His horse's hooves, once they hit the blacktop, made a hollow noise in the snow, muffled and deep.

Money. He breathed the smell of it in deeply, becoming fully aware of the existence of vast quantities of the stuff and what it could mean in relation to himself.

That it should even make a difference in love, he had never supposed possible. Yet, there it was, the realization that now he would get to enjoy Susie as his girlfriend all because he would be sure that money came his way...one way or another.

But it would take more than what was contained in his tin can under the hay bale. Although, he supposed, even his savings would have been sufficient eventually. It just might have taken him longer to get there.

Now though, things were suddenly and swiftly different, possibly coming much sooner than he had imagined. This very Sunday Susie Burkholder might very well be riding beside him after the singing. That look in her eyes would be his to enjoy. He would call her his own—his girl.

This did put things in quite a different light. Maybe money was more important than he had ever supposed. His father said that it wasn't important, and Luke had always leaned in that direction himself. The advice was, after all, coming from a deacon of the church and his father. Thus it ought to bear quite a bit of weight.

Now though, he had seen with his own eyes, felt with his own heart, some of the things that money could do. It had brought the idea of love to him, the love of a girl who wanted him. He was sure he would not have entertained the notion if it were not for the presence of money. Plenty of it, he reminded himself.

Too much money, his father often warned, was dangerous. Well, this must not be too much yet because it was causing good things for him. He let the memory of Susie's eyes run all the way through him. How would it be to have her beside him in his own buggy? He wasn't sure, but his mind enjoyed trying to get a firm hold on it.

"Susie," he said the name softly, as his horse's hooves hit the blacktop, pounding away in the snow. Why had he never fully noticed how beautiful her name sounded before? That was because of the money too, he reasoned. *How strange,* he thought, but that was what had happened.

Yet fear pushed at him. If it was money that was responsible for his newfound notions, then maybe money could also take away one's happiness. Was that not possible? He clutched himself with both arms, nearly jerking on the reins in the process.

He pushed the thought away, afraid it might be true and decided that for now he would have to play it safe. He would take the package to the post office and buy the proper postage. That way, wherever this package was going to, Emma would receive no inquiries as to why it had been opened en route.

I could take it home and let Mother open it. She could get it back together without anyone being able to tell. Startled at the thought, he considered this for a moment. That would be a way to cover both of his bases, and he might come out the best in the end.

Just when he was at the point of turning east on 900 instead of west toward Milroy, he remembered Emma. Could he really betray her trust? Was it fair after all she had done for him? After she was responsible for his little savings account in the haymow?

No, he would not betray her. Tomorrow he would need to go back to work for her, and with this on his conscience, it would just be too hard. *No, Mother would have to find some other way around this problem. I will not open the envelope or take it to Mother.*

Pulling on the reins, he turned left, then right on 100. Ten minutes later he was at a stop sign with the buildings of Milroy within his sight. Waiting for two cars to pass, he slapped the reins and pulled out onto the state road, hugging the right shoulder—driving half on and half off of it to make more room for passing vehicles.

The state road was always dangerous, and in snow like this, it was extra precarious. He considered turning on his flashers, but that would use up battery power. Instead, he would just keep his eyes open, and when headlights lit up his rear mirror, he would turn the flashers on for a short time.

But no headlights appeared until he was in the center of town, and by then the cars had to slow down anyway, so he left his flashers off. When Luke reached the post office, another buggy was already tied to the hitching post, so he pulled up beside it.

After climbing out, he tethered his horse, picked up the envelope from the passenger seat, and headed up the walk. With so many Amish in the area, he gave no thought of who might be inside until he swung open the post office door and saw her.

Susie was standing beside the counter with her mother, while a package was being weighed by the clerk. Turning, she saw him and quickly lowered her eyes. He thought for sure she would keep them there, but she must have caught something in his face because she looked up again.

He smiled at her. A smile he meant to convey meaning. This was his day. The Lord Himself must be smiling from the heavens for so many things to be going in his direction.

Susie blushed, the first time he had ever seen her do that. It made him feel like a man—like an important person. It was a feeling he liked very much. Stepping up to get in line, he held the envelope in front of him, still looking at her blushing face now turned away from him.

Her mother, a stout short woman whose brown hair showed no signs of gray yet, turned around, apparently sensing his presence. "Hello, Luke," she said with a smile. "We weren't expecting to see you."

"No," he allowed, "I wasn't planning on coming into town, but Emma wanted this envelope dropped off. She was afraid the mailman wouldn't be making his rounds, what with the snow and all."

"Must be important," Nancy said, "to have to be mailed today."

"I suppose so," he told her, keeping the address covered with his arm. It was none of Nancy's business whom Emma was writing to, and he would keep it that way.

He felt a great boldness come over him, and he wondered if all people with money felt like this. He looked in Susie's direction, meeting her eyes, now turned toward him fully.

"Can I speak with Susie? Outside maybe?" he asked Nancy.

Nancy raised her eyebrows. "I suppose. The clerk isn't done checking this in. Go on," she replied and motioned to Susie.

As if frozen to the spot, Susie made efforts to become unthawed, her body moving slowly. Luke noticed it, his heart skipping a beat. He had never known that a girl could be so attractive. "We'll be just a moment," he said to her mother.

She nodded as if she understood.

Luke led the way, and Susie, finally thawed, followed. After they had walked a few feet outside, he stopped. Glancing ahead, he saw that no one was coming up the sidewalk, which was just perfect. It was as perfect as this day had started out to be, like the Lord God Himself was truly in it.

Susie was looking at him, questions in her eyes. He cleared his throat, a little nervous after all. "Can I take you home from the singing this Sunday?" he asked.

He felt like lowering his gaze as her cheeks distinctly gained color right in front of him. Her lips moved and her hand came up to her mouth. "Me?" she finally got out.

"Yes," he said, feeling calmer, "I want to take you home. Will you?"

"Oh, yes!" she gushed, her tongue becoming unloosed too quickly, too suddenly. Then she remembered she was an Amish girl. "I mean... yes...if Mother doesn't object."

"Do you have to ask her?" Luke asked.

"Well, no. Not really," she said. "It's just that I'm so surprised."

"Okay...well, it's a date? I'll see you then." He smiled at her again. "You know what my buggy looks like, don't you?"

"Of course." She was sorely flustered. "I mean. I can find it."

"Sunday night," he told her, raising his eyebrows, "after the singing."

He turned to go back into the post office. As he turned his back and left her standing there on the sidewalk, Nancy was just coming out, and he held the door for her.

"Have a good day," he told her in passing.

"And you," she responded, wondering what had transpired until she looked at her daughter's face. "He asked you," she stated more than asked.

"Oh, *Mother,*" Susie whispered in awe, "can you believe it? I have wanted this for so very long. I was beginning to think it would never happen."

"Just control yourself," her mother said. "You have a long ways to go yet. This is just the first date. Trouble and love go hand in hand it seems. You just remember that."

"But he *asked* me!" Susie placed her hand on her heart. "I can't believe it."

Nancy muttered something, which Susie was hardly listening to anyway. Luke watched them climb into the buggy, a smile on his face. So this was how it felt to be a man.

"Can I help you?" the clerk asked him, as if her voice was coming from a distance.

"Ah, yes." He brought himself back sharply. "I need to mail this envelope. First class."

Taking the brown envelope, the clerk carefully weighed it. "That will be four dollars and fifty cents."

Luke fished in his pocket for the money, gave her the five dollars, and took the change. Emma would be expecting the fifty cents and a record of the transaction tomorrow, so he took the receipt and carefully placed it in his billfold. She liked things done that way, proper and in order.

Chapter Fifteen

"There! That's done." Rebecca breathed a sigh of relief, turning off the gas oven. On the counter beside the window sat the six pecan pies, cooling and looking like inviting faces turned upward toward the world.

"Why did we make so many?" Mattie asked.

"It's the way it turned out," Rebecca told her. "You had a little extra dough, I think."

"Ach! Lester can eat two himself," Mattie said, justifying the matter.

"He has better sense than that," Rebecca replied, confident in her father's good judgment. "I suppose they can always be put to good use somewhere."

Mattie chuckled. "How true." She glanced toward the kitchen door. "I know what we can do with one. Take one and run it across the road to Edna's. She doesn't get out much, what with her arthritis and all. I'm sure she can use it."

"But I have to help chore. It's almost time for that."

"I know. Go anyway. You'll be back. If not quite in time, Matthew can help. He needs all the practice he can get, with you leaving on Saturday. Here, throw this to the chickens on the way out."

Rebecca reached for the slop bucket after the pecan pie had been carefully placed in the plastic holder. Slipping on her heavy coat and boots, she stepped outside. Setting the pie holder gently on the ground, she used both hands to upend the slop bucket and pour its contents inside the wire chicken enclosure.

The chickens tried to dodge the falling pastries, then pranced back to greedily peck them from the ground. A few ended up with pastries on their backs and getting pecked, their indignant squawks adding a discordant sound to the beat of beaks on frozen ground.

Rebecca looked grimly at the ruckus, leaving the slop bucket set on the ground. The main road was already plowed when she got there, so it was an easy matter to walk the few hundred feet west to Edna's driveway. The driveway had not been plowed yet, and Rebecca sunk into the snow. Her father, who normally cleared Edna's driveway, must not have gotten to it yet.

Knocking on the door, Edna answered immediately, her smile radiant. "Oh my, I saw you coming, and I was sure you would never make it in all that snow," she exclaimed, her black shawl wrapped tightly around her shoulders. Still spry at seventy, Edna's white hair was tucked tightly under her head covering, her shoulders stooped.

"Dad didn't get to the driveway yet," Rebecca commented, answering her smile.

"Yes. He has so many things to do. Harold would do it when he comes for chores. Though with only a shovel, it's a little too much."

"Dad's glad to do it," Rebecca assured her. "We'd even do your chores at times, if Harold can't make it."

"Oh, it's all too much to ask," Edna told her. "There aren't that many chores anyway. Harold just sees that the horse and cow are fed. I half think I could still do them myself except on snowy days like this."

"If you need help some Sunday morning, do let us know," Rebecca told her.

"Ach! That's not necessary yet. Your mother send something over?"

"A pecan pie," Rebecca said, lifting the lid so Edna could take a peek.

"Oh my! A pecan pie," she proclaimed. "The Lord must have made those the very first day He worked, to help Himself along the rest of the week."

"You think so?" Rebecca chuckled, used to Edna's ventures into theology.

"Well! You never know," Edna allowed. "They are sure good. Did you make them today?"

"Just out of the oven," Rebecca told her. "Mom didn't have time on Saturday to make enough for all week. We had to catch up today."

"Yes. That's how it used to be," Edna said, a faraway look in her eyes.

Rebecca ventured, "Mom thought maybe you could use the pie for your visitors this week."

"Well! I guess I could," Edna allowed. "I suppose they won't think I can't do my own work anymore. It certainly would help out."

"Mom wants me to go to Leona's this Saturday."

"Oh! A baby?" Edna guessed.

"Yes. It's due next week. The latter part, I think."

"How are you going?"

"Mom said there's a load coming through from Holmes County. They're going on out to Milroy Saturday morning. It might be the same people you are getting."

"Yes, it could be." Edna's face brightened. "My brother Mose is along. Wants to come out and visit. He and his wife Elsie. Then they go on to our sister in Milroy."

"Who are the others?" Rebecca wanted to know.

"I'm not sure," Edna said. "Mose got up the load. So probably folks with relatives or connections in both places."

"Well," Rebecca drew in her breath and said, "I must be going. It's already past choring time."

"Matthew helping out yet?" Edna asked, as they stepped toward the door.

"Just starting," Rebecca replied. "He'll get broken in next week when I'm gone."

"That's good," Edna said. "Learning to work must never be lost.

It keeps a man or woman close to their God. The young ones should learn that as soon as possible."

"It's hard sometimes, though."

"No one said it wasn't," Edna agreed. "Just necessary."

"It does seem so," Rebecca allowed, opening the door and stepping outside. "Enjoy the pecan pie."

"Yes. I will," Edna assured her. "Tell your mother thanks."

"Okay," Rebecca replied, walking quickly down the driveway and then up the hill. She picked up the slop bucket at the chicken coop and deposited it on the kitchen doorstep, not bothering to go inside. Then she headed out to the barn to milk, thinking that Matthew would be glad to see her coming.

Chapter Sixteen

Stepping out of the post office, Luke got into his buggy and headed home, his head full of happy thoughts. Always before, he had kept thoughts of girls at a distance. Now though, it felt like the floodgates had opened, the waters pushing hard downstream.

The snow was slowing. His horse flicked its ears to get the last flakes off, jerking its head down as far as the reining strap allowed to complete the job.

So he would finally be having a girl, other than his sister, in his buggy. *Nearly twenty,* he told himself in surprise, now that he thought of it. *I should have done this a long time ago.*

How old is Susie? he suddenly wondered. He did some calculations, concluding she was also twenty. *A few months younger though,* he added quickly. That was important to him. Older would not do. Vague images appeared in his mind—her wrinkled face—while his hair was still black, her walking with a cane while he was still throwing out the hay by hand.

He pushed those thoughts away. She was not older than he was. "So why is she not taken already?" he wondered out loud. "Twenty's old already for an Amish girl." Running his memory again, he recalled no time when he heard of her ever having had a date. *That's strange,* he thought. *I wonder why? Was she waiting for me?* He smiled at that thought, slapping the reins to get more speed on the back road.

He continued smiling to himself, letting thoughts run through his mind of Susie turning down wildly handsome prospects in her wait for him. No, that was hardly the reason. She was simply plain looking, he decided. That likely had as much to do with it as anything.

That thought didn't faze him as much as he supposed it should. *What good was a good-looking girl if she didn't like you? Not a lot,* he supposed. There was no sense in pursuing what couldn't be caught. Anyway, Susie suited him just fine. "As sweet as the morning's dew," he muttered, a phrase from somewhere he couldn't recall. Yes, that was what it was.

Then the same force that released him in Susie's direction now drove him past her. Pushing at him like a train on the tracks rolling across the open fields of Indiana, the thoughts came unbidden and forceful. *Wouldn't money make a big difference in the consideration of the type of girl I wanted?* He pondered the question, letting it drive him upright on the seat of the buggy.

He ran it through his mind. *Did money have anything to do with me asking Susie out?* The answer was "Yes." Without a doubt it had everything to do with where he was now. Could it then go even further? The more he thought about it, the more certain he became, and the more certain he became, the more the thought took a hold of him. *Why not get a beautiful girl, now that I have money, or the near certainty of it?*

Nervous at the very notion, he let the thoughts continue. Thoughts that were to him unholy and blasphemous ran unchecked through his mind. Ones he would never have gone close to before were like horses set free from the barn after a long hard winter, kicking their heels in excitement. Visions of girls, good-looking ones, their heads turning in his direction, smiling at him, self-consciously brushing their stray hairs back under their head coverings when he walked by, played in his mind.

Then fear struck as a strong feeling of unease gripped him, and he brushed his forehead with his gloved hand. What was he doing, thinking this stuff? Must God Himself not be angry, real angry with him?

Then another thought struck him like a blow to his chest. *What if Susie knew about the money?* The horror of the thought went all the way through him, but surely that was not possible. *How could Susie know I will come into money soon?*

Then he knew that it *was* very possible. She *could* know. She could know quite well. It was widely known that Emma had received all of the inheritance, her brother having left it all to her, and now her health very questionable. She could die soon, and everyone knew it. And certainly everyone, including Susie's family, knew Emma had three farms, free and clear. From there the conclusion any reasonable person could have was that when Emma died, she would be passing the farms and her money to immediate family.

So Susie might have been waiting for me because of this. His joy gone, he now stared blankly at the snow through his buggy's storm front. Feeling an ache in his back, he shifted on his seat.

"Confounded money," he said out loud. "A blessing and curse," he added, quoting something from memory but not sure from where. *Surely she doesn't know.* He stared at the snow again. *Then why had she been waiting so long?*

"Because she's plain," he shouted, causing his horse to jump, double its speed, and throw him back against the seat. Amusement hit him as he clutched the reins. *I am really being stupid, that's what I am. So what if she's seeing me for the money, which she probably isn't?*

He let the memory of her eyes at the post office return, and decided finally that she was not. The longer he thought on it, the more sure he became.

But she was *plain.*

There *were* prettier Amish girls he knew. And shouldn't he think more about them? There would always be Susie.

I should keep my options open until I'm actually married, he told himself. Yes, he would keep his options open. In the meantime there was no reason to deprive himself of Susie's company on Sunday night and in the weeks to come. The experience would be beneficial, if for no other reason. Having dated someone before was not a stigma against you, provided you were the one who quit. That he would be the one, if it came to that, he had no doubt.

Plus Susie's sweet, he thought, the smile returning to his face.

Slapping the reins, he urged his horse on for the last few hundred yards to his parents' driveway. It would look better to be moving fast when he approached home. Not that his father would say much about speed, but his mother might.

"Time spent poking on the road is time wasted," she had told him often.

That it was, he was sure, slapping the reins again for good measure.

The snow had quit completely as he pulled into the driveway. Stopping at the barn, he unhitched the horse and took it inside. Luke then pushed the buggy under the lean-to, making sure the doors were both shut. With the wind blowing, it could easily move snow inside, especially overnight.

Not seeing his father around, he walked toward the house and entered by the utility room door. Leaving his coat and boots, he opened the kitchen door and felt a wave of heat greet him. His mother must have supper on the way.

"Hi," he said, before he even got halfway through.

"Shut the door," his mother said, bending over the oven. "It's cold outside."

He grunted his acknowledgment, closing the door gently behind him.

"So how was Emma?"

"Same as always," he replied, not feeling like volunteering anything more.

"Did you see anything unusual?"

"No…and there were no visitors. It was snowing," he said.

"Did you have a chance to ask about the car in her driveway the other day?"

"Yes," he nodded. "Tried the best I could. She wouldn't give me any information. Just said it was someone she had asked to come out to the farm."

Rachel sighed, "It never was going to be easy. I knew that from the start. We just have to do what we can."

"She gave me an envelope to mail at the post office," he said. What he had done might as well be dealt with here and now.

There was no response from the stove as his mother carefully lifted the casserole out, heading to the surface of the stove.

"It was addressed to a lawyer's office in Anderson," he said nervously.

The casserole clattered down heavily, its hot contents spilling over the edge. She turned to him, eyes gleaming.

"You didn't mail it, did you?"

"Sure. I had to," he said, struggling to keep his gaze from dropping to the table. "I work for Emma."

"You checked what was inside first?" she stated more than asked.

"No," he said, hanging his head in shame.

"You mean you had a chance like that and didn't open the envelope?" she said, her voice low. "What did I just tell you this morning? If you didn't have enough nerve to open it, why didn't you bring it home to me? You could have mailed it tomorrow. Gone back this afternoon even."

"Maybe I should have," he admitted, "but I just didn't."

"I'm ashamed of you," she said, her voice still low.

"It won't happen again," he said. "If I ever get another chance, I won't pass it up."

"You realize how serious this is?" she asked, her eyes full on him. "Our money may be gone forever if Emma foolishly follows my father's example."

"Surely she won't." He raised his eyes.

"She had better not," she said, putting her hands on her hips and facing Luke. "I can't believe you'd pass up an opportunity like that. This had better never happen again."

"It won't," he said, with images of Susie or even someone else somehow coming to mind. "I'll open it next time. That, or bring it to you."

"You had better hope there is a next time," she replied, still looking at him.

He nodded and left, raising his face to the cold as it hit him when he stepped outside. The feeling stopped the rush of blood in his head and dulled the shame he now felt in his own failure to live up to expectations, and he had yet to tell his mother about Susie.

What would she have to say about that?

Chapter Seventeen

Rebecca began planning for her week in Milroy in earnest the next afternoon. The morning housework completed and not yet time for the choring, she went up to her room to plan. It was a wonder that her parents let her have a room of her own, what with her siblings. And she so loved having it to herself.

Entering, Rebecca paused. All around her were the sights and smells she was used to. The dresser sat near the window, its dark stained oak polished to a dull gloss, worn from age. The bed supposedly matched the dresser but no longer did. Due to some previous owner's attempt to refinish it, the bed's new color was close, but it no longer had the same aged look as the dresser. Someday she would refinish it right. But that would be when she and John were gone. Her mother might object to refinishing the wood, claiming that it was being too worldly, caring what things looked like.

Looking around, the scent of old pine floors, still sweet from when she had refinished them last year, reached her. Her mother had not objected to that, although she had put her foot down when stain was suggested. Varnish was good enough for any Amish girl—plus it would look better she had said.

Now she would be leaving her room for possibly a few weeks, and she couldn't shake the nostalgic longing stirring in her. Even if for just a short time, soon—when she and John were married—she'd leave it forever.

She sighed and wished there had been more warning about this trip. But babies are that way she supposed. One just kind of went with the flow of things.

Will I have babies someday? With John? She felt a flush creeping up her neck at the thought of it. Those were things best left to the Lord. She must think of something else because there was already enough to do, just to get to their wedding day.

Bringing her mind back to her room, she thought of all she needed to do before her trip. There was the family laundry that needed to be completed so that her mother would not be burdened with it too soon. Their regular wash day was on Thursday, leaving only two days between wash day and her departure.

Running through her inventory of dresses, she settled on taking two Sunday dresses and three weekday dresses. That should be plenty to last the two weeks she might be there. The work dresses could be rotated, the fairly new one with the two older ones, which showed some wear. With the good dresses, one could be worn the first Sunday and the other the next.

It would not work to have someone think she was so poor as to have only one Sunday dress. This could easily happen if she wore the same dress twice in a row. Beyond that, if for some reason she had to stay for the third Sunday, it would do to repeat the dress from the first Sunday. No one would think ill of that.

Her mind turned to the one big thing she must do while in Milroy: the final break with her past. She would need to find time and offer a reasonable explanation as to why she needed to visit the schoolhouse and the Moscow bridge.

Supposing that there would be some time available, she ran the scenario through her mind. Surely Leona would not need her constantly. Since school was in session, she might need to visit the schoolhouse in the afternoon or early morning. The bridge could be handled in-between sometime.

And then too, she would want to try to see Emma. Not that she had anything to do with her resolve regarding Atlee, but a visit with her would be most pleasant indeed. If at all possible, it would have to be worked in.

She wondered where Emma lived by now. Was she still on her brother Millet's old place? Rebecca grinned at the thought of how Emma had obtained that property. *What a ruckus that had been.*

Rebecca wrinkled her brow, wondering if Emma was still able to live alone on the farm. She was surely old by now. Rebecca's image of her was the same as from when she was in school. She could see her at the chalkboard in front of the classroom or reading stories in front of the school after lunch hour.

She was a great teacher. No one else had came close. Of course, she smiled, *there never was anyone else in the first grade.* Young Mary Mast tried her hand at teaching that year, barely lasting the year out. Rebecca could still see her white face on the day she caught the eighth-grade boys cheating on the first quarter math exam.

Mary had noticed the similarities in the boys' test work and asked the five boys if they had cheated. All five shook their heads, looks of astonishment on their faces.

"We wouldn't think of doing something like that!" David, the oldest, declared, turning his head away as if he could hardly bear the insult.

Mary had taken a deep breath. Finding the courage somewhere, she continued the inquiry. "But most of the answers are the same."

"Not all of them," Jacob commented, his voice quivering a little.

He should probably not have shown this sign of weakness becasuse a few streaks of red returned to Mary's white face.

"You will all stay after school this afternoon," Mary pronounced weakly.

"*All* of us?" Martha, the youngest of the two girls, asked, bewildered.

"No. Just the boys," Mary said, with a little firmer tone this time.

All five looked at each other, then at Mary, as if contemplating what damage she could do to them. David cleared his throat but said nothing.

With that, Mary had proceeded with the lesson of the day, and nothing more was said about it. At noon, though, little Timothy went across the road to Emmett Yoder's place with a note, and later, at five minutes till three, just before school let out, a buggy pulled into the school yard. Surprised students stared out of the windows, watching two Amish men climb out and tie their horse to the hitching post. The one was their minister, Emery Mast, his beard snow white and flowing halfway to his waist, and the other was James Troyer, a farmer, his pant legs still sporting straw from the bales he had been spreading for his cows after morning chores.

Mary quickly announced that it was time to dismiss. The clock on the wall still read two minutes shy of three, but no one was doing any more school work anyway.

"You are dismissed for the day," Mary told them. "Please stand and file out."

They all did except the five eighth-grade boys, whose eyes were all firmly glued on their desks now. As Rebecca filed by, she noticed the resignation to their doom written on their faces.

Reports the next day claimed that all had been soundly spanked. This could well be imagined with either Emery or James—both school board members—wielding the dreaded *pattle,* which was known to be stored in the bottom of teacher's desk. None of the five boys, though, would discuss the matter with anyone, keeping glum faces all day. After that Mary had never been quite the same—her starry-eyed innocence gone. Emma came the next year and taught Rebecca for her remaining seven years.

Yes, if at all possible, she would have to visit Emma.

Opening her closet, she took down the suitcase from the top shelf, dusted it, and then leaned it against the far wall of the closet. It would stay there until Friday morning when she would pack. One suitcase was all that was going. In the van with so many other travelers, there would only be room for her to take one piece of luggage.

Glancing at the alarm clock, she noticed that it was approaching choring time. Matthew would be helping tonight, taking on greater responsibilities in preparation for her leaving.

After walking downstairs, she put on her work coat and boots. Her mother was not around, likely in the basement, perhaps getting canned fruit for supper. When she got to the barn, she found Matthew already there with a frown on his face.

"Choring's no fun," he said, knowing that complaining was useless but needing to say it anyway.

"You're growing up fast," she replied, squeezing him on the shoulder. "You'll soon be a big man."

"I'm not choring all the time, though," he told her emphatically.

She chuckled. "No, you don't have to. There will be plenty of other things to do."

"Like what?" he asked.

"Oh," she wrinkled up her face, as if in deep thought, and replied, "You can take girls home from the singing."

"Like John does with you? Ugh!" he said, making a face.

"Let's see. Maybe Margaret?" Rebecca continued. "She's in your grade."

He kept making his face, but she saw the interest in his eyes. "Girls," he said, his face and his eyes contradicting each other, "they are ugh!"

"Well, whatever," she told him. "Now, let's see if you can pick this milker on and off the line by yourself."

She brought a milker from the milk house and he tried, the muscles in his arms taut. The milker went on the line and back off with enough ease to assure her he could do it. "Don't let it touch the floor until you have it on the cow," she said, watching the hoses dangle dangerously close to the concrete floor.

He nodded, keeping the milker on the wire until the cows would come in. "I can do it," he said firmly.

"I'll help you until I leave," she said. "You should be fine by then."

"Of course," he said, "I'm a boy."

"Girls are just as important as boys," Rebecca said, giving him a lesson she figured he needed. "They're just good at different things."

"Ya," he said, seemingly mulling that thought, and then dropped it willingly when their father opened the barnyard door, letting the first of the milk cows come in.

Chapter Eighteen

Rebecca woke up before the alarm clock went off, the chill of the early morning having again crept into the room. Swinging her feet out of bed, she found the vent and opened it. The warm blast she was expecting did not occur. Mother was obviously late getting to the kitchen.

Reaching for the clock to turn its face toward her, she shut off the alarm, when it showed five minutes till official get-up time. Thoughts of a few more minutes of sleep vanished when she remembered that today was the day of the sewing. It would be a busy day before she would see John tonight and tell him of her departure for Milroy on Saturday.

If he knew what she intended to do while in Milroy, would he object? Well, there was certainly no need to tell him. It might hurt him too much to know she hadn't quite gotten over her first girlhood crush.

She tensed, thinking about it and knowing that she would always be a little nervous until this problem was resolved. One thing was for sure—the ring would go with her to Milroy. It would not stay here. God would help her, she hoped. She took the ring gently out of the drawer and slid it into the folds of the suitcase.

But for now, the chores needed to be done. Matthew needed to be awakened if there were no signs soon of movement from the boy's room.

Donning her housecoat, she opened the door, stepped across the hall, and quietly opened her brother's door. "Matthew," she whispered, "time to get up."

There was silence.

"Matthew," she whispered louder.

When there was still nothing, she walked over to his bed and shook his shoulder.

"Go away," he muttered.

"It's time to get up," Rebecca said.

"I'm too tired," he replied. "Go away."

"If you don't get up," she said, still whispering, "Dad will have to holler for you."

That produced a stirring under the covers. "I'll be coming," he said.

"You'd better be," she told him. "Now get up!"

"Go away," he repeated, but the covers kept on moving so she left, closing the door behind her.

She was almost to her room when she heard the familiar hiss of an approaching lantern. The door at the bottom of the stairs opened, allowing a shaft of light to brighten the stairs.

"Is Matthew up?" her father asked.

"Yes," she said. "I just woke him."

"Good," he said, closing the door, returning the upstairs to a blessed darkness. Rebecca's room was solid blackness except for the faint outline of the distant window. She felt for a match in the top drawer and lit the kerosene lamp. Noises across the hall assured her that Matthew was indeed up.

When, moments later, the boy's door creaked open, followed by footsteps on the stairs, she was glad for it. Matthew was well on his way to carrying his share of the responsibilities. That would help everyone, including Rebecca.

When she went downstairs to head for the barn, Rebecca heard her mother in the kitchen. In the barn, she found Matthew sleepy eyed, but already hanging one of the milkers on the wire and waiting for Lester to bring in the cows.

"You have to feed them too," she told him.

He grunted and moved toward the feed shoot. She held up her hand. "I'll get it this morning. You can do it tomorrow morning just for practice. Starting Sunday night, it's all yours."

"Quit reminding me," he said through a crooked glare, his one eye still pasted half shut.

Rebecca chuckled. "You'll have to get used to these early hours."

"It'll come fast enough," he said dryly. "Just be quiet and let me do my work."

"I'll be quiet if you do it right. If not, I'm going to let you know."

He shook his head, too tired to bother with a response.

Rebecca went into the milk house for warm water to wash the cows' udders, as the sound of their low bellows filled the barnyard.

By six thirty she left for the house, having sent Matthew in earlier. The smells of breakfast greeted her at the door. She caught sight of Matthew already at the table, looking hungrily at the food. A bowl of scrambled eggs sat in front of him, kept warm by the plate resting on top. If breakfast were delayed too many more minutes, Rebecca knew her mother would move them into the oven.

Biscuits, also ready and on the table, could stand a little cooling off, but those too would go back into the oven if Lester didn't show up in a few minutes. The gravy bowl sat open, steaming heavily and ready to pour. Mattie was keeping her eye on the kitchen door.

"Your father coming?" she asked, looking in Rebecca's direction.

"He's right behind me, I think." She glanced at the door about the time it opened.

"I'm sure hungry," Matthew said loudly, hoping to make his father hurry.

"Good work makes for a good appetite," Lester said, heading for the wash basin. "I'm coming."

"Can I start now?" Matthew asked but did not receive an answer.

He knew good and well there was no starting until prayers had been said.

"Your father's coming," Mattie said, implying a little wait.

Lester dried his hands on a towel in the utility room and entered the kitchen to take his place at the table. Once there and without a word, they bowed their heads. It was early morning and silence was the chosen form of prayer, befitting the hour when man's words should be few in the presence of his Maker.

"There's a van across the way in Edna's driveway," Lester said for the benefit of anyone who was interested, as he waited for the scrambled eggs to reach him.

"Probably the load from Holmes County," Rebecca said. "Edna's brother is along."

"Edna tell you that?" Mattie asked.

"Yes, when I took her the pie. He's the one who got up the load."

After they had made the rounds, Mattie set the bowl of eggs on her end of the table and placed the plate back over them. "I wasn't told that, but it works out real well. They can pick you up right here on Saturday morning."

Rebecca nodded, the reality of the trip becoming ever more apparent. "The sewing is this evening," she said. "John's going to be surprised when I tell him about my trip."

"I suppose," Mattie agreed. "He'll understand."

"Tell him you're moving back to Milroy," Lester said, straight-faced.

"Now, why would she want to do that?" Mattie asked…then smiled when she caught sight of his poker face. "He's just teasing you, Rebecca."

"I thought so," Rebecca replied. "He just wants to make trouble."

"Now why would I do that?" her father grinned. "Aren't you having enough trouble as it is?"

Rebecca started at her dad's words. In fact, she *was* having enough trouble dealing with that long-ago promise. She grabbed the biscuit bowl and stuck it under Matthew's nose. "Take another one," she said.

"I've had enough. I still have half of one," he protested, gently rubbing his stomach, "and I'm full already."

"She's just teasing you too," his mother said, giving Rebecca a questioning look and letting it pass.

"They're just having the normal problems," Mattie said in Lester's direction.

"It's to be expected," he said. "We do have good young people though. They do seek to walk in the will of God and church."

"There's *always* trouble with girls," Matthew spouted off suddenly, his mouth full of his wisdom and the last of his biscuit. "I'm just going to leave them alone."

"You just go ahead and do that," Lester chuckled. "It'll all come to pass for you soon enough. Things that can't be helped."

"I'm going to be *without* trouble," Matthew pronounced. "I'm just going to do chores and make lots of money. That's what comes from leaving girls alone."

Rebecca lifted the biscuit bowl, pretending she was going to bring it down hard on his head. He never winced, as she stopped a hair's breadth short.

Lester grinned and chided his son. "Well, you wouldn't want to miss out on the good times, now would you?"

"There aren't any," he said wisely. "Girls just create a bother."

"Now, now." Mattie patted his head. "Take it easy. You'll be going down that path soon enough. You'll need all the help the good Lord can give you."

"So why would I want to go down that path at all?" he asked.

"It's just the way it is," Mattie said. "The Lord so decreed it. So it will always be."

"Maybe He'll change His mind this time," Matthew ventured.

"I doubt it," she said. "It will all come in its own good time. Now stop thinking about it. It's not good for you."

"How's school?" Lester asked, as Matthew scraped the bottom of his plate for the last of the gravy, then licked it off his fork.

"It's okay," he said. "This is Fannie's first year teaching. She doesn't know much."

"Watch your mouth," Rebecca told him sharply.

"It's true," he protested. "She has a hard time explaining my arithmetic problems. She doesn't see the whispering that goes on. It's hard to study with that."

Lester and Mattie looked at each other, raising their eyebrows. Children were children they knew, but new teachers needed instructions sometimes too.

"If there's any problem, I'm sure it'll be taken care of," Mattie assured him. "In the meantime, make sure you mind and do your work well. We want you to get good grades."

Matthew nodded his head, yawning sleepily. "I'd better get ready for school," he said.

"You still have time," Mattie told him, turning to Rebecca. "Call the rest of the children. You can start with the dishes then."

Rebecca did that from the bottom of the stairs, waiting to repeat the call if there was no noise from her sisters' room. The shuffling of feet on the wood floor was what she was waiting for. Leaving the stair door open, she went back to the table to pick up a handful of dishes and carry them to the sink.

Matthew was slowly sliding out of his bench seat when she came back for more. She whispered to him, "Bring those math problems home. I'll see if I can help you with them."

"You would?" he asked, raising his sleepy eyes slightly.

"Sure."

He frowned, thinking about it, his mind refusing to function at full strength. "I might," he said, coming to the end of the bench and standing up, "if it gets too hard."

She nodded as the rest of the family came down the stairs and Matthew moved quickly to get out of the way. Then, while her mother oversaw their breakfast, she washed and dried the dishes they had used so far.

"What's on the list for me to do while you're at the sewing?" Rebecca asked when she was done.

Mattie thought for a moment. "Have you got your packing done?"

"As much as I can," she replied. "Wash day is tomorrow. I can't really get packed much before that."

"What if it rains tomorrow?" Mattie asked herself as much as anyone.

"I can move wash day to Friday," Rebecca suggested.

"I suppose so," her mother agreed. "In that case, why not start with the week's cleaning of the upstairs? Your room can be done Friday before you leave. The others can be done today."

"Anything else?" Rebecca asked.

"You can decide that for yourself. Just do whatever will help me out next week when you're not here."

Silence then fell between them as the flurry of the day began. The school children had to be sent off to school, the rest of the dishes needed to be washed and dried, and then Mattie herself would have to leave for the sewing.

Rebecca offered to harness the horses, which her mother accepted. While she was out in the barn, Matthew came out to hitch his horse to the buggy. At eight thirty, she helped the children climb into the buggy with Matthew. He drove the new single buggy Lester had purchased just last year for these occasions when both the school children and family needed transportation. By nine o'clock Mattie was in the old single seater on her way to sewing.

Chapter Nineteen

That evening John pulled into the Mullet place, a smile playing on his face. He was going to see Rebecca again. The warmer weather had turned a little brisk, but he still had his buggy door open to enjoy the evening. It seemed like ages since Sunday when he had asked her to be his wife.

She said yes, he remembered. *Can it be that it was only on Sunday?* "That it was," he said out loud, bringing his horse to a stop by the barn. All around him were other buggies, some still being unhitched, others already parked neatly in two rows.

With more buggies behind him, the rows would soon be getting longer. He pulled his horse to a stop, turned the wheel slightly, and hopped out.

"Good evening," he said to Will Yoder, who had put his horse in the barn already and was walking toward the house.

"Good evening," Will replied. "Weather turned a little chilly."

"That it has," John agreed. Will was a farmer. He lived just west of the Keims, and occasionally when it worked out, he and his sister would bring Rebecca to the midweek youth functions. Otherwise Rebecca would have to drive by herself. He wondered if Will had brought her tonight, a little jealousy teasing his feelings. Before he could ask, Will answered, "I brought your girl."

"Oh." John tried to sound uninterested, but the subtle jealousy reared its head. *This is foolish,* John reminded himself. Will was two years younger than Rebecca and well-known to be sweet on one of the Wengerd girls. Yet the idea of another boy in the same buggy with Rebecca bothered John.

"She's leaving on Saturday," Will said.

"Leaving?" John couldn't keep the astonishment from his voice.

Will looked up in surprise. "You mean she hasn't told you?"

John tried to keep his head. Will would, of course, have expected John to know.

"No," he said simply. "This is the first I've heard of it."

"When did you see her last?" Will stepped back as John took his horse out from under the buggy shafts.

"Sunday," John said from the other side of his horse.

"Strange she didn't mention it." Will shook his head, puzzled. "She's going out to her aunt's house in Milroy. Her aunt's having a baby."

"I haven't heard that either," John replied and started toward the barn. There was no use staying around and letting Will see how shocked he was.

"A baby," Will was saying, for some reason feeling a need to rub it in. "She probably knew it for awhile already."

"I know," John said over his shoulder, irritated. *Why had Rebecca not said something?* The question burned in his mind. *Was this why she had acted so nervous when that van from Milroy passed us at the bridge? Surely not. What could going to her aunt's to help with the baby have to do with being afraid? Was she hiding a secret?*

Will walked to the house, while John led his horse toward the barn, through the double doors, and found an empty space in the stalls. From habit he memorized the place and position so that he could find the horse in the dark.

Walking back, two more buggies were coming in. He stepped to the side to let them pass. Both of them held teenagers from the west district, but at the moment, he wasn't interested. All he could think of was Rebecca's leaving and not telling him. He took a deep breath and entered the house.

With the fading winter light, gas lanterns were already lit, hanging from the ceiling. Two large stitching quilts were set up on the living room floor, colorful patterns already hand sewn in. Amish youth milled all around, both boys and girls running the threaded needles through the quilts.

He paused just inside the door. With so many people there, no one noticed him, which he was glad for. He wanted to see Rebecca, and his eyes scanned the room in search of her. In the light of the gas lanterns, the shadows danced this way and that, made even more pronounced by the movements of so many people.

Her dark hair caught his attention first. Longingly he looked at her. How lovely she was—so graceful as she stuck her needle underneath the quilt, and then back up again. With a smooth motion, she snipped off the end evenly, then repeated the motion. Her head was moving in conversation with someone beside her, but he couldn't tell who.

Waves of feeling came over him, and he wished he could tell her how he felt, but that wouldn't be appropriate.

Moving carefully he ventured forward.

She saw him before he got to her place by the quilt.

"Hi," she said, her voice straining above the surrounding hum of conversation. She smiled at him, turning her face fully toward him, her eyes shining.

"Hi," he replied, taking the spot she made open for him by the quilt.

"Here's a needle and thread," she said, pointing out an available one.

He nodded, taking the needle and preparing to use it. But how was he supposed to ask her about this trip she hadn't told him about in the middle of all these young people?

She solved it for him by moving her head closer to him, her body leaning against the side of the quilt frame, her brow wrinkled up. "I have something I need to tell you."

"Oh," he said. "Maybe I already know."

"You couldn't," she said. "I just learned of it on Monday."

He found it hard to keep her gaze, with the feelings their nearness caused in his chest, his fear fading away. He dropped his eyes to the quilt and asked, "So what is it?"

"I have to go to Milroy. My aunt Leona's having a baby. Mom just decided the matter over the weekend and didn't tell me till Monday. I know it's a real surprise. It was for me too, but I need to go."

"Will told me outside," he said. "Just that you were going on Saturday, of course."

"Oh," she responded, wrinkling her brow again, "I didn't think he would see you before I did."

"So how long are you staying?" John glanced around to see if anyone else was noticing their conversation. No one was, all of the others deep into their own conversations.

She leaned closer, having moved away to reach her last stitch. "A week after the baby comes, I suppose. You know how babies are. They come when they want to."

"Some of them," he commented wryly. "My older sister had a real time. Went two weeks overdue."

She made a face at that. "If Leona's goes that long, I'll never come home." She hesitated a moment before adding, "I'll be looking forward to seeing you again."

"I hope so," he said quickly, glancing around again to see if anyone was listening.

"They're not listening," she whispered, causing the person next to them to turn around and glance at them.

"Don't whisper," he said in a normal tone, chuckling. "They'll hear *that*."

She laughed softly. He listened to the sound, letting it thrill him with its lightness.

"You still have friends in Milroy?" he asked, keeping his eyes away from her. "I guess you'll have time to visit," he said. "Your old friends, I mean."

Yes, I hope so," she said, carefully running the needle through the quilt again.

He knew he shouldn't ask the question, but his earlier bout with jealousy goaded him. "Any old boyfriends you'll see?"

"Of course not," she said. Then she added, "Well, the two-date guy might still be around, but I don't know. You shouldn't be asking things like that again. You just asked on Sunday. I told you then."

Still, John sensed she was not telling him everything. There had been that fear. Was it anything to do with her life in Milroy?

"I know," he said. "To be honest, it just seems like there's something you're not telling me."

She took a deep breath. There was no way she was going to tell him everything, but maybe she could she tell him a little. If he had really sensed her fear, it would be necessary to say something. She let her breath out slowly. "A schoolgirl crush in the sixth grade. He went Mennonite." Then she added calmly, as inspiration struck, "You probably had those too."

To her surprise he smiled. "Ya, that I did. I suppose we all did. We grow out of those. No Mennonites for me though."

"So, now you know," she told him.

He nodded, bending over the quilt. "So hurry back. I'll miss you."

"I'll try," she said, coming to the end of her line of stitches.

Not long after, they both stood back as their quilt was folded up and removed and chairs were brought out, along with popcorn and apple cider. John pulled up a chair for Rebecca before getting one for himself.

An hour later, the gathering over, John helped Will hitch up before he left himself. Mainly he wanted to see Rebecca up to the last minute.

Standing by the buggy, he waited until Will's sister Wilma came out with Rebecca following. "Have a good trip," he told Rebecca.

"I'll be back soon," she said and then climbed in, and to John's satisfaction, seated herself on the outside of the seat, away from Will. Wilma then got in and waited until Will was seated to sit down in the middle.

John smiled to himself as Will's horse jerked, and they took off into the darkness, the taillights of the buggy twinkling at him.

Chapter Twenty

On Saturday morning, Rebecca got up with the sound of the alarm clock. Within moments her father hollered up the stairs for Matthew. Life at home without her was already taking shape as Matthew, not Rebecca, would be doing the early morning chores. She stood listening to Matthew's footsteps on the stairs, their sound amplified in the morning stillness.

Responding to a sudden whim, Rebecca hurriedly dressed and headed for the barn. Opening the door, she was greeted by the familiar warmth that came from the animals and the smell of hay and grain mixed with the background odor of barnyard manure. This was what she had come out for, letting the sensations and smells flow over her. Silly of her, she knew, but she would miss even this.

"You don't have to chore this morning," Matthew said, catching sight of her coming through the door. "Mom said so. You're leaving."

"I know," she said, heading for the feed shoot and the nearby shovel, then throwing feed into the first few stanchions from where she stood. "I'll just be out for the first round."

He shrugged his shoulders as the first line of cows marched in. Rebecca hurried to finish with the last stanchion slot. That cow was already in place, mouth open and its tongue expectantly waiting for the grain. Almost before the feed hit the ground, the cow lowered its head and licked greedily.

She helped attach milkers on two cows, waited till those were done, then repeated the motion. Finally she said, "I'm leaving now." Matthew simply nodded as she went out the door.

"What were you doing in the barn?" her mother asked when she got back into the house. "They're picking you up in forty-five minutes."

"I had to take one last look," she said, smiling.

"You're not leaving for long, silly. You'll be back in two weeks or so."

"I know. The whim just hit me."

"Get changed then. I want you to have some breakfast before they come for you."

Rebecca quietly went upstairs so as not to awaken any of the other children. Having a grouchy child on hand expressing its displeasure at being deprived of a few precious minutes of sleep was not preferred at the moment.

Changing into her traveling clothes, Rebecca brought her suitcase downstairs and set it by the front door. Mattie had prepared a plate of food for her in the kitchen and waited silently as Rebecca bowed her head in prayer.

"So how am I coming back?" Rebecca quickly asked, as she began eating.

"First we'll have to see when the baby comes," Mattie said. "After that, maybe there'll be another load coming back."

"And if not?" Rebecca asked, her fork cutting into an egg.

"You can always use the Greyhound."

"Does Leona know that I'm coming?"

"I mailed her a letter on Monday morning. I'm sure she was expecting that you would come. She knows me. Figures I would send you, I expect."

Rebecca lifted the last of the egg to her mouth, adding a bit of toast. "I'm going to walk across to Edna's now," she announced.

"They'll pick you up here, I'm sure; if you'll wait."

"No. The suitcase isn't too heavy. I'll just walk." She rose from the table, adding, "Early mornings are such a beautiful time of the day. I'd enjoy the walk over."

"That they are," her mother agreed. "Clear your dishes before you leave though. Matthew and Lester ought to be in soon."

Picking up her plate and silverware, Rebecca deposited them by the sink.

Across the room, her mother opened the oven where she had been keeping the eggs. She took them out and set the plate on the table. There they sat in their pale yellow glory. Rebecca enjoyed the warmth of the kitchen and the good breakfast smells as she brushed past, leaving the washcloth in the sink. *This is home,* she thought as the emotions wrapped themselves around her.

"I'll see you, then," she said, forcing herself to go into the living room to get her suitcase and head for the front door.

"Have a good trip," her mother replied, following her to give her a hug. "Tell Leona hello for all of us."

"I will," she said, releasing herself from her mother's arms. She then opened the door and stepped out into the morning light just appearing on the horizon, the air crisp and clear. It was going to be a beautiful winter day—the snow from the recent storm still on the ground. She hoped it would stay till Christmas, but it was unlikely. A warm spell was sure to come through before that.

The chickens clucked when she went by, a few out in the yard already, their necks bobbing in the dim light. By the time she reached the road, she could see that lights were already on in Edna's house, and as she approached the house, she heard the sound of the engine. The van was warming up. Just then the dome light came on as the van door slid open.

"Good morning," she said to whoever was on the other side.

"Good morning," a man's voice answered, his head appearing out the van window as she approached. "You're up early." His beard was nearly white, voice gravely, his eyes not visible in the dawn light.

"Are we about ready to go?" she asked him.

"Just about," he said as he stepped down from the van. "Name's Elmer. Edna's my sister." He offered his hand.

She took it in a quick handshake. His fingers felt cold, as she supposed hers did too. "I'm Rebecca Keim from across the road. Catching a ride, I guess."

"Yes. Someone did say we were picking up an extra passenger. Well, there's plenty of room. We're just about ready to go. I thought we were coming over to pick you up, though."

"I wanted to walk over," she said. "It's such a beautiful morning. Saves time this way too. Can I help with anything?"

"Us old people can always use help," he allowed. "The good Lord knows. I reckon my Elsie has our suitcases ready. You might help her get them to the van. Our driver was staying here too. She just started the van a little bit ago, so it would warm up."

"I'll go see what I can do to help," Rebecca said, setting her suitcase on the ground.

"You go on in," he said. "I was just making sure the van was cleaned out a bit. Should have done it yesterday, but I forgot. Elsie reminded me this morning."

"Here, let me help with that," she said, not waiting for a reply. She climbed in the van and did a quick pickup of some paper and other traveling debris. Glancing behind her, she saw Elmer walk slowly toward the house, open the door, and disappear inside.

After the van was clean to Rebecca's satisfaction, she went into the house.

Elmer was coming from Edna's spare bedroom with two suitcases. Edna and a lady she assumed was Elsie were clearing the kitchen table. A Mennonite looking woman, thirty years old or so, was seated, talking with them.

"Good morning," Edna called out, greeting her from where she was standing. "Elmer said you were outside." She wiped her hands on her apron. "Elsie, this is Rebecca. She's the one from across the road, who brought us the pecan pie. Rebecca, this is Elsie, Elmer's wife. Over here is Mary Coblentz, who is driving the load."

"So, you're the one who baked the pecan pie!" Elsie exclaimed.

"Mom and I," Rebecca said.

"Well, it was among the best," Elsie assured her. "Pecan is Elmer's favorite."

After a few moments of casual conversation, Mary said, "We really must be going. There are two more stops to make for the others."

Minutes later they were gathered by the van, exchanging goodbyes.

Mary was in the back, making sure all the suitcases fit. "We'll have to rearrange suitcases as we pick the others up," she said to Rebecca, closing the back. Together they waited for Elmer and Elsie to finish talking with Edna.

"I hope my suitcase isn't too much," Rebecca said.

"No, you Amish all travel pretty light," Mary said.

Elmer and Elsie climbed into the van, and Rebecca began to follow, but Mary said, "Rebecca, why don't you take the front seat beside me?"

"Oh! I wouldn't want to do that," Rebecca objected.

"I'm sure no one will mind." She stuck her head over the seat. "Elmer, okay with you if Rebecca rides in front?"

"No matter to me," he said. "She'll keep you company."

"See?" Mary said to Rebecca. "Now get up here."

Reluctantly Rebecca got in, finding the experience unnerving. She had never ridden in the front seat of a van. That was always reserved for her father or mother when they hired a driver.

Mary started the van as Elmer pushed the side door shut. Moments later they were on their way, turning right at the main road, crossing the little open bridge, and rattling across the Harshville covered bridge.

Chapter Twenty-one

The sun was just cresting the little hamlet of Harshville, sending out strong steaks of light, as Mary accelerated the van to negotiate the hill. Rebecca saw her foot tightening and wondered what it must be like to know how to drive. *Would it feel evil, maybe sinful? Would it feel as if one was free, or would it be even a greater bondage to the things of this world, as the old folks claimed?*

"You born around here?" Mary interrupted Rebecca's thoughts, turning left on the Duffy road.

"No," Rebecca said, "in Indiana."

"In Milroy, where we're going?"

She nodded.

"My parents were Amish. Way back," Mary volunteered, pulling into a driveway. "Our first pickup."

"How many stops have we got?"

"This one and one more. It's not a full load," Mary said, so accustomed to Amish ways that she no longer considered it strange having to explain why she was driving with less than a full load. To any Amish person paying for a taxi, especially on long trips, an empty seat was considered a great wasted expense.

An older couple appeared, he carrying their one suitcase. Rebecca caught a glimpse of the man's face as he approached, his black hat pulled down low over his ears to ward off the morning cold. His eyes looked kind as they caught hers in the brightening morning light. He nodded and glanced away to make sure his wife found the step into the van.

"Good morning," the wife said cheerfully, once inside. "The Lord has given us another great day for travel."

"That He has," Mary agreed, getting out to help and setting their suitcase between the seats. "I'll pack it better when we pick up the Yoders," she said.

They nodded and took their seats.

"You sleep well?" the woman asked Elsie.

"Ach! Ya!" Elsie replied. "Elmer's sister always has a good bed ready when we visit. Good food too."

The man, who had just gotten in, chuckled. "Martha, on the other hand, is not the best cook in the world. But an old body doesn't need it like it used to."

"Our daughter can cook just fine," the wife retorted.

"Now, now," he said, stroking her arm, "I wasn't meaning anything by it. Or about your cooking either. It's just not one of Martha's strong points."

"Well, I suppose that's so," his wife admitted, settling back into the seat. "She always liked farming better."

"There you go," he told her. "Each of us has a strong point. With twelve children, it's best not to be too good at cooking anyway. Cheaper too."

Mary smiled at their conversation, as she backed out to the main road and turned south back toward Wheat Ridge Road. Turning left she drove through Unity and pulled into another driveway a ways out of town. There, another couple appeared. And while Mary was packing all the luggage securely behind the backseat, the new woman, her face round and cheery under her white hair and head covering, said to Rebecca, "I didn't know you were coming along."

Rebecca smiled, turning around in the front seat, "I didn't know I was going either. Not till Monday. Mom just made her mind up then to have me go to Milroy. My aunt is having a baby. I'm helping out."

"When's it due?" the woman asked.

"End of next week."

"So you're going out early?"

"Yes," Rebecca said. "Getting there early, just in case the baby comes sooner."

"Well, it's good to have you along." She motioned toward her husband. He nodded, his face sober and withdrawn, unlike his wife's cheerful expression. With his thumbs through his suspenders, he seemed to be studying the rising sun over Wheat Ridge.

"Well," Mary said, climbing back in, "now we're on our way."

Esther turned around in her seat to speak to Elsie, as Mary got on the road again, heading west now. Once she got on 247, Rebecca decided it wouldn't interfere with her driving to ask, "You're Mennonite?"

"Yeah," she said, "Conservative Conference."

"I wouldn't know what that means," Rebecca said hesitating.

"Believe me, I don't either. Not half the time. It's just a way of telling ourselves apart. I don't like labels much myself. Holmes County has every flavor and variety of our people."

Not sure if she was including Amish in her comment, Rebecca asked, "You consider Amish in the family too?"

"Sure," Mary beamed. "I have several good Amish friends. Went to school together at Highland Heights, outside Berlin."

Rebecca raised her eyebrows. "Amish people go to public schools?"

"Sure. Some of them do. Not all. Like I said, they come in all shapes and sizes."

"That's sure different from what I know," Rebecca allowed. "Are you married?"

"Nope. Never was."

"Ah," Rebecca said, finding herself feeling surprisingly comfortable around this Mennonite she had only met a few minutes ago, "you're good looking enough."

"Well, thank you!" Mary gushed in a decidedly un-Amish fashion. "That's nice of you to say. Stokes a girl's self-esteem a little. I can always use some of that. I've had my chances at marriage. Decided not to, I guess. Too involved in mission work."

"Really?" Rebecca asked in surprise.

Mary noticed her tone. "Lots of the Amish support our outreach too."

"Oh!" Rebecca was again surprised. "Like where?"

"I usually spend half the year at a mission in Haiti. The other half in the States. Amish mostly support it with money. We have an auction every year for the outreach. Sometimes some of the young Amish people come along for a trip on a work project—Amish and Mennonites."

"I see," Rebecca said uncertainly. "Well, my dad says the Lord is in the saving business."

"That He is," Mary said, apparently missing the Amish take on that statement.

Rebecca decided she should make sure there was no misunderstanding. "Ah," she cleared her throat and continued, "He's a great God. Dad says He can do wonderful things by Himself. We just tend to mess things up when we try to help Him."

"Well," Mary said, "God can do things by Himself. He does, I know. He also wants us to help Him. Work *with* Him."

Rebecca was astonished at such boldness in offering help to the Almighty. It must have shown in her face.

Mary laughed. "I know. The Lord wouldn't need our help. He could do it all by Himself. But I think He wants us to learn something in the process."

"But we make so many mistakes," Rebecca ventured, glancing back over her shoulder to see if anyone was listening to their conversation. No one seemed to be. Esther's husband, Chris, was dozing in his seat.

"Well, that's true," Mary allowed. "Maybe that's part of the process. Anyway, it's something I love to do."

"I see," Rebecca said, even though she was not sure how such a thing was possible. Going to a foreign country every year was not even in her realm of possibilities. She had no idea whether or not she would enjoy it.

The time sped by as the two women shared occasional small talk. Then, after a lengthy silence, Mary rather boldly asked, "You seeing someone?"

Rebecca knew she was going to blush, even before the redness spread on her neck. "Yes."

"Serious?" Mary asked, glancing at Rebecca's flushed cheeks.

Rebecca nodded, keeping her eyes straight ahead.

"I've been thinking more about it lately," Mary's voice took on a confessional tone. "There's a real nice local man in Haiti. Converted by the mission when he was younger. His wife died last year. I thought I saw something in his eyes the last time I was down there. Set me thinking about it."

Rebecca's eyes must have become as big as saucers because Mary laughed out loud when she saw them.

"A *native?*" The question just popped out of Rebecca's mouth.

"Yes. Why not?" Mary said. "They're people just like us."

"Ah." Rebecca wasn't certain of that at all. "They don't look like us."

"No. They don't. But they live and die like us."

"But *marrying* one...do you think that's wise?"

"Well," Mary tilted her head and replied, "that's a good point, I suppose. They're so poor down there. His name is Marcus." Mary paused to glance at Rebecca.

She nodded. "The name sounds usual."

"He pastors one of the local church groups from the mission. I guess that makes him one of the upper crust down there. That's all fine and good until you compare it to American standards. Then it all changes. Not that I think myself better than them. Not at all. It's just that I'm used to things. Refrigerators. Electricity. Cars. Washing machines. All of that."

Not used to thinking along those lines, Rebecca just lifted her shoulders in puzzlement. It was a world removed from any she knew.

Mary continued, "I suppose he might want to live like I do. Unless I want to live like he does, which would be an option, I guess. I think if I want to marry him, I should live down there with him."

"You think you could do that?" Rebecca asked.

"That's the big question. I must say," Mary said rolling her eyes, "it does hold its fascinations, don't you think?"

Rebecca let the breath out that she had been unconsciously holding. "What a complicated world."

"That it is...but then it isn't," Mary allowed. "We just need to find our way. Or the Lord's way actually."

"That's true," Rebecca said, thinking of the ring in her suitcase. That was nothing quite like this, but she still needed God's help. She needed a way through it. But a schoolgirl crush had to be easier than deciding whether to marry such a strange person from a completely different culture. She took a deep breath at the very thought of it.

"You think...Marcus...is serious then?" Rebecca asked.

"Yes," Mary said.

They drove along in silence for a few minutes, each lost in her own thoughts.

"Hey, I never expected to say all that," Mary finally spoke up. "This has been a pleasant surprise. I think the Lord sent you along to brighten my day."

"I don't know about that," Rebecca said quickly, again astonished at how easily Mary assumed the Almighty's plans and her particular place in it.

"You think we should stop for lunch?" Mary asked, glancing at her watch.

"I don't know." Rebecca was not particularly hungry. "Can we make it to Milroy before twelve?"

Mary did the calculations in her head. "I don't think so. Besides, no one knows exactly when to be expecting us. They won't have lunch ready."

"That's true," Rebecca said.

"Hey," Mary hollered toward the back of the van. "You want to stop for lunch?"

After some quick consultations, the answer "Yes" was hollered back by Elmer.

"Where?"

"Anywhere."

"There's an Applebee's up ahead."

Again the quick consultations and a "That's fine" came from Elmer.

Mary began to slow down.

She grinned and said, "That was quick enough," as she took the next exit and pulled into the Applebee's parking lot.

Chapter Twenty-two

An hour later they were on the road again.

When the hum of conversation started behind their seats, Mary asked, "So what's your fellow like?"

Rebecca, not quite used to this direct approach, blushed again. "John works at his uncle's business on Wheat Ridge."

"So what does he look like?"

Rebecca hesitated. This experience was unnerving, but she decided it would be rude not to answer the question. "Well, he's taller than me," she began. "A little lighter haired. Although not blond. His hair curls when it's wet." She then laughed at how easy it came out.

"Oh! So how do you know that?"

"Well, it rains, you know." Rebecca blushed seriously now, not believing she was telling someone this. "We were getting ready to leave from church. The wind blew his hat off when he was hitching up the horse. I saw the hat roll across the yard." She chuckled. "Thankfully, his horse stood still while he ran after the hat. When we got in the buggy, I could tell. The edges curled where they stuck out from under his hat."

"So you like him?" Mary asked.

"Yes," Rebecca replied, "a lot, I think."

"He's Amish, of course."

"Most certainly!" Rebecca said. "Mom and Dad wouldn't want me dating someone who wasn't."

Mary raised her eyebrows. "Have you ever thought of doing that?"

"No!" was her instinctual response.

"Did you ever want to?"

Why did Mary have to ask so many questions? "Well, I've never really considered it. Besides, I really do like John. More than any other man I've ever met."

"That's a good enough reason," Mary allowed. "So you're going to marry him?"

"Yes, I hope so." She felt a blush threatening again.

"That certainly makes things easier," Mary said a little wistfully.

"You ever think of marrying a Mennonite boy?" Rebecca asked, thinking she might need nudging in that direction.

"I have. It's too boring, somehow. Maybe I just haven't met the right boy. Although it's getting a little late for that."

"Well, marrying a native would sure be something," Rebecca allowed. "I'm not sure 'exciting' is the right word. 'Different,' maybe."

"A challenge," Mary said. "A real challenge. I would need all of the Lord's help I could get. Plus, if it's love, it would be wonderful, wouldn't it?"

"Like between me and John?" Rebecca asked, then blushed deeply at her own words. Feeling a need to explain it, she added, "I like him a lot, I guess."

"There's nothing wrong with that," Mary assured her. "I just hope I feel like that someday. You know, all certain and fussy."

Rebecca smiled at the image, not sure it fit her, but unoffended.

An hour or so later, Mary announced, "Looks like we're here. There's the sign for Milroy. Where shall I drop you off?"

"On through Milroy," Rebecca said, watching the familiar farmland from her youth roll by. "A few miles on the other side. You turn left onto 500."

The first buildings in Milroy came into Rebecca's view with the memories associated with them: the gas station where she would go with her dad to buy kerosene for the farm, the post office where Mattie would take her when they had packages to mail, and the little grocery store on the other end of town where they would shop sometimes. Their major shopping had been done in Rushville, where things were cheaper. Here and there a few Christmas decorations were up on the buildings, their red, green, and blue lights turned off in the daytime.

Rebecca was silent as she watched the passing landscape, the memories coming thick and heavy. A buggy passed them, but Rebecca couldn't see who was in it. *Probably wouldn't know them anyway,* she told herself.

"You know this area?" Mary asked, watching Rebecca.

"I grew up around here," Rebecca said. "Went to school just ahead." She pointed as the Flatrock Amish schoolhouse came into view. "We need to turn here."

Across the field, the schoolhouse's white siding was shining in the sun, its yard, with the softball field out back, empty.

Memories of days from long ago came rushing in…games she had played in this very place, and, of course, memories of Atlee. She could see him even now, swinging his bat and running to first base.

"You went to school there?" Mary looked across the fields, as she turned left onto 500. "They have some of those schools at home. I never attended, though…and I always wondered what it would be like."

"Depends on the teacher, as much as anything, I think." Rebecca turned her head for one last look as they drove past. She could almost see Emma in the doorway, vigorously swinging the bell after the noon hour.

Then breaking her reverie, a shiver went through her as she remembered what she must do while she was here. *Why had my promise never bothered me while we were living here? It was surely John's proposal that brought it all back.*

"You had a good teacher?" Mary asked.

"Yes. I did for the last seven years at least. Her name was Emma,"

Rebecca said almost reverently. "I plan to look her up, if I have time. I haven't seen her since we moved. Not much before that either, except at church. It's funny how you miss people more once they aren't around."

Mary nodded. "How true. That's why we should remember to value those closest to us. They are the ones we will miss the most once they're gone."

"Turn left here. The house on the left. That little white one."

"Stephen & Leona Troyer," Mary read aloud the name on the mailbox as she pulled in.

"My uncle and aunt," Rebecca said.

"Is this where Rebecca gets off?" Elmer hollered from the back.

Rebecca answered by opening her door and stepping down. There didn't seem to be anyone around.

Mary opened the back of the van and gave Rebecca her suitcase.

"Thanks for the ride. I guess I need to pay you for my share."

"Sure." Mary knew the routine. Taxi service came by the mile, divided by the number of passengers. Pulling out a notepad, she walked up to the van door, checked the odometer, and made calculations. After telling Rebecca the amount, Rebecca paid Mary from the money her mother had given her. The payment made a small dent in the sum, which would have to last throughout her time spent in Milroy.

"Thanks," Rebecca repeated.

"It was good to talk with you. Maybe we'll meet again sometime."

"I hope so," Rebecca said, meaning it. "If you're here for church tomorrow, maybe I'll see you then."

After Mary left, Rebecca took a long look at the house before walking toward the front door. The single-story ranch home was English built. Leona and Stephen had purchased it ten years ago. Apparently it had been a good deal, or Stephen would not have bought it. English property was purchased with the full realization that it would take money and effort to convert it to Amish usability.

Stephen had since turned off the electric power at the transformer at the end of the driveway and taken down the main electric lines. On the inside of the house, he left all the switches and plugs alone. The result was a slightly English looking home, both inside and out, but still within the *ordnung*.

Rebecca knocked on the front door, waited a minute, and knocked again. The sound of footsteps came faintly from inside, followed by the door opening and her uncle standing there.

"Oh! It's you," Stephen said. "Good to see you." He smiled a welcome, stepping aside so she could enter.

Stephen was tall and thin like her father. Leona, on the other hand, was unlike her sister, much more on the plump side.

"Leona's in bed," Stephen said. "She's not been well the past few days. Fannie took the children last night, just to give us some relief and quiet around here. She'll bring them back late tonight."

"Did Leona get the letter from Mom saying that I was coming?"

"On Wednesday," he said. "That was one of the reasons we took the offer from Fannie. She will take the children again during the baby's delivery. Go on now and see your aunt. She's been waiting."

As Rebecca reached the door of the bedroom, Leona's weak voice greeted her. "I'm so glad you could come, Rebecca."

Rebecca went right up to the bed and began fussing over Leona's pale look and bulging stomach under the covers. "You don't look well at all. Are you okay?"

"Yes," Leona smiled and replied weakly. "The midwife was here before lunch. She thinks it's just exhaustion, mostly. I've been trying to keep the house going, but now you're here...and I'm so glad you came before the baby arrives."

"I suppose Mother knew," Rebecca mused, glad now for her mother's instincts. "I guess sisters know," she added.

"Yes." Leona nodded weakly. "With you here, a great load is off my shoulders. Stephen hasn't had a decent meal in weeks. The poor man."

"I'd be glad to fix his meals," Rebecca assured her. "That's what I'm here for. You just tell me what to do. The things I don't see, of course. What about yourself? You want anything?"

"Some chicken soup," Leona muttered resignedly, relief in her voice. "I know that sounds silly, but that's what I'm hungry for."

"What about Stephen?"

"Something with meat in it. And potatoes maybe. We don't want to overburden you the first evening you're here."

"Don't worry," Rebecca assured her again. "You just stay in bed. I'll start on the supper right away."

"Just you being here has made me feel better already. I'm getting up for awhile," Leona announced firmly.

But Rebecca was still skeptical. "Are you sure?"

Leona slowly swung her feet out of bed and onto the floor, testing, finding her footing, and standing with both hands on her stomach. "I do declare it must be twins."

"You think so?" Rebecca asked, her eyes wide.

"No," Leona chuckled. "I was just saying so. The midwife says it's just one. A *big* one though."

Rebecca followed as Leona made her way to the living room where she chose the couch with a view into the kitchen. That was where she stayed for several hours, sipping the chicken soup Rebecca brought her. She watched as Rebecca prepared a meat casserole for Stephen's supper, asking family questions as fast as she could think of them.

Stephen was served his supper at five thirty, just as darkness was starting to fall. He expressed his deep gratitude, retiring afterward to the living room with Leona while Rebecca did the dishes.

She watched the darkness deepen outside the kitchen window, praying silently that God would help her through the next week and the hard work ahead. And yes, that He would help her with that other problem. Surely He would, seeing that He had brought her back to Milroy at this perfect time, just after John's proposal.

Fannie came a little after eight with the children, who after being inspected and questioned by their mother, went straight to bed.

Later, as Rebecca lay with her eyes closed in her bed, she couldn't help but think of memories of the ring, the Flatrock schoolhouse, and of a young boy named Atlee. Now, John seemed distant, as if he didn't fit in this world, *her* world, as it used to be. That feeling brought the fear anew. What would happen to her while she was here? Could she forever be free from the promise she had made? She wished with all her heart she knew.

Getting up, she walked to the window again and looked out into the darkness. There was nothing to be seen, just the faint distant outlines of trees against the dark sky. It crossed her mind to forget the whole thing. Why not just stay here and do her duty, helping Leona. Let the bridge keep its memories. Let these woods hold their secrets. She would simply not have to be a part of it. Yet, she *was* a part of it all because her heart was betraying her. Longing for something it had once known, unwilling to let go, hanging on to the promise she had made.

Standing by the window, the darkness of the night deepening both inside and outside the house, she told herself, "No, you will need to go and see. Then maybe you will let go."

She said the words, feeling faintly hopeful and comforted by the thought. Turning back from the window, she slipped under the covers, pulling them tightly up against her chin, and soon fell asleep.

Chapter Twenty-three

Luke spent an unsuccessful week watching in vain for any sign of the lawyer's return to Emma's. Of course, he told himself, this highbrow lawyer could come anytime, day or night, whether he was there or not.

But then an idea occurred to Luke.

It was on Tuesday night, just after the big snow on Monday. No strange car had appeared all day, so when his chores were done and as he was getting ready to leave, he implemented his plan. At the place where he hitched up his buggy—a place where it was not out of the ordinary for him to be—he spread snow across the driveway.

He carefully spread the soft snow in a thick carpet across the driveway. He tapered the edges off to make them look completely normal. Then after he was hitched up to his buggy, he drove across it himself to test his plan.

Glancing out the buggy door and using his rearview mirror, he could see that the test was a success. The pile of snow across the driveway recorded perfectly his horse's hooves and the thin buggy tires. It would do the same for an automobile because anyone coming in would have to drive across the snow to reach the walk to Emma's front door.

Telling his mother later, her smile had been reward enough. "I'm glad to see you take this serious, Luke," she had said.

By Wednesday evening there had been no mark left in the snow, but now with no fresh snow, he would have to carry more snow from a distance. Emma would surely notice and wonder what he was up to. So, instead, he simply smoothed out the dirt on the driveway in that spot. When it occurred to him that the freezing temperatures would turn the dirt solid, he walked back to the barn, returning with several handfuls of cow feed in his pockets. He glanced at the house windows, saw no one, and then spread the feed across the smooth dirt. It would have to do.

There also had been no more envelopes either placed in the mailbox or given to him to take to the post office. He would have known, he was sure, even though Emma took the mail to the mailbox herself. He made a point of being near the front barn about the time Emma walked to the end of the driveway. There had been no brown envelopes in her hand on the trek to the mailbox all week.

This morning though, Emma had gone to the mailbox early, while Luke was still in the back lot carrying out a round bale of hay for the cattle. Frantically, he watched her walk down the driveway, her arms swinging vigorously as was her custom. It was as though she was glad to see each new morning, heading out to embrace it, face wide open.

He felt like shoving both sticks of his New Holland forward and tearing down the driveway after her. *That,* he told himself *was exactly the wrong thing to do.*

Of course, it occurred to Luke that Emma could easily have been mailing smaller letters to the lawyer. It would not always have to be a large brown one, would it?

When he went home, he didn't tell his mother about these new concerns. That night, lying in bed, he had a headache just thinking about it all. *Money, money, money.* Why was something so important so difficult to obtain? It seemed to him that it should all be a little easier. This was their inheritance, as his mother had once again reminded him earlier in the evening.

That things were turning out this way was cruelty itself. He could see it in his mother's eyes and could now feel it in himself as well. It was just so wrong, and no one seemed to care. *God certainly didn't.*

He shuddered at the thought and at his presumption of thinking it. "Sorry," he said into the darkness, "I didn't mean it. Of course You care, even though we can't see it. You are giving Mother and me the strength to do all this."

No doubt, he told himself, *that is what it was.* It was God who had given his mother the wisdom to suspect what was happening again. If she hadn't, who would have known until it was too late again? And who might Emma be giving the money away to, anyway? If Rachel or he just knew that, maybe then something more could be done.

The responsibility rested heavy on his shoulders. He never knew money could be this troublesome. The weight pressed upon him until he could barely breathe.

Finally, unable to sleep, he got up, pulled on his jeans and a flannel shirt, and quietly made his way down the hall, tiptoeing past his parents' bedroom door so as not to awaken them.

He wasn't sure what to do. It was too cold to go outside, as much as he wanted to take a walk somewhere and think. He thought maybe the couch would hold more peace than his bed. As he opened the stair door, he was startled to see a dim light glowing from the kitchen.

Softly he tiptoed forward. The kerosene lamp was sitting on the kitchen table, its flame casting a dancing light into the room.

Stepping fully into the kitchen, he saw his mother. She had a chair drawn up against the far wall within arm's reach of the table. Her hands were in her lap, her hair hanging loose, her face half lit by the lamp.

"Mom," Luke said softly.

She turned her face toward him so that he saw the weariness in every line.

"What are you doing up?" he asked.

"Thinking," she said. "You can't sleep either?"

"I was worried. Couldn't breathe. Thought the couch might be more comfortable." He pulled a chair out from the table and seated himself.

"About the money?" she asked.

"Yes. What else? It shouldn't be this hard."

"I know," she said, letting her face fade into partial darkness again. "*Da Hah muss drinn havva fa uns.*"

"No, Mom. The Lord must be on our side," he said, but a worried look crossed his face.

"We must have sinned."

"We didn't do anything," he protested.

"Maybe someone in the family did," she said, sounding as if she believed it could be.

"You mean...Dad?"

"No. Someone else in my family. It would have to be. It was my father who didn't leave us the money. Yes, surely the Lord is against us."

"No, Mom. The Lord is with us, helping us."

"How do you figure that?"

"He showed you what was happening. You were right about Emma contacting a lawyer. I think the Lord wants us to be warned, so we can do something about it."

She let out her breath slowly, turning her face so that the lamplight flooded it again. Her long dark-brown hair, with its few streaks of gray, hung full across her shoulders, dropping down under the edge of the kitchen table. "Maybe that's it. I don't know. It's just so hard. If it's the Lord, He must want us to walk through the hard times."

"That's right," he assured her.

She sighed. "That would just be like the *Da Hah.* If there has been sin, there must be atonement with suffering. Perhaps it's *our* suffering that's required."

He shuddered, sitting there beside the table, the night pressing in on the window. Only the small flickering flame of the lantern seemed to stand against it. *Even that flame,* he thought, *so feeble and frail. Like us. We too must stand up for what is right. Whatever it takes.*

"We must do our part," he said out loud.

"That does seem to be what it's coming to. This cannot be allowed to happen again."

He nodded. Feeling the need to spill his secret, he added, "I am taking Susie home tomorrow night."

"Susie Burkholder?" Her voice sounded resigned.

"Yes."

"She has been looking at you for some time already."

"I know," he chuckled.

"What made you change your mind?"

"Not really change it," he corrected her. "I just decided it was time."

"The money?" she asked.

"Yes, that. It just seemed like I could now."

"I suppose that's how it is," she ventured, looking at him now, her face still partly in the shadows. "What if we don't get the money?"

"But we *must,*" he half whispered.

"Yes," she allowed. "We must. There may yet be a lot of work. This has just started, I'm afraid."

"I know."

"You had better wait to get married until this is settled."

"Will it be that long? Emma may die soon."

"And yet she may live. We must do what we have to do."

"All right," he said, but not for the reason she thought. He had already realized that with money, he might actually dare ask Ann Stuzman, the dark-haired eighteen-year-old from the other district, to let him take her home. Without money, he wouldn't dare. That was just how it was.

Yet, at eighteen and with her looks, he supposed she wouldn't last long before being snatched up. With that in mind, haste was necessary in arranging this matter with Emma. Not just in secret, but it needed to be brought out into the open that she would leave the farms to the rightful heirs.

"You'd better get to bed," his mother said, interrupting his thoughts.

"I suppose so," he heard himself say, pushing his chair back from the table.

Once upstairs, he cautiously lay down on the bed, and five minutes later, he dozed off, thoughts of money and Ann Stuzman still going through his head.

Chapter Twenty-four

Rebecca awoke from habit at five thirty even though she had set the alarm for six. Six was when Leona suggested she get up because that would be early enough to prepare breakfast for the family.

"Nothing fancy," Leona had told her. "On Sunday mornings we just cook oatmeal and make toast."

Rebecca rolled over, trying to sleep till six, but it was no use. The newness of the house and the day's duties were simply too much. She climbed out of bed and immediately was impressed by the warmth of the room. Last night she hadn't noticed it, but this morning it was pronounced. Tonight she would have to find the register and close it before retiring. A warm room was not meant for sleeping—at least not for a Keim.

She clicked off the alarm clock before leaving the room and stepped into the dark kitchen. Not knowing where to find any of the gas lanterns, she returned to her room for the kerosene lamp. It would have to do for now. By its dim flickering light, she found the box of Quaker Oatmeal, a suitable pan, and began heating the water. The toast would have to be made in the oven, but she would wait until the last minute so it would stay warm.

Hearing a door open down the hall in the direction of Leona's bedroom, Rebecca wasn't surprised when Leona appeared in the doorway.

"You need more light in here," Leona said.

"I'm okay."

"Stephen will be up in a minute. He'll get one for you. Did you find everything?"

"I think so. Am I too early with breakfast? I'm just making oatmeal as you suggested."

"A little early." Leona attempted a smile, her face and hands swollen. "Stephen goes out to get the horse ready about now. We get the children up at six thirty and eat at about a quarter till seven."

"I'll turn off the burner, then," Rebecca said as she reached for the knob. Already little bubbles were appearing on the bottom of the pan, which settled down quickly with the heat removed.

Leona slid with a groan into a chair by the kitchen table. "Babies are sweet, but they do come the hard way. Too bad I never remember this agony for very long after it's over with."

"It's that bad?"

"Yes, dear, it's that bad. At least now. But like I say, I'll forget as soon as the baby comes. It's funny though. We women long for babies. Then when we get like this, we think never again."

"So why do you do it again?" Rebecca ventured, thinking of Leona's already large family.

Leona sighed. "I ask myself that sometimes. Then I know. When this child, whether it be boy or girl, comes out and I hold him or her on my poor abused stomach, there is simply nothing like it. The joy of being the mother makes us forget the pain. Having the power to create such a wonder as a baby is beyond words, Rebecca. To see the years—even eternity—stretch out in front of you and to know that this child has life because you birthed him...well! That changes everything."

Rebecca was silent, thinking about another pain. *Would I have wanted to meet John if I had known the trouble ahead? Was there an ending coming that would make it all worthwhile?* She surely hoped so.

The door down the hall opened again. Stephen came out, disappeared briefly, and then returned, accompanied by the hiss of a gas lantern.

"You want it in the kitchen or the living room?" he asked, holding the lantern low so it wouldn't blind their eyes.

"Here," Leona said. "We can move it if we have to."

Stephen lifted the lantern to its hook on the ceiling. As he let it go, it swung a few times before coming to rest.

"How are you feeling?" he asked Leona.

"As well as can be expected."

"Are you going to church?"

"I don't think I should," she said, squinting at him. "Not the way I look. Plus, sitting for three hours could be a problem."

"That's what I would think," he said. "You're holding up well so far. There's no use taking chances. What if it comes while we're all at church, though?"

"I can stay with her," Rebecca volunteered from where she was standing by the stove.

Stephen nodded. "It makes no difference who, just that someone should stay with her."

"I'm not helpless," Leona protested, glancing down at her rounded stomach. "I've had seven others, you know."

"Someone should stay with you," Stephen told her firmly.

"But it's Rebecca's first Sunday here. She should be able to go to church."

"I'll be glad to stay," Rebecca repeated. "Really."

"No," Leona decided, glancing up at Stephen from her chair. "We'll let one of the younger ones. Thomas can stay home. He can run over to tell Mrs. Spencer if anything starts. She can come and get you."

"Thomas will be fine," Stephen agreed.

"Good. Then that's decided."

"I'll be a little late for breakfast," Stephen said, glancing at the kitchen clock, having been delayed by the talk.

"What? Five minutes?"

"Something like that."

"Okay," Leona said as Stephen left.

Rebecca pulled a chair out from the kitchen table and took a seat. She might as well sit down until it was time to get the children up.

Leona glanced around conspiratorially at the dark house before asking, "Now that we're alone, are you still dating that John fellow your mom mentioned?"

"Yes." Rebecca was glad the gas lantern was not showing her full face. Her relationship with John was not something she wanted to talk about at the moment.

"Serious?" Leona asked.

"Yes," Rebecca said, keeping her answer short.

"I remember when you lived here in Milroy, you and Atlee used to be so sweet on each other." Leona's face looked as if she was seeing a faraway dream. "It was during your school years. I told myself, if there was ever a case where a couple would be matched up for life, it was you two."

Rebecca said nothing, feeling a chill going all the way through her. *Had Atlee and I been so right for each other? Was I supposed to be with him instead of John? Does Leona know what she is saying? Perfect couple?* Determined not to show her feelings, she held perfectly still.

"I often felt it was such a shame his parents went Mennonite. Several years before you moved, wasn't it?"

"Sometime around then," Rebecca replied, struggling to keep her voice calm.

"Your mother didn't seem to have any problem—you being with him on Saturdays sometimes. I was just at the point of mentioning something to her." Leona waved her hand sympathetically. "I know you were both young...weren't doing anything inappropriate. But you were getting older. But then his parents left, and that was the end of it. Did you get to tell him goodbye?"

"Yes," Rebecca said, sure that her voice was trembling now, "on one of the last days he was in school."

"Well," Leona commented, her voice full of sympathy, "we all have our first loves. Too bad this one didn't work out." Then catching a glimpse of Rebecca's face in the light of the gas lantern, she relented. "Oh! I'm sorry, Rebecca. I didn't mean that the way it sounded. Really, I wouldn't want to imply anything about you and John. I haven't even met him. He's probably even better for you. Please don't think anything of it."

"Atlee and I did spend time together," Rebecca said. "I understand why you see it that way."

"We'd better get breakfast on the way," Leona said, suddenly distracted and, much to Rebecca's great relief, grabbing the edge of the table with both hands to rise. "I'll wake up the children."

Rebecca went to the stove and turned the burner back on. The flame came on in a soft blurb of noise. While the water was heating, she set the bread on the oven racks. From what she figured, a dozen pieces would be a good start. Just before the water boiled, she turned the oven on, then poured the dry oatmeal into the pan of hot water. Wanting it to boil for three minutes, she kept track of the time by the minute hand on the kitchen clock.

As if on cue, the seven sleepy-eyed children showed up and took their places around the table. Rebecca set out plates and bowls for them, keeping an eye on the toast in the oven.

"You know how to make toast?" the oldest girl, Lois, asked, her blue eyes still not awake. "Mom burns it sometimes."

"I think so." Rebecca smiled. It had been awhile since she had been around her cousins, and she had been looking forward to it. "But sometimes I burn it too. It's a tricky thing to do."

"I suppose so," Lois allowed, as Rebecca opened the oven door to flip over the toast. The upper side was already golden brown.

"See," she told Lois. "I waited a little too long to turn it. Now we have to take it out before the bottom is quite done."

"That's better than burned," Elmo, the oldest, offered.

"Well, we can always scrape it off if it burns," Rebecca said, "but I will try to not burn it."

"I think you're going to make a good breakfast," Lois said. "Are you staying all of next week?"

"Yes, very likely. And if the baby doesn't come on time, maybe longer."

"I hope he comes early," Elmo ventured. "That way he might be born on my birthday."

"Oh," Rebecca said. "When's your birthday? Let's see. I should know. But I don't think I do."

"Guess," he said.

"Friday?"

"Nope. Almost. It's Thursday," he said. "And I know when yours is."

"Someone must have told you."

"Well, ya," he admitted. "I heard Mom mention it the other day to Fannie. They were talking about how many of the cousins were twenty-one. You will be the sixth one."

"Yes, I'll be twenty-one," Rebecca said, "but I didn't know I was the sixth."

"You are though," Elmo assured her. "It's a real important date. Lots of things happen when you turn twenty-one."

"I suppose so," Rebecca allowed, a cold chill running up her spine. *The promise. Would he actually come back?* And perhaps most importantly, *Do I want him to?*

Remembering suddenly, she bent down and yanked open the oven door. Already the toast was past done, little shimmers of smoke spilling from the oven. She grabbed each piece in turn and placed them on a plate on top of the oven.

"You burned them," Lois said, disappointment in her voice.

"I don't think so," Rebecca said quickly, picking the last piece of toast out of the oven.

"Not bad enough to have to scrape," Elmo concluded, after lifting himself up on his chair for a closer look at the plate of toast.

"Are you children complaining?" Leona asked, just coming in from the bedroom and pulling a chair out for herself.

"No. I just about burned the toast," Rebecca said, glad there was an excuse for her face, which she was sure was fiery red.

Stephen opened the door and joined them.

With no preliminary gestures, they bowed their heads for prayer, then passed the pan of oatmeal around. The older children helped themselves, while Rebecca made sure the younger ones didn't take too much.

As Rebecca served up little Leroy's portion, he wrinkled his face and said he wanted more. Leona told him he could have more when he had finished his serving. Not totally satisfied or convinced that his mom knew what she was doing, he waited with his spoon in the air while Rebecca mixed in the milk and sugar. The moment she was done, he was dipping the porridge hungrily into his mouth.

Chapter Twenty-five

When breakfast was finished, Rebecca simply stacked the dishes before going to her room to change into Sunday clothes. By the time she returned, the children were seated in the living room waiting. Stephen was already outside, and Leona was in bed resting.

"Ready to go?" she asked the children. They answered by rising as one and silently following her out the door.

She took a backseat with two of the girls, two others got in front with Stephen, and Elmo stood behind her, between the backseat and the end of the buggy, with another of his brothers.

With Stephen slapping the reins to get the horse going, they silently drove out of the driveway and turned right onto the state road. Looking out of her side window, Rebecca caught another glimpse of the school across the fields. It looked lonely on a Sunday morning, as if its bustle of children was seriously missed. The roof was worn, she noticed, surprised that it had not been repaired yet.

"Are they going to fix the roof on the school anytime soon?" she asked Elmo, who was watching with his chin on the backseat.

"There was talk of doing it last fall," he said. "They decided to get through another winter."

"It looks worn," she said, taking one last look.

Elmo shrugged, offering as explanation, "It doesn't leak." He then added, "Church is at Raymond Yoder's place."

Rebecca nodded. She knew where that was—only a little way up 400. *Close enough,* she thought, *where Stephen could be reached easily if Leona went into labor.*

Hopefully that would not happen. Leona seemed fine in the kitchen this morning, so surely labor wouldn't set in suddenly. Then again, babies had their own minds concerning these things. She leaned back on the seat, listening to the sound of the horses hooves on the pavement and relaxed.

After pulling into the driveway at the Yoder's, Stephen stopped to unload the female passengers at the sidewalk. When Rebecca climbed out with the two girls, Elmo hopped over the backseat and sat down for the short ride out to the barn.

The house was as Rebecca had remembered it, a simple two-story house, built in a style long since gone by the wayside. Its slate roof spoke of age and expense no Amish person would go to with present-day prices. The whole place had a feel of long ago and a slower pace of life.

The barn had received a new coat of red paint last summer, from the looks of it. Its upright barn siding looked refreshed, as if it appreciated another chance at this age. Hay hung out of the corners of the second-story double doors, making the mow appear full and overflowing.

Leading the way, Rebecca went into the washroom. There they left their shawls and bonnets. Surrounded by other women who had just arrived, the group slowly moved into the main part of the house, where the greeting began.

Finding a place against the wall, Rebecca stood among a group of young women she knew from her years growing up. This morning she was receiving a considerable amount of attention from her friends who had missed her.

Looking out the window, a van pulling into the driveway caught Rebecca's eye. She recognized it as the one Mary drove yesterday. A feeling of delight filled her at the thought of seeing Mary again.

Five minutes later, Mary worked her way slowly into the kitchen with Elsie and Esther in front of her. Rebecca was reluctant to show Mary too much enthusiasm right there in front of everyone. Being obvious friends with Mennonites, unless they were your immediate relatives, was not a good idea. So she took care to give Mary the same smile she gave the two Amish women.

It was Mary, though, who stayed beside her and whispered, "How are you this morning? You get settled in?"

"Ya. But Leona's not here today. The baby's too close to coming."

Mary nodded, pulling the sleeve of her dress up to glance at her wristwatch. Rebecca saw its gold face shine before Mary quickly drew the sleeve back over it, obviously aware of Amish sentiments about anything resembling jewelry.

"When does the church service start?"

"Nine."

"That's what I thought. And lasts three hours."

Rebecca nodded.

"Hard benches?"

Rebecca raised her eyebrows.

"Just as I remembered, but it's been awhile."

"You can't speak German, can you?"

"No."

"Then you won't understand much either."

"I thought that too."

Women were looking their way, so Rebecca knew that this conversation was going on too long. Even with her visitor status, there were limits, and one limit involved long conversations prior to the church service.

"Sit with me," Rebecca whispered, seeing the men already filing past the outside window heading for the living room door.

Mary readily agreed by following her when the girls got in line behind the women to file in. Rebecca felt the eyes of the boys on her, as she and Mary took a seat on the second bench back. A glance at Mary's face almost made her break into a smile, but she caught it in time. It was obvious that Mary enjoyed the male attention.

Three hours later, Mary stuck tightly to Rebecca on the way out. When Rebecca volunteered to help serve tables, Mary followed suit. So it wasn't until the third change of tables that they finally got a chance to sit down and eat. The now nearly empty tables stretched into the living room and the main bedroom—a few young boys sat on the other side of the room at the men's table, several girls further down from them.

A few women were taking care of the last ones to eat, but no one was paying much attention to this visiting Mennonite and Amish girl, who seemed to know each other well. Surrounded by a sense of privacy, they got down to the business of preparing their peanut butter sandwiches.

"So what was it with the boys this morning?" Mary asked Rebecca, grinning. "Makes me glad I'm single. Do you think that blond boy, about twenty-five or so, might ask me out? He had nice blue eyes."

"I doubt it," Rebecca chuckled. "You're Mennonite."

"Does that make me sinful?"

"No. Just undatable."

"Well!" Mary, in mock indignation, lifted her nose in the air.

Rebecca would have giggled if she were at home, but she wasn't. She was a visiting Amish girl, sitting at the table after church and eating, so she simply shook in silent laughter.

"Well!" Mary repeated, having to smile herself.

"I thought your eye was on the native in Haiti."

"It is. I was just looking."

"Is Marcus better than this Amish boy?"

"At least he would dare to date me."

"I guess you'd need to date to get married."

Mary made a face. "Not always in Haiti. They have spiritual marriages with their spirits."

"Really?"

"Yes. It's part of their custom—voodoo."

"But the church people don't, surely?"

"No, not the church people."

"Have you ever seen these spiritual marriages?"

"No. I wouldn't go to one of the meetings. It's said that they have a service of some sort. Then the person who is to be married to the spirit has convulsions. I guess they don't know any better. They really do need the gospel message."

"Is that why you go down there?"

Mary nodded. "There's just so much need. You can work all day and still feel like you just started."

"This native...Marcus. Aren't you afraid he might fall back into his old ways?"

"No, he's been a Christian for quite a long time. He and his wife were married in a civil ceremony even before they became Christians. That's unusual down there. He's a pretty upstanding fellow."

"Sounds pretty unusual," Rebecca said, pulling back from the table as one of the older women with a coffeepot offered them refills. They both accepted.

"So, do you know yet when you're going back to Ohio?" Mary asked.

"No," Rebecca said, "just after the baby comes."

Rebecca noticed Stephen heading out to the barn for his horse. "I have to go soon," she said, nodding in the direction of the retreating Stephen. "I sure hope Leona was okay today."

"I'm sure she was. Rebecca, it's been nice talking to you again. If I'm around I'll give you a ride back home."

"What are the chances of that?"

"Not much." Mary laughed as Rebecca rose to her feet.

"When are you going back?" she asked, seeing Stephen bring his horse out from the barn.

"Tomorrow morning."

"Have a safe trip."

"Goodbye, then," Mary said as she turned to leave.

Rebecca gathered up the two girls and helped them find their bonnets and shawls. They came out just as Stephen pulled up. Elmo was in the front this time, with two of his brothers standing behind the seat.

~

Leona was seated in the recliner when they walked in the door.

"Are you okay?" Rebecca asked.

"Yes, nothing has happened yet."

"You want anything special? Can I make you lunch?"

"No. I'll just nibble on whatever you have for supper."

"That would be the casserole from last night unless you want me to make something fresh."

"No," Leona said, "tomorrow will be a big enough day. I'm afraid you'll have to do the wash."

"I was expecting to," Rebecca said.

"I haven't gotten things caught up very well, I'm afraid," Leona said apologetically.

"That's what I'm here for," Rebecca replied, assuring her. "We'll just keep you as comfortable as we can and have a nice quiet evening."

"I'll be glad when this is over," Leona groaned, her hands on her stomach, glancing around to see if any of her children were in earshot before she said it. None were, and so she groaned again for good measure.

"I'll be right back," Rebecca said, heading toward her bedroom to change into work clothing. When she came back, she brought Leona another pillow from the hall closet and then went into the kitchen to make popcorn and warm the casserole in the oven.

"Oh, Rebecca?" Leona's voice came to her. "Did you want to go to the singing?"

"No. I'm fine," Rebecca assured her. "No problem at all."

It would be as comfortable an evening as she could make it for the family, even though she was missing Wheat Ridge and her own room at home. But to her surprise and horror, she realized she was not missing John. That discovery left her cold.

Chapter Twenty-six

The singing was almost over in the home where church had been that morning. It wouldn't be long before someone led out in the closing song. The clock showed it was five till nine. That morning he had been watching Rebecca Keim, but she hadn't given him so much as a look.

It made him mad. When he thought about it, Rebecca was just the kind of girl he really wanted—slim, dark-haired, carrying herself with class, her smile like a ray of sunshine. But he had seen her on the trip to Harshville, down by that bridge with a young man. Was she going to marry him? Or was she still free?

And what was Rebecca doing here anyway? And with that Mennonite girl? Rebecca came from this community, so she was probably visiting. The other girl could be the driver of the van that was parked outside, although that didn't make a lot of sense. Most hired drivers were elderly men or women, not young like that girl all done up in English clothing.

Mennonites had no sense at all with things like that. She had no right to be in their church service, tormenting him and, no doubt, others too. But what could one do? At least she wasn't here every Sunday. That would be torture.

Anyway, he deserved someone like Rebecca or the Mennonite. Certainly he deserved more than Susie. She had been looking at him all morning, and he was tired of it. Couldn't she see that it was all a little too much?

Maybe it wouldn't have been as bad if Rebecca and that Mennonite girl hadn't been there this morning to pour salt into his wound. And on the very evening he was to take Susie home...*plain* Susie, who had suited him just fine before, he reminded himself.

He could have been happy with Susie, would have, in fact, if he hadn't thought about what more money might do.

Looking into Susie's eyes would never be the same now, having just been reminded of what he was missing. And would continue to miss without the money that would rightfully be his and his family's.

He glanced over at Susie. Her eyes too were on the clock. She saw him, and her cheeks flushed momentarily. He should have been delighted, and would have he told himself, if Rebecca had stayed home where she belonged instead of wasting her dad's money with a stupid visit.

It seemed he saw money everywhere these days. Saw its influence on people—the decisions they made and the actions they carried out. Saw it in people's eyes when they looked at him. Saw it in town on Saturday at the gas station where he stopped to fill the gasoline can for Emma. Everywhere someone was spending money, hiding money, taking money—everyone except him.

This would all change once his mother had her way. Of course, he would do his part, when and where he could. Then he would have what was his.

He took a deep breath. The hands on the clock just crossed nine o'clock, and someone started the closing song. He would soon have Susie in his buggy, his first date. Someone so plain and common. He swallowed hard.

Well, he supposed, that was the hand dealt to him, and one he would have to take. Just like the hands of the men he shook in front of the barn every Sunday morning. Some of those hands were hard and calloused, while others, the hands of those who worked in shops, were not quite as rough.

Thinking of hands, he found himself calculating how much each man behind the hand was worth. Never having thought about it much before, it took a little doing. He had to remember what each home looked like, how many horses they owned, and what the rumors implied about how much debt remained. Sitting there, he came to the conclusion that the farmers were coming in last. A raw chill ran up his spine.

That he was a farmer shamed him till he almost said out loud, right there surrounded by the young people, *I will prove I'm not poor. This is one farmer who will not have to endure this shame.*

The last notes of the song died away. Soon it would be time to go. Time to stand up, knowing that a girl would soon be doing likewise. She would be following him outside, getting into his buggy, allowing him to drive her home. In spite of his anger, the emotions swelled up in him.

Momentarily he forgot about the sight of Rebecca and her English girlfriend from earlier in the day and was lost in the pleasure of this thought. When he rose to his feet though, just after Johnny Mast did, it all came back in a rush. Following Johnny, he walked out.

Johnny's girl was Susan Hershberger from over in the other district. Her father, Ben, owned the Hershberger Harness Shop north of Milroy. Ben was one of the men, Luke had calculated, who almost had his place paid off. Susan was their third girl, tall for her age, her thin face framed in the blond hair that was tucked under her white head covering.

Luke caught a glimpse of Susan, as she sat in the front row, when he walked by. She had the same look on her face for Johnny that Susie had for him. Anger rose up in him. *Why did a girl like that not care for me? They would, if they only knew,* he thought.

If they only knew that three farms were in his family—farms that were paid off and debt free. Surely with that knowledge on his side, he would be able to get whomever he wanted. Walking toward the door, feeling more and more frustrated, his hands clenched into tight fists.

Tomorrow he would go to Emma and demand that she name the

proper heirs and have this over with. It had to be that way. He could not hold off any longer. Time was slipping away from him, and beautiful girls were being snatched up right under his nose.

As soon as he arrived for his daily routine, he would march right in and confront Emma. She would see it too, understanding that what he was saying was right.

And then he realized he would never do it because his mother would not permit such a thing.

Johnny, walking in front of Luke, held the door momentarily so it wouldn't slam in his face. Smiling, Johnny nodded when Luke's hand reached out for the door. Luke attempted to make a smile cross his face but couldn't—his anger forbid it.

"No girl tonight?" Johnny said, glancing at Luke's face and taking a guess at his obvious displeasure.

Luke wanted to yell, wanted to tell him that he too could get the good-looking girls. That Susie was just a temporary thing. That he was as good as Johnny was. That money was in their family too. But none of that would do, so he simply said, "I'm taking Susie home."

"Really?" Johnny lifted his eyebrows, the light from the living room still reaching his face. "I thought you'd never get around to taking a girl home."

Luke felt the anger boil again, but he took a deep breath.

"She's not too bad," Johnny said, the shadows almost covering his broad smile.

Luke still said nothing as he stepped out the door and turned to close it.

"She's about right for you." Johnny's voice came from the darkness in front of him. "Glad to see you two together."

Luke wanted to tell Johnny he was worthy of much better than Susie. Worthy of a beautiful girl like Johnny himself had, but the words stuck in his throat.

"Have a good evening," Johnny said cheerfully, his shape barely discernable in the darkness.

They walked in silence to the barn, Luke following at a distance, Johnny marching ahead. Once in the barn, they went in different directions to find their horses. Luke took his time in the stall, where he had tied his horse, to let Johnny get out of the way.

When he heard the shuffle of horse hooves in the straw and Johnny's cheerful "Goodnight" at the barn door to another boy coming in, he figured the coast must be clear.

Luke led his horse out and found his buggy, only to discover Johnny preparing his own buggy just two spaces away. Ignoring him, Luke walked by and waited until Johnny took off.

There was no hiding the shiny oiled look on the black buggy even in the dark. Johnny had a buggy to match his girl and a sleek horse, which held its head high. They made a grand sight when the light from the kitchen caught them at the end of the sidewalk, light shining on the black canvas.

Luke wearily lifted the shafts on his buggy and led his horse into place. He would pull over to the house and pick up Susie for the ride home. His first date.

Chapter Twenty-seven

Forcing thoughts of Rebecca, of Johnny's girl, and that Mennonite girl from his mind, Luke focused on the task at hand. He might as well enjoy this evening. There might not be much money in his family, but there was more than what Susie had. He simply had no need to feel ashamed around her as long as she was all he had…for now.

Finding his courage and good humor rising, he pulled his buggy up short by the sidewalk. Where was Susie? Why hadn't she come out? Didn't she recognize his buggy? What an embarrassment. If his girl, on her first date, had to be told how to find his buggy, then this grievous thing would reduce him to the lowest of the low. It would be something to hang his head over; something spoken about in low voices at the singings.

Almost on the verge of panic, he willed himself to keep looking up the sidewalk. Another buggy was already in position behind him, its horse pawing the air in anticipation, the occasional piece of gravel flying up against the dashboard of the buggy. It would not be long before everyone saw what was going on.

To his great relief, a girl's figure appeared around the corner of the house. There was no way to tell exactly who it was, what with the bonnet pulled tightly around her face, the shawl, and the darkness. It was the shape of Susie, but it was also the shape of a dozen other Amish girls. He was about to panic again, thinking that it might be the girl heading for the buggy behind him. This would only add to his shame.

She veered to the left, disappearing out of sight behind his buggy.

This could still mean anything. It could just as easily be the girl going to her boyfriend's buggy as Susie coming to his buggy. For the horrible three seconds of waiting, he saw doom hanging over him, shame completely overrunning this whole evening.

Susie's hand appeared before anything else. She grabbed the side of the buggy, placed her foot on the step, and gracefully, with the balance perfected by a hundred such maneuvers, came through the door to sit beside him on the seat. Only the edges of her shawl brushed his legs.

The relief shot through him like a stimulant. His voice carried his intense pleasure. "Good evening."

"Good evening," she said, more than matching the intensity of his voice. This was her first date, longed for and anticipated until at times it had turned into that hopeless despair a person feels about things that may never happen.

"You liked the singing?" he asked, searching for anything to say at the moment.

"Oh, it was nice, I guess," she said shyly. "I was thinking about when you would take me home."

She distinctly leaned toward him until her shoulder pressed against his arm, her eyes looking ahead in the darkness. This was much better than he had imagined. He pulled himself up in his seat, feelings of manhood flowing through him.

"I saw you watching the clock," he said. "I'm glad you said yes the other day at the post office." He laughed a little, pleasure now filling the place where his anger had been.

There was no response from Susie, just an increasing of the pressure on his arm. They drove out of the driveway and turned north toward her place.

"Where were the visitors from today?" he asked, as he let his horse pick up speed.

"I didn't know all of them. Most came from Holmes County." Her voice came from beside him, thrilling him with its nearness. Now he remembered how much he had wanted her with him, for this moment, all to himself, his girl.

"I think they all have family here," he offered. "At least Rebecca Keim does." The name was no more out of his mouth than he wished he hadn't said it. Glancing at her in the darkness, he waited for the shoulder to draw away, but it did not.

"Her aunt is having a baby. She's here to help."

"I see." The subject really held no interest to him, other than not wanting to see her on another Sunday to torment him with her presence. "So when is the baby due?"

"This week," she said, now drawing herself up straight on the seat, away from him and pulling her shawl tighter, as if she were cold.

"You cold?" he asked, reaching for the buggy blanket under the seat. Giving the black robe a shake to undo it, he wrapped one end around his legs and offered the other side to her.

"A little," she said, taking the offered end and wrapping it around herself. In a moment she pulled it up higher on her chest. "Are you always this interested in babies? That's really sweet of you," she mentioned in a half-whisper.

His mind spun in desperation, searching for a response. "I was just wondering how long Rebecca would be around," he said. Whatever her response was, it would be easier than pretending an overwrought interest in babies.

"Oh," she said simply, "you knew her from school?"

"We all did. She was a grade ahead of me."

"Do you know what grade I was in?" she asked.

"Mine, of course," he said, smiling even though she couldn't see him. This was going quite well.

She breathed deeply, as he pulled in the reins to turn into her driveway. Parking by their barn, she waited in the buggy. He hopped out and tied his horse, making sure the rope was tight—he wouldn't want to come out and discover his horse had gone home by itself. With that secure, Luke walked back to the buggy, where Susie was already on the ground waiting for him.

In the hushed darkness, he allowed her to lead them toward the house. Her shawl switched against the bushes at the end of the walk, their still silhouettes barely visible. That was something he admired about this place. They might be poor, but the place was well-kept. Nothing like how the English kept their lawns, just a line of green bushes behind a split rail fence. Appropriate and tasteful. If he had to stay poor all his life, Susie might be a good wife to have. Trained, as she would no doubt be, in making the best out of little.

He would still need to check if she was a big spender. Even with money, a big spender would be out. It was indeed something to keep in mind.

She was holding the front door open for him, so he brought his mind back to the present. "Your parents keep the place up nice," he said.

"Yes. Mom is good at that."

He couldn't help himself, and so he replied, "You're probably learning too."

She laughed, her voice low and bubbly. "I hope so."

Stepping past her, he wasn't surprised to find both her parents still up. That was the kind of people they were. And he was glad. It made him feel welcome.

"Hello," he said smiling.

"Good evening," James, her father, replied, nodding at him and glancing up from reading *The Budget.* He was a short man with a beard still black as coal and blue eyes that shone when he was interested in something. Luke noticed they were shining. Nancy, seated on a chair beside her husband, only smiled at him.

Susie, who seemed at a loss with what to do, finally cleared her throat and said, "I guess we'll sit in the living room."

"Ah, sure." With that decision made, Luke took a seat on the couch.

"We were just ready to leave." Nancy looked in James's direction.

"Oh! Ya," he muttered, laying *The Budget* on the floor. He rose and nodded his head again before heading toward their bedroom in the back of the house. Nancy followed right behind him.

"Well," Susie sighed, letting out her breath as her mother disappeared around the corner. She then came over and sat beside Luke on the couch. "It's so good to have you here," she said softly, adding, "finally."

Luke settled into the couch, a feeling of contentment going all the way through him. Was this the way it felt to have a girl? He supposed it must be, since that's the way it was with Susie. Feeling completely confident, he reached out without any compunction and laid his hand on hers. When she blushed violently, he squeezed her hand gently for just a moment, then let go.

The pleasure was all he had ever thought it would be and more. He felt a wave of emotion for her, thinking that perhaps he would still date her even when he came into the money, the thought bringing him more pleasure than he had expected.

She rose to her feet, her face still red. "Let me get you something to eat."

He nodded and watched her go toward the kitchen.

She returned moments later, carrying a plate of cookies and crumb-sprinkled brownies with little swirls of caramel on top.

"Chocolate chip?" he asked, glancing down at the plate.

She nodded, a hopeful look on her face.

"I love those," he assured her as he took one of the cookies.

"Would you like some orange juice?"

"Yes," he said, the words coming out almost in a croak. He coughed to cover it up.

She returned to the kitchen. Meanwhile, all thoughts of her plainness left Luke's mind. He felt like a man in her presence, the wonder of it filling him to overflowing.

When she came back, he asked, "You're not going to eat one?"

"No," she said. "I've had enough food for the day. Plus I'm nervous."

"You don't have to be," he said warmly, yet delighted that she should be nervous around him.

She took her seat beside him again, watching as he ate another cookie.

The conversation turned to the recent snowstorm and what might be ahead weather wise. They discussed the weddings in November and who they knew would probably be marrying soon. By eleven o'clock, Luke told Susie he had to be going, stood up, and walked to the door. Since that was a little early, a cloud crossed her face, but it disappeared when he asked her if he could see her again.

When she said yes, he squeezed her hand again before stepping out onto the porch. As he untied his horse and drove out the lane, he caught himself whistling a tune he had heard at the gas station last week. It was an English tune, forbidden really, but he decided that this was a special occasion.

Going down the road, a cloud soon crossed his mind. Tomorrow he would have to face the money problem again. Money, Emma, and his mother, which had seemed so far away only moments before. He decided he would let it stay that way, pushing everything but thoughts of Susie out of his mind.

Chapter Twenty-eight

On Monday morning Rebecca was determined to prepare a full breakfast and have it done in time for Stephen to eat before catching his ride to work. That was at six thirty. It was now ten minutes till six. She was watching the bacon at the moment, making sure it didn't burn.

The water for the oatmeal had been measured, poured into a pan, and set on the burner. The eggs she would do last. That way they would not have to be kept warm—as she would need the oven for the toast.

She looked up when she heard footsteps in the hall. Leona groaned as she came into the kitchen.

"You don't have to make so much breakfast," Leona protested, coming over to survey the frying bacon.

"Now, you just sit down," Rebecca replied. "I can handle it."

"I know, but I don't feel too bad this morning." Leona kept her place at the bacon pan, testing and flipping the pieces with a spatula in one hand, her other hand on her extended stomach. "A lot of activity," she stated flatly, as if she were speaking to the whole world, "but no signs yet." Then she gasped. "Oh! Stephen's lunch. I forgot to tell you about that."

"What goes in it?"

"No, you're not going to do that yet. Here. You take over the bacon. I'll fix Stephen's sandwich and throw in some other things."

Rebecca decided it was better to go along with Leona and stepped in front of the pan of sizzling bacon. Leona took over a corner of the kitchen table to make the sandwich, moving at a surprising rate of speed.

"When do the children have to get up?" Rebecca asked, turning on the burner for the water.

"Six thirty or so. Stephen eats before they do on weekdays." Leona slid the sandwich in a plastic bag and from there into a lunch pail. "He's probably coming right now," Leona said, hearing the sound of footsteps. When Stephen entered the kitchen, she told him, "We're almost ready."

He nodded and took a chair, but then noticed Leona making his lunch. Rising, he went to the cupboard and handed her a bag of chips and some cookies. As Leona packed the extra items, Rebecca placed the bread in the oven to toast.

"Can you still work outside in this weather?" Leona asked Stephen, as he sat down again. Returning to the bacon pan, she took a piece out and held it up in the air for inspection. Satisfied, she placed it on the plate, quickly removing the rest.

"We have metal to put on a pole barn. I imagine that's what the boss will try to accomplish first. If there's ice on the boards, we'll likely move over to the Westmorland job. There's inside trim work there."

"Will the work last all winter?" Leona asked.

"I think so. If not, we may have to drive a little farther. There's work there for sure."

Leona sighed. "With the baby coming, it would be rough if you were out of work."

"I've thought of that. Last winter we had a slowdown. It looks better now. Especially with the amount of trim work the boss claims is coming up."

"You don't have to worry about things like this, do you?" Leona asked in Rebecca's direction.

"No. Not money right now," Rebecca said. "Other things."

"It's always something," Leona sighed wearily. "When I deliver this baby, I'll sure be thankful."

"Is the midwife checking on you again?" Stephen asked.

"No, not until the baby comes. When she was here on Friday evening, she said things look well enough to wait until the baby is on its way."

"That's something to be thankful for," Stephen assured her. "The Lord has been good to us with all the births."

"Yes," Leona agreed, setting a plate in front of him. Rebecca already had four eggs fried and was taking the toast out of the oven. "We count ourselves blessed. No matter how it turns out, He knows what He is doing."

"I have enough eggs done for Stephen," Rebecca said, from in front of the oven. "The oatmeal's ready too. Why don't you start?"

"No, we three are going to eat together," Leona said. "Make four more eggs. That doesn't take too long. Then we can eat."

"My ride'll be here," Stephen said.

Leona changed her mind quickly. "Wait on the eggs, Rebecca. Come sit down, and we can have prayer. Then Stephen can eat while you make some more eggs."

Rebecca stopped in mid-air, an egg in hand, her arm raised. She quickly put the egg back into the carton and took a seat at the table. They bowed their heads together for a few minutes. When Stephen lifted his head, Rebecca moved back to the stove and cracked four more eggs into the pan.

By the time those were done, Stephen was already eating his oatmeal, having gone through the four eggs, bacon, and two pieces of toast. Leona, who was waiting for Rebecca before starting, took two of the eggs from the plate when Rebecca brought them over and sat down. "I'm hungry this morning," she said. "Is that good or bad?"

"I wouldn't know," Rebecca said, sliding the other two eggs onto her plate.

"It's good," Stephen said with conviction. "I think it's going to be another easy birth."

"Don't say that, " Leona gasped. "Such things are best left unsaid.

If good is coming, it will come in its own time. We shouldn't try to encourage it."

"I wasn't," Stephen protested. "I was just observing. Either way, you'll be okay."

"I hope so. My! I wish this would be over." Leona glanced down at her bulging stomach.

"I can imagine," Stephen said quietly.

"No, you can't," she told him. "You've never given birth to a child."

He grinned. "I hope I never do."

"Don't be smart," she retorted. "It's not fun."

Stephen leaned over the table to squeeze her hand. "It'll soon be over. Then we will have another blessing in our home."

Gravel crunched on the driveway outside, as headlights came streaming through the front window.

"Your ride's here," Leona said.

"Have a good day," Stephen said to both of them. He took his lunch pail and went out the front door.

While Rebecca fried more eggs, Leona woke the children. They gathered around the table, rubbing their sleepy eyes.

"I want plenty of bacon," Elmo declared, awake enough to voice his request.

"You will get three pieces. Only three," Leona said.

He grunted his dissatisfaction. "I need more than that to do my chores."

"Then you can eat more oatmeal. That's better for you anyway."

"It doesn't taste as good as bacon."

Leona shook her head. "None of us can always have things that taste the best in life. You might as well learn that now as later."

Elmo shrugged his shoulders, having heard that lesson before.

"So how's school going?" Rebecca asked Lois.

"Oh, okay," she ventured cautiously. "I got a hundred in English last week."

"That's because she's a *girl,*" Elmo said, reaching for the eggs. He slid three onto his plate.

"There's nothing wrong with English," Rebecca replied before Leona had a chance to speak up. "Everyone should learn it."

Elmo snorted. "Some of the boys draw ugly faces on their English workbooks." He laughed at the thought. "Henry has a huge dragon on his. It's breathing fire and roasting a girl."

"That's horrible," Leona gasped. "Doesn't teacher pay any attention to what you boys are doing?"

Rebecca, with a little more recent school experience, chuckled at the description. "How does the picture look?"

"Come to think of it, it was a pretty good drawing," Elmo said. "The dragon had real long spines, all the way up in the air. They hung down right at the end. His fire went out in a great swoop and swirled right around the girl. The girl looked like," he glanced at Lois, with a grin on his face, and turned to whisper in Rebecca's direction with his hand on the edge of his mouth, "Lois."

"The wicked boy," Lois snapped. "He's always in trouble. Now he's making fun of me."

Leona was gasping again. "I can't believe you. Both of you. How can you talk like that? It's not right."

Elmo shrugged his shoulders again. "I was just answering Rebecca's question."

"You ought to say it better," Leona said.

"I just told it the way it was. I didn't know there was a better way."

Leona sighed, piling the last of the eggs onto the serving plate as Rebecca shut the burner off.

"Do you know why I asked you about the drawing?" Rebecca asked Elmo.

"No," he said, a fork full of eggs halfway to his mouth. As he paused, egg dripped back onto his plate. He quickly completed the trip, chewing while he waited for the answer.

"Because apparently Henry is good at drawing. Which could be considered just as girly as English."

Elmo's face lit up with glee. "I never thought of that. Wait till I tell him."

"Don't do that," Rebecca said. "There's nothing wrong with being able to draw."

"You just said it's girly. What boy wants to be girly?" Elmo said.

"I didn't say it's girly. I said it could be considered as girly as English. The point is—neither is girly. They just are what they are. If a boy can do either well, then they're boyish."

Elmo was still grinning. "I'm still going to tell him. Wait until he hears this. He'll never draw again."

"You will do no such thing," Leona said, glaring at him. "You will behave yourself. Leave such things alone. If Henry can draw, you ought to be glad for him instead of trying to get him to stop."

"This is all getting too complicated." Elmo put the last of his eggs in his mouth and reached for the oatmeal. "You always complicate things all up."

"That's so you can learn," Leona said. "Most things in life aren't simple."

"They are if they're just left alone." Elmo topped off his oatmeal with a large spoonful of brown sugar and slowly stirred in some milk.

"Well, you children will learn what's right. You will all grow up to be decent church members like you ought to be. Now finish your breakfast and get going with the chores. There's no sense being late. See, it's already after seven o'clock."

"Okay," Elmo mumbled, bent over his oatmeal, "I'll not tell Henry anything about his drawing."

"The rest of you, gather up the wash from your rooms. Make sure your rooms are straightened up before you change for school. I'll pack your lunches."

"You think the wash will dry on the line today?" Rebecca asked, as she began clearing off the table.

"I thought of that too," Leona muttered. "I sure hope so because I don't have a place for it inside, and we *have* to wash."

She wrinkled up her face and said, "Rebecca, I'm so glad you could come early."

Chapter Twenty-nine

Watching the children walk down the road toward school, swinging their lunch pails, brought back memories for Rebecca. Elmo walked behind the younger ones, who ran ahead, as if he already felt his responsibilities as the oldest of the family.

"They do grow up fast," Leona said from nearby, having walked up to watch too. The two smallest boys, Leroy and James, were leaning on the front window.

"I was just thinking about walking to school," Rebecca said. "It's funny how the simple things make the memories."

"Yeah," Leona agreed. She smiled at James and Leroy as they tired of watching out the window and went into their room to play. "Yet it's probably times like this that will bring tears later. Simple things. I rarely have time to watch them go. You think the Lord sometimes gives us trouble so we'll slow down and notice what's really important?"

Rebecca frowned. "I don't know. You know more about those things than I do. There does seem to be plenty of trouble in life."

"You have trouble?" Leona laughed at the thought. "You haven't even had children yet."

"No, that's true," Rebecca allowed, thinking of her own trouble.

"I guess the Lord gives us what trouble we need," Leona concluded.

"You think He gives us the strength to bear it?" Rebecca asked.

"Always has for me," Leona said. "I don't know what everyone else would say, but that's been my experience. And I think the plain life has less trouble in it too. I don't know how the English handle it with all the things they have going."

"I don't know either," Rebecca agreed. "Not that I know that much about it."

"I don't either. God help us once we think we know everything."

Rebecca chuckled, "You think that's ever going to happen?"

"No. But, oh my! I shouldn't even say that. Like the preacher said on Sunday, *Wer denkt, dass er steht, Acht geben, damit er fällt.* Let him who thinks he stands, take heed lest he fall."

"It's a scary walk. This God thing."

"But He helps us. He always does."

"You weren't there on Sunday," Rebecca said, changing the subject. "The English driver was there. Her name is Mary. She's an older girl—thirty or so, I would guess. Never married. Mennonite."

"That's surprising. The drivers are usually older people."

"Yes, I know. But Mary isn't. I got to know her a little on the trip. She's a missionary in Haiti."

"You didn't get to know her *too* well, did you?" Leona raised her eyebrows. "Don't want any of that Mennonite rubbing off on you. You're doing fine mission work right now just by helping me out."

"That's what Dad would say," Rebecca agreed, then continued. "Mary goes down for lengthy stays in Haiti. Six months at a time. She's thinking of marrying a native."

"Oh, no!" Leona's eyes got big.

"Yes. Isn't that something? She's not that bad looking either. Said that Mennonite boys just never interested her. Something about being too boring."

Leona gasped. "Now I have heard everything. I thought Mennonite life would be mighty interesting. What with all the modern things they have."

"Just goes to show that everything gets boring after awhile, I guess."

"So is she actually going to marry this native man? What if he runs away on her?"

"She seems to think he won't. His name is Marcus. He's been a Christian for a while already, she said. Pastors one of their churches down in Haiti."

"Is he divorced?" Leona asked with suspicion.

"No, his wife died not that long ago."

"Well, that sounds a little better. He might be more stable than most, then."

"She didn't say she was going to marry him—just that he had been looking at her."

Leona gasped again. "Well, I would think so. A white woman has no business down there in the first place. I hope you haven't gotten any ideas from her." She glared at Rebecca. "You wouldn't, would you? Go Mennonite?"

Rebecca laughed. "Of course not!"

"You never know. One has to be careful when making friends."

"Mary's nice enough."

"*Those* are the dangerous ones." Seeing the look on Rebecca's face, Leona quickly changed course. "There are nice Mennonite people who are just fine. I know some. Although we have been blessed not to have too many as relatives, that's when you are most tempted to let go of your convictions."

"You say we don't have too many in the family," Rebecca stated and then asked, "Why do you think that is?"

"The blessing of the Lord, I guess. It sure takes His help to stay true to the faith even without having Mennonite relatives trying to persuade us." Seeing that the breakfast cleanup still needed doing, Leona said, "Well! We had better get busy. The day is wasting away."

"I think I saw the washing machine out in the garage, didn't I?" Rebecca asked. "That's what you're using as your washroom?"

"Yes. But if it's too cold out there, just leave the door into the house open. There's only one register in the garage. We keep it open just enough so things don't freeze."

Carrying the hamper that the girls had filled, Rebecca stepped into the garage, leaving the door open behind her. The brisk cold would have been bearable, but this definitely made it more pleasant.

Empting the hamper onto the floor, she went back for more. Five hampers later and with wash all around her, she began sorting things out—whites and linens together, colors, pants in a separate pile.

Stopping as soon as she had a pile big enough to start a load, she turned the dial on the back of the Maytag, dumped in a cup of soap, and waited until the tub had filled with warm water—little bubbles from the soap forming one on top of the other. She watched them float, her eyes glancing every now and then at the water level because there was no automatic shutoff. It would be nasty work to mop up the floor if she neglected to turn the water off on time.

When the level of the water was just right, she turned the knob to off, stepped back toward the gasoline engine, and choked and started it. On the second jerk, it roared to life, filling the garage with its racket. Stephen must keep things in shape, she thought, watching the little motor vibrating.

Stepping over the extended muffler, which took the fumes through the outer wall of the garage, she grabbed the handle, which tightened the belt that stretched from the motor to the Maytag, and pulled it down. Things snapped into place, the washer sprang to life, and the noise lessened a little as the motor pulled on the load.

To the roar of the motor and the swish-swish of the Maytag, she sorted the remainder of the clothing. With the heat generated by her own movements and that of the motor, she soon shut the door to the main house. That racket had to carry into the house pretty loudly, she figured. Now that it was warmer, Leona might be grateful for a quieter version of washday.

With the load done, she stopped the plunger by disengaging it with the pullout button on the side. She then swung the wringer into place and set an empty hamper behind it. The two rollers churned without a sound when she turned them on. Ivory colored and made of soft rubber, they squeezed every drop of water from the clothing she fed through.

They could be murder on fingers if one got caught in them. Nothing would stop their roll except the on and off lever or the safety release on top, which was not obvious to the eye of untrained persons. Many an Amish child had his first introduction into terror when his hand followed the piece of wash into the wringer.

If mother was around, it was usually just a matter of a serious scare. If not, the entire arm would enter up to the shoulder. The machine would then spin on the armpit until the child's screams brought an adult who knew how to hit the safety bar. First and second degree burns were not unknown from the experience.

With the hamper full of clean wash, she placed a box of wooden snaps on top of the clothing and set it away from the washer. Before heading outside, she refilled the machine and started another load of wash.

Stepping outside, the sun was already climbing fast and trying to heat things up. From what she could tell, it would only get better. Behind the house and to the south of the garage was the wash line. Its three wire strings were dripping from melting frost.

She took out the first pair of pants and shook them in the morning sunshine. Pleasure ran through her as she pinned the pants onto the line. There was something primitive and satisfying about the moment, increased by each item that got snapped onto the line.

When the hamper was empty, the line hung heavy from the load, its contents unmoving in the morning cold. Little shimmers of steam rose from the first few pieces as the sun caught them in its warmth. She took a deep breath, taking a moment to rest and run her eyes down the line of clothing. In that moment, standing there and looking at her wash, she felt feminine—like a woman, like the world was made for her, like she belonged here among children, home, and love.

Oddly, there was no particular man associated with her thoughts, just the nebulous feelings of being held close by strong arms. Moments later, she remembered her duty with a start and reached down and into the hamper.

Back in the garage, she found the next load of wash almost done. She waited for a few minutes, then pulled the button out to shut it off. From there it was back to running dripping wash through the wringer and hanging it out on the line. By eleven thirty everything was on the line, and she was ready for lunch.

Leona had prepared two sandwiches and had set them on the kitchen table with glasses of orange juice.

"My, you are a fast worker," she exclaimed.

Rebecca smiled. "And tired," she replied

"Well, I would think so. I have the sandwiches fixed. When do you think the wash will dry?"

Rebecca thought about it and said, "I would say late this afternoon."

"You think it will dry completely?"

"Maybe you'd better go out and see," Rebecca said doubtfully. "I think it will. But Mom is always better at knowing those things than I am."

Leona nodded. "I'll go out and look after we have something to eat. You certainly need it more than I do."

"But you're feeding someone else," Rebecca said.

"And what about us? We're hungry too," James piped up.

"Yes, I suppose you are," Leona chuckled, taking a seat and motioning for Rebecca to take one too.

As they ate, Rebecca decided to pose the question she had been harboring since she arrived.

"Do you think I could visit the schoolhouse this afternoon? Before the wash is dry?"

Leona thought, did a few calculations, and replied, "I don't know why this wouldn't be a good time. I figured you would want to visit sometime. The boys are behaving themselves, at least for now, the wash doesn't get dry till around four or so, and that would give you plenty of time. We can't possibly put it all away tonight at that hour, but once it's inside, we can take our time tomorrow. I hope I'm well enough to help then."

"I'll do it myself if you're not," Rebecca assured her.

Leona nodded. "I'll go out and take a look at the wash. This afternoon may be the best time for you to walk on over to the school."

"Well, finish your sandwich. I'm not in such a hurry," Rebecca said.

So Leona did take her time, grinning openly at her rounded stomach when she was done. "I hope he's satisfied. Now, let's go see about that wash."

Chapter Thirty

Leona carefully stepped down the two steps and into the garage, gasping as her foot landed on the concrete floor. "I guess we could have gone out the front door, but this is closer."

"You don't have to come out at all," Rebecca assured her.

"Ach! Ya! It does me good. I've been in the house way too much—baby coming or not." Leona opened the outside door, breathing the cold air in deeply. "I *need* this."

Carefully Leona walked around the back to the wash line. Touching the first few pieces of wash and brushing her fingers over them, a pleased smile crossed her face. "They're already drying quite well."

"That's what I was hoping you would say," Rebecca said.

The verdict was the same with the other lines and also on the farthest end, which Leona insisted on checking also. "I need the exercise. Maybe it will hurry things up."

"Will you be okay then for an hour or so? What about Leroy and James?" Rebecca was still concerned.

"Oh! Ya! I'll watch them. You go on up to the school. It will be three o'clock or later before everything's dry. The girls can help you carry the wash in when they come home."

"I'll go right away then," Rebecca replied.

As Leona went inside, Rebecca took a deep breath and began her walk toward the school.

Out on the road, she stayed close to the shoulder in case a car came, but the road was empty.

To Rebecca's right, she noticed that the English farmer had recently worked the field. It was plowed under, the rows of soil fully exposed to the wind and weather. To her left were the hay fields of Emery Stoll, if she remembered correctly. She could see his place coming into view at the corner of 500 and the state road.

Emery's farm had a prosperous look to it—a red-roofed smaller barn on 500 and a large two-tiered brown one on the state road. The white two-story house was in a typical Amish rectangular shape, but without a front or back porch.

Behind that was the schoolhouse, its worn roof looking no better than it had on Sunday. In the back was the baseball field. She could see children bursting out of the back doors for their lunch-hour playtime, having just finished eating inside.

Quickening her pace, she wanted to arrive in time to watch. Thinking of cutting across the fields as she would have done when younger, she decided against it. If someone should see her, it would look strange indeed to see a nearly twenty-one-year-old Amish girl walking across a hay field in the middle of the day.

But she wanted to do it—badly wanted to do it. Why did big people no longer do what they wanted? Now they had to consider how it looked. When she had been younger, she wouldn't have thought about it for a minute. Then, she was sure, anyone seeing her would have thought of her as adventurous, courageous, maybe even seen a sign of a bright future in a child who took the straight way to her destination. Now, it was different. She was an adult.

Walking as quickly as she could, her breath was soon coming in short jerks. This would not do either. Sweating under her coat would make for a miserable time watching the ballgame behind the schoolhouse. Taking off the coat was not an option either because it was simply too cool for that.

She wanted to watch the game because it would take her back to another day when she and Atlee had played on this very ground. Back then when the sides were picked, the captain who picked Atlee would usually pass on a boy for his next pick in favor of her.

It was highly unusual for any girl to be picked until the best of the boys were already chosen. But the risk was usually taken because of her reputation as a first baseman. She consistently caught the balls Atlee threw to her from his position as shortstop. Groans would sometimes break out at the pairing, but the opposing captain was not about to waste his pick of a boy by choosing her without Atlee.

She smiled at the memory. She enjoyed it…yet why did these memories make her afraid somehow? Was it that they inevitably led to memories of the promise? Was this what she was afraid of?

With renewed courage, she walked on. She would just have to face what might lay ahead and go wherever the fear was hiding. And then it would be over, wouldn't it? Comforted, she slowed down as a car passed her.

As she resumed her speed, she remembered that this was where she and Atlee had walked so many times. Right here but in the opposite direction of course…so many years ago now. He, a freckle-faced, brown-haired boy, blue eyes shining—and she with her thin knees pumping up and down under her dress as she tried to keep up with him.

"Hurry, Rebecca!" he would say on a blustery afternoon with rain clouds threatening. "I have to get home to my traps."

"You checked them this morning," she would tell him, knowing how conscientious he was about getting up early, lest an animal suffer all day from being trapped the night before.

"But they move around more in bad weather."

"Well, then you just have to go fast on your own. I'll walk with the other girls."

"Ah," he would say, regret in his voice and blue eyes, but he would hurry on. He would quicken his pace and leave her behind to walk with her older sister and friends.

She watched him go again even now in her memory, her heart aching. But was that something to be ashamed of? Everyone had known about them. Even Leona remarked on the couple they made. Nothing was hidden. Hadn't it been a perfectly normal first love? The kind everyone had—one that would pass with time? But why had it not passed for her? Why couldn't she leave it behind as others had? And leave it behind was what she must surely do. A new life, holding promise and hope, lay in front of her.

Resolutely she turned into the schoolhouse circle driveway, gravel crunching under her feet. Shouts from behind the schoolhouse were already beginning as the game got into full swing.

Before she walked around to the back, she took a good look at the front of the schoolhouse. This was *her* school, her school and Emma's. That was how she would forever see it, she supposed. It looked common and plain enough now, but without much effort, it became a grand structure, mighty and tall, seen from the height and mind of a sixth grader.

Glancing through the windows as she went by, it looked the same. More desks were lined up in the central open room, but they were either the same desks or more just like them. Little desks for little students and larger ones for larger students. The same blackboards hung on the front wall with white chalk set in the trays underneath and erasers hanging half on and half off.

Today's assignments were still being written in large letters across the blackboard on the right side, just as Emma had done.

She grimaced, feelings from the past sweeping over her. Emma's voice sounded in her ear in answer to a math question from long ago. "You can do it. Just add all the numbers together and divide by the amount of numbers you used."

Even now the terror of the math book still bothered her. Much as she liked Emma, no soothing teacher's voice could ever quite overcome that. Numbers had a way of getting away from her, disappearing somewhere in the brain. But with Emma's assistance, she achieved a B average, even in that dreaded subject.

Rounding the corner, she walked across the rest of the driveway and onto the grass beside home plate. Intent on the game, the children paid her scant attention other than the closest ones muttering "Hi."

A teacher she knew walked up and welcomed her. Betsy Yoder had been in her grade in school—a short girl with a ready smile. Rebecca hadn't known she was teaching but wasn't surprised. Betsy could get a hundred in math class without even trying.

"I didn't know you were coming by," Betsy said smiling.

"I didn't either," Rebecca replied. "With Leona's baby coming, it's hard to tell how the week will go. I had a chance to come up while the wash is drying."

"How's Leona doing?"

"Better today. Ate a good breakfast and lunch. Good enough to stay with Leroy and James." Rebecca shrugged her shoulders. "I don't know if that's a good sign or not."

"I don't either." Betsy motioned toward the older girl standing off to the side. "Rebecca, this is Martha." Martha, her head covering pushed to one side, straightened it quickly at the mention of her name and nodded in their direction. "She's from Daviess County. She's come up to help for two years. The other teacher is Barbara. I think you know her. She's from the east district. She went to Milroy Amish School, but we won't hold that against her."

"She missed out on Emma," Rebecca said passionately.

"I know," Betsy agreed. "You want to play?"

"Ah, I don't know," Rebecca said.

"You used to play first base, didn't you? With Atlee at shortstop."

Rebecca felt like blushing but simply said, "Yes. And he was a good thrower."

"That's true," Betsy allowed. "So will you play? Because then I can play too. The children don't think it's fair with an extra teacher on a team, but with four we'd be even."

"Why not?" Rebecca felt a grin spreading across her face. "All I can do is break a leg."

Quick consultations were made between the three school teachers—the smiles on the children's faces expressed their agreement. The more teachers playing, the better with them, provided it did not produce an obvious advantage for either side.

Rebecca went with Betsy's team. After a whispered conference between the captain, a burly eighth grader with hair sticking out in all directions, and Betsy, Rebecca was placed in her old position on first base.

"I'm no Atlee," Betsy whispered to her, motioning toward shortstop, "but I'll try."

The first batter was a young girl, who looked to be eight or nine. Timidly she placed the bat on her shoulder and warily eyed the ball, her little head covering nearly tipping over her left ear.

"Easy does it," Barbara yelled at the pitcher.

Doing his best to be fair and knowing full well he would catch grief for a hard throw, the pitcher sent a slow floater over the plate. The girl swung mightily, her bat wobbling, and missed.

No one made a sound—either a cheer or a jeer. It would have been considered inappropriate. She got ready to swing again, knowing it was better to miss three times than to fail to swing. Honor lay in trying and in learning from her failures. Success was a thing to be earned, wrestled from the hands of fate or from the ground if you were a farmer.

The pitcher sent another floater, and this time the batter connected, surprise written all over her face. It flew almost straight up into the air. Choruses of "Run" propelled her forward, dragging the bat a few feet before she dropped it. But it didn't matter after all. The pitcher caught the little pop fly.

Resigning herself, the girl hung her head and turned back. No one said anything, even in encouragement. Tomorrow she would do better. That was the faith that undergirded all they did. Time, they all had learned, didn't make things better by itself, but it allowed for another try, and that was where their hope lay. She was one of them because she tried, not because she failed or succeeded.

The pitcher tensed and got ready for the next batter, an athletic boy with more muscle than fat. Making no attempt to be nice, the pitcher threw a fast underhand pitch. The batter squinted, brought his bat around and, with a solid whack, hit the ball way over second base.

He was almost at first base before the ball landed, despite the best efforts of the outfielders to catch it. Taking his opportunity, he easily made it to second and then to third.

What looked like a ten-year-old boy was up next. He sent a grounder between first and second. The outfielder ran with all his might, scooped it up, and threw it to first, but the boy was already safe. The runner on third had run for home, making it easily.

Next up was another girl, a little older and taller than the first one. She got a hit on the first pitch. It went right to Betsy at shortstop who, after catching the fly ball, threw it to Rebecca on first. The boy on first was halfway through his run to second, but now was out as Rebecca tagged the base. Three outs.

As the fielders made their way up to bat, Betsy whispered, "Was I as good as Atlee?"

"No," Rebecca said without hesitation. "But it was good."

"You wouldn't think anyone could be as good as Atlee."

"No." Rebecca chuckled. "I probably wouldn't." Her laugh came easy and relief spread all the way through her. Maybe this was being put to rest once and for all. *Thank the good Lord,* she thought. *He led me here.*

Two innings later, Betsy disappeared into the schoolhouse and came back out to ring the bell. All playing stopped on the sound, and the children streamed into the schoolhouse. Betsy made a point of coming back out and asking Rebecca, "You're staying for a while, aren't you?"

"I have some time. Will I disturb anything?"

"Of course not," Betsy said. "I'll get you a chair for the back. You can leave when you're ready."

"I'd love to stay a bit," Rebecca agreed, as they followed the last of the children inside.

Barbara was already standing in front, holding a storybook as the last stragglers came in from the bathrooms and drinking fountain. Betsy led Rebecca to the back and found a chair for her plus one for herself. Together they waited for Barbara to begin the after-lunch story.

Listening to her read, Rebecca was sure Barbara wasn't nearly as good as Emma was, but maybe that was just her memory. Perhaps to her, no one could sound as good as Emma.

Barbara's voice rose and fell for the next fifteen minutes as she read two chapters from *Treasures of the Snow* by Patricia St. John. Everyone seemed as attentive as Rebecca had always been when Emma read the noontime story.

Closing the book, Barbara called her fourth-grade English class up front. Betsy did the same for the fifth graders in the back. Martha, at the moment, was answering questions from the children who raised their hands.

Rebecca remembered that Atlee had rarely raised his hand. He was smart as a whip. Yet he had never made her feel as if she was less because of the grades she received.

Barbara's class was having a problem understanding the difference between adverbs and adjectives. They turned their little heads upward as she explained and wrote sentences.

"But they're the *same*." Rebecca heard the plaintive little voice from all the way in the back, where she was seated.

A student two rows away grinned at the sound, then went back to his work.

Barbara's lips were moving as her hands wrote, but Rebecca couldn't hear what she was saying. Half interested, she thought of moving closer, and then decided that would be interruptive. Getting up to leave was one thing, but sitting closer could interfere with the learning taking place.

Instead, she turned her attention to Betsy's class, which was attempting to write short stories. From Betsy's comments, she gathered that previous efforts had already been made but lacked satisfactory results.

"You have to focus on your grammar, punctuation, and spelling. Not just on the story line," she was saying. "Some of these stories could be good stories. But the words have to be spelled correctly. You don't ask, 'Why's the matter with you today?' Instead, can anyone tell me the correct way to say it?"

"I don't know." The offending boy glumly shook his head, his round face stricken. "That's how we say it at home."

"You don't talk English at home. So don't blame it on your parents," Betsy told him, which caused Rebecca to grin. It was true, but it was Betsy's spunk that amused her. *She's doing better than I could.*

"Does anyone know?" Betsy asked.

Two students raised their hands. Betsy pointed and asked one of them, "How do you say it?"

"What's the matter with you today?" came the prompt answer.

"Why would you say it that way?" the boy asked. "It doesn't sound right."

"Why don't you think it through?" Becky instructed him. "Let's say that you hurt your knee. Just bumped it maybe. You are limping when you walk in here. As you walk in, do I know what is wrong with you?"

"No," the boy said, "I would have to tell you."

"That's right. First you have to find out what is wrong before you can ask why it's wrong. So," Becky held her pencil out in front of her as a pointer and continued, " 'why' can't be used if there is an unknown. Now I could ask you why you are limping. But I cannot ask you why your knee is hurt until you tell me, or I see it. Is that clear?"

"I guess."

"What about the rest of the class?"

They all nodded, indicating they understood.

"So let's go back. Rewrite your stories. Work on your spelling, punctuation, and grammar. You can use the dictionaries for spelling, if you have to."

Rebecca was startled by the sudden thought that she had nothing planned for supper back at Leona's. *Am I supposed to make something or not? Surely Leona would have said something, unless she was planning on doing it herself.*

That was probably it, she figured as she settled back into the chair. But she couldn't get it out of her mind. Suppose she was wrong, and Leona wanted her to make supper. There was simply not enough time to tend to the dry laundry and prepare supper if she didn't hurry back immediately.

Rising, Rebecca gave a little wave to Betsy and left. The students barely raised their heads as she went by. Out on the road, she stepped briskly toward her responsibilities. She breathed in deeply, glad she had gone to the schoolhouse.

Entering the house, she was surprised to find Leona in the kitchen.

"You shouldn't be up and around," Rebecca said. "Where are Leroy and James?"

"In the garage playing," Leona said. "I feel fine. Here take the slop to the pigsty out behind the barn. I have the potatoes almost ready to mash. You can help with that if you want to."

"You're making the whole supper." Rebecca was horrified. "Why didn't you tell me? I could have helped. That's what I came for. I wouldn't have traipsed all around the schoolhouse."

"Oh yes, Rebecca, you need that time," Leona said. "That's important too. I would've let you know if I needed help. Now take the slop out. Then you had better start bringing in the wash."

Walking to the pigsty, Rebecca emptied the bowl over the fence. She then walked by the clothesline and found the clothes dry and soft to her touch.

She returned to the house and told Leona the clothes were ready.

"That's great," Leona said, "but first I need help with the corn and salad. Also, would you mash the potatoes for me? I can make the gravy. The girls can help you bring in the wash when they come home. We can get to the ironing tomorrow."

"However you want to do it," Rebecca said.

For the next hour and a half, they worked side by side. When the girls walked in from school, Leona told them to get changed and help Rebecca.

They were not going without comment first, though. "Mom," Lois whispered to Leona, "have you ever seen Rebecca play softball? She can catch like a boy."

Rebecca grinned, having overheard the words even with their whispered delivery.

"Oh, I wasn't that good."

"Oh! She was!" Lois insisted. "I was just waiting to see her at bat. Her turn never came up."

"Okay, change!" Leona told Lois. "I'm sure Rebecca was good, but the wash is waiting."

When the girls reappeared, Rebecca took them with her. They returned one by one with hampers of clean wash, while Leona held the front door open for them. When everything was in, they began folding what didn't need ironing.

"You girls start putting things away," Leona told them almost as soon as the last piece was folded. "You know better where everything goes than Rebecca does."

Finally all that was left was the pile of ironing. "We'll do that tomorrow," Leona said. "Let's get supper on now."

When Stephen arrived fifteen minutes later, they were ready with supper. He seemed appreciative of the menu, but said little about it.

That evening Rebecca stretched her weary body out on the bed, thankful for how the day had gone.

"Tomorrow the bridge," she said to herself before falling asleep, "and then this problem will be over."

Chapter Thirty-one

The next morning Leona came into the kitchen groaning. She was dressed for the day, but her hair still hung over her shoulders.

"You have no business being up," Rebecca said, from where she was standing at the oven.

"You're right," Leona agreed, pulling out a chair from the kitchen table, then changing her mind. "I think I'll take the recliner for now. Maybe I can help set the table when I get the children up."

"I'm fine," Rebecca assured her. "I got up early enough, so there's time."

"We'll see. In the meantime, let me get this bloated body into a soft chair."

Moving as quickly as she could, Rebecca had breakfast ready and set out on the table by the time Stephen appeared. The eggs, bacon, toast, and oatmeal were a welcome sight. He seated himself and bowed his head in prayer. Rebecca stopped her movements by the oven until he was done. In the silence of the prayer, she heard Leona go down the hallway to call the children.

While Stephen ate, Rebecca prepared his lunch, relying on memory as to what Leona had put in the day prior. The sleepy-eyed children showed up about the time Stephen was ready to leave.

"Mom's getting close," he told them, focusing on the two oldest, Elmo and Lois. "If the time comes while you're at school, Rebecca will have someone pick you up after school is out and before you walk home. Whoever picks you up will take you to Fannie's. Elmo and Lois, you watch over the younger ones."

"Why? Is mom sick?" eight-year-old Verna asked, standing beside Stephen, her eyes full of concern.

"No," Stephen said, pressing her hand. "She's not sick. There's another baby coming to live at our home."

"Where's he coming from?" Verna asked, not at all sure about this. "Do you get him from town?"

Stephen smiled at her. "No. The baby's coming from God."

"Oh!" Verna thought for a moment. "That's nice of Him. I guess."

"Yes," Stephen agreed, "it is."

When he was gone, Verna whispered to Lois, *"Vi brink Da Hah da glay one?"*

"In mom's stomach," Lois whispered back, pointing to her own.

Verna's eyes got big, but she said nothing more.

Leona came in to eat with them, and Rebecca noticed that Verna had a hard time keeping her eyes off her mother's protruding middle. She raised no more questions, though.

With the children gone and the dishes washed, Rebecca set up the ironing board in the living room. With two flat irons, one heating on the burner while she used the other, she tackled the waiting pile of wash. Leroy and James contented themselves with playing on the living room floor.

Speaking from the recliner, Leona insisted, "Bring me the pieces of clothing after you've ironed them, and I will fold them."

"There aren't too many."

"I know. It will make me feel useful."

Complying, Rebecca set up an upside-down hamper beside the recliner and brought her some Sunday handkerchiefs to fold once she ran the iron over both sides. The weekday ones had already been put away yesterday.

With her two irons and spray bottle of water, the ironing proceeded smoothly. Rebecca worked in silence, broken only by the sound of hot metal sliding on damp cloth, steaming on the wet spots. Leona dozed off in the recliner.

Rebecca set aside several small items in case Leona awoke and wanted something to do. But when she was done with the last piece, Leona was still sleeping. So Rebecca finished the folding herself and carried the last pieces into the bedroom closets.

Finally, having thought about it most of the morning, she went to her own bedroom, dug among the folds in her case, pulled out the ring, and slipped it into her apron pocket.

Working quietly in the kitchen, she fixed four sandwiches and placed three in the refrigerator. Finding a small carrying case in the pantry, she put the other sandwich and a pint jar of water into it. It would be her picnic lunch, of sorts.

Leona woke with a start when Rebecca approached the recliner, much to Rebecca's gratitude. She would have felt awkward having to awaken her aunt, but Leona needed to be told that she was leaving.

"Are you finished?" Leona looked around. "I dozed off, I guess."

"Yes, I'm done," Rebecca said. "I was wondering if it would be okay if I went for a walk down by the bridge for a little while. If it's not too taxing for you to watch James and Leroy, I'll be back in time to fix supper. I'm taking a sandwich along, and I left three for you and the boys in the refrigerator." Then she added quietly, half hoping Leona wouldn't hear it, "Today's my birthday."

Leona rubbed her stomach and said, "I guess I did forget your birthday with all that's going on. I'm sorry. But sure, go. The baby's not coming just yet, I don't think. It shouldn't be too bad. Maybe we can bake a cake tonight for you. The children would like that."

"I'd better be going then."

"Is that where you and Atlee used to go?" Leona's face lit up with a smile.

"Yes," she admitted, hanging her head.

"Don't dream too long then." Leona's smile contradicted her words. "Life moves on. We have to go with it."

How could Leona know what was in my heart? Or was she just guessing? "I know," Rebecca agreed.

~

She left the house and turned south on the road. A brisk five-minute walk brought her within sight of two homes at the junction where she would turn right toward the bridge. Two cars sat in the driveway of the first place, their red and white contrasting colors off-setting each other.

From what Leona had mentioned in passing, this was where she was supposed to go to call when the baby came. An older lady, Mrs. Spencer, lived here with her two grandchildren. This arrangement, from what Leona had told her, benefited both parties and allowed Mrs. Spencer time to do some taxi driving for her Amish neighbors. The tan-colored house had a Christmas tree in the window, lit even at this hour of the day, sparkling with a star on top. A massive green wreath with bright red ribbons was hung on the front door, creating a warm welcome. Rebecca decided she already liked Mrs. Spencer, even without having seen her.

Without any Christmas decorations, the place next to Mrs. Spencer's looked almost Amish, but the overhead power line running to the house gave it away. Rebecca decided it must be English too, and maybe they were just late in putting up their lights.

Turning right at the junction, she began looking for things that reminded her of the past. There was nothing she wanted to miss, not because of some morbid fascination but because she wanted to come to the root of her memory of Atlee. *What had it really been like and what had we really done?* she wondered. *Was this hold he had on my heart something I could get rid of—and get rid of today—or was there something else behind it all?*

The West Skating Rink Road was rather featureless along this area. A lone tree or two stood, casting shadows across the road. Other than that, plowed and shorn bean fields lay on either side.

A single building sat near the road. She couldn't remember what purpose it served. She guessed it was a toolshed. Whatever it was, it sat alone, as if forgotten by the world.

Atlee had not brought Rebecca down here often. He kept several underwater traps along a stretch of the Flackrock River. Because the trapped animal would quickly drown, he didn't have to come down here every day to relieve its misery—the cold water preserved the game for a day or so.

On that Saturday so long ago, she remembered that it had started out similar to this day—first cool, then warming up to a comfortable temperature. She had followed Atlee to the bridge, after her mother had given permission. It was here they had walked together. As usual she tried her best to keep up, yet that day he hadn't seemed as impatient with the slower speed Rebecca required.

As they made their way off the road and into the woods, she thought perhaps their shadows caused her to be able to see him better. He had been just ahead of her, swinging his two empty traps in rhythm with his step.

He had turned to say, "I hope I have a big muskrat today." A big grin spread across his face. "They've been bringing a real good price. The fur man told me yesterday that a big one would be almost double the normal fee." He made a face, his freckles moving. "I've just caught little ones so far this winter."

She felt the wind move in the trees as she heard her own answer, "You're making good money, are you?"

His blue eyes twinkling, he glanced at her. "I don't know. I can always do better."

But she knew, she just knew that he was making good money. He was so much bigger and smarter than she was. He knew how to read a stream and determine where the best place to set his traps was. He knew when to head home because a storm was coming, timing it just right so they didn't get wet. He even knew how to make Emma laugh when she didn't want to.

Rebecca had never told Atlee what he was good at. Atlee no doubt knew, but did he know how he made her heart skip a beat? Did he know what his blue eyes were beginning to do to her? Did he know about the strange quiver she felt in her stomach when his hand brushed hers as they walked side by side on the road? No, she supposed he couldn't know. It was just the way it was, and she had never found the time or words to tell him.

The road took a sharp turn, and she could see the bridge ahead through the trees. Her steps quickened. The bridge still looked as massive as she remembered it, stretching wide across the Flatrock River.

Coming up to the entrance, she stopped and read, "E.L. Kennedy 1886," written in a half circle across the top. The county must have hung the small green Christmas wreaths on either side—they were too high off the ground to be the work of a friendly neighbor perched on his pickup truck.

Other things looked much the same. On the right side of the bridge was a little path going down to the river. Glancing around to make sure no one was looking, she jumped the guardrail and carefully made her way down the path.

In a rush of memories, she walked to the water's edge. The Flatrock River was swift-flowing here, its waters seemed to be in a hurry to get where they were going. This was where Atlee had kept one of his traps. Right in the deep water over there. She could remember it so clearly. And that day.

This was also the place where she had planned on eating her lunch, but the rush of the moment was overtaking her. She now knew where this was going. She willed it to stop, and yet at the same time allowed it to continue. Was this not what she had come here for? To know, to face, to understand, and to meet Atlee if he came?

She saw it all as if it were yesterday. Atlee had walked down to the river ahead of her, his black hair shining in the sun. He had checked his trap and found nothing. Silently he had returned to where Rebecca stood. She remembered wondering why there was no look of disappointment on his face. *Was he not looking for his big one?* She had then thought they would continue walking farther down the river, but instead he had paused in front of her. Then he put his hand in his pocket. He looked like he wasn't thinking about muskrats anymore.

She had looked at him, puzzled. She heard his voice clearly, even now, coming to her from across the years.

"Ah, Rebecca, there's something I need to ask you."

"Yes?" She raised her eyes to him, questioningly.

"You know we're moving after Christmas. You know that, don't you? I'm going to another school."

She had nodded, knowing but not understanding.

He fumbled in his pocket. "I found this the other day." Slowly he pulled out the ring. It sparkled in the sunlight, just as it still did. "Rebecca, I would like to ask you something."

His eyes first went to the bridge beside them, then back to her eyes. They burned with an intensity she had never seen in them before. Yet she had not looked away, letting his fire come into her, burning in her chest.

"Promise me something, Rebecca." His voice quivered, but it did not break. "I know that we're still young. I have no control over our leaving Milroy. But will you promise me you'll keep this ring till you're twenty-one?"

She responded slowly, not understanding, whispering, "Why?"

"Keep it for me, Rebecca. I will come back for you then. From wherever I am. When we are of age, it will be different. Promise me you will keep it—that you will wait for me before you ever decide in favor of someone else."

She gasped, her breath barely coming. Then slowly, she had reached out, her fingers brushing his as she took the ring. "Yes, I promise," she said in the rush of her emotions, so quietly she hoped he would hear… hoped that she had actually spoken the words.

She now knew she had loved this boy with everything in her heart. That there was no corner of it she would not have given to him. She had seen the years, the miles of life stretching out, and knew she had wanted to walk them with him. She had known it with every fiber of her beating sixth-grade heart.

She also knew her breath was barely coming any more as the running water in front of her came into focus again. Forcing herself to breathe, she lifted her face skyward as the tears came.

Chapter Thirty-two

It seemed to Rebecca that time was standing still on the banks of the Flatrock River. The trees above her, stripped of their leaves, were her silent witnesses. Rebecca now knew why she was afraid. It was because she had loved, and loved with all of her heart.

She hadn't asked for it, hadn't searched for its embrace, nor longed for its agonies. It had come unbidden and taken its place without her ever having been aware of it. Yet, when it came to her, she hadn't asked it to leave or barred it from staying. Instead, she had promised.

This was her sin, her transgression. Was there forgiveness for it? She contemplated the thought. Her mother and Leona would understand if she told them. They would think it a thing of the imagination, a fancy of the youthful heart.

John, whom she had barely thought of, would easily overlook this too. His soft brown eyes would hardly be troubled with a schoolgirl crush, as he would call it. She could almost hear his laughter, as if she were telling him a silly story, hardly worth mentioning.

No, what she was afraid of was her own heart. Could it forget? Could it believe that better things were ahead? Having once given all, could it give as much again? Could it ever really make place for another? She had thought so. That was why she had forgotten Atlee and turned her love to John. But now she was no longer sure.

How could something so sacred, so pure, so all-giving have gone away, driven like the leaves before the wind? Why had she lost this? Did God know something she didn't? Was Atlee really coming?

Her mind searched vainly for an answer, perplexed in its search. Was there anyone she could talk to? Anyone who would really understand?

The wind blew softly in the trees above her, the warm sun reaching down between the bare branches. Yet it hardly reached her where she needed it the most. And what of God? Did He really know her heart? He must for He had made it. He made everything...and if so, then He too had made this love.

Feeling weak she thought of her sandwich, the hunger in her body distasteful at the moment. Searching the riverbank, she found the grass still thick enough to sit on. She finally sat down and ate her sandwich, its bread dry in her mouth. She let the surroundings hold her—the stream with its water in a hurry to move on, the rattle of a car crossing the Moscow bridge.

"You said you'd come," Rebecca said softly, "when I turned twenty-one—you said we'd meet here. You promised." She whispered, "Today I'm twenty-one. I've returned and kept my promise."

Then it occurred to her that it was Atlee arriving in the car on the bridge. Surely he had remembered. He was coming, and this was no longer something in her heart or her head but in front of her, right here in plain sight.

Rebecca stood up, waiting, listening to the sound of the automobile clattering across the covered bridge. *Atlee was coming...but then what if it wasn't Atlee? What if it was just some local farmer who would wonder what an Amish girl was doing out here all by herself?*

She hardly could tell the farmer the real reason—if he stopped to ask. She hardly could tell herself that she had come here because long ago she loved a boy and was now waiting for him to return. It had been eight years since she had heard from or seen him, but they promised to meet each other on her twenty-first birthday.

Her anticipation and excitement were fast fading away. What had seemed like a good idea—one she couldn't go on without knowing the answer to—no longer seemed so grand. With this birthday she was of age, now considered an adult and capable of making her own decisions. The sudden reality of it was staring her in the face.

She gathered her courage. Atlee had said twenty-one because he hadn't wanted to force his hand and make her choose while her parents were still her guardians. His consideration of her and the foresight that had taken still moved her deeply, but now differently.

This was a love she could not treat lightly. The emotions from only moments before were now turning into the present-day Atlee and the Mennonite world he represented. Their weight was heavy on her.

To love the Atlee who was coming, to take that wild leap, now shook her deeply. This moment was not quite as she had imagined it, the whole experience disconcerting and unsettling.

The approaching car was driving a thought toward her with an intensity directly associated with its nearness. She could hear the car slow down as it exited the bridge. Atlee. Would she even recognize him? His face, once so soft in its first hint of maturity, would now be hardened into early manhood. There might be a beard or a shadow of one on his face, if he had followed his parents into the world of the Mennonites. He would be different certainly. Where he had been a boy, now there would be the look of that other world in his eyes—the world of men—where they often walked alone, walked in their strength, and walked with the desire to pull what they loved into their orbit.

She shivered. If it was him—Atlee—then that would mean he had been waiting all these years for her, had planned and was now implementing his singular love for her; perhaps having turned down other girls while thinking of her and waiting to meet her this morning.

That she had taken a different path in life was apparent, but that was not what loomed so large in her eyes. It was *his* waiting, *his* preparation for this visit. These thoughts rose like a mighty mountain. This would not be a small matter anymore.

Flattering as Atlee's return would be, it was now frightening in its implications. If this was Atlee, then this was it. There would be no turning back. She was as good as Mennonite and married to him. Saying "No" was an option completely removed. Atlee might not demand it from her, even with the immense love he would obviously have, but she would demand it of herself.

Rebecca saw she had come to a place she had not thought to go. Her motives had been wrapped in innocence, but this wouldn't spare her now. The love of such a man would be a steel band pulling her in and demanding, not by words but by its very existence, her complete loyalty.

She gasped as she saw the driver. He looked toward her and slowed the car. His hair was black. His face appeared young, but she couldn't quite see his eyes.

As the car came to a stop, the driver rolled down his window and called out, "Can I help you?" His voice reached her, the face of the young man now appearing clearly. "Do you need a lift?"

"Atlee," she said because that was all she could think to say, caught up in the intensity of her feelings.

"Atlee," he repeated, his face puzzled. "No…Derrick. I live back in town."

Dimly comprehending her mistake, she felt the red rush to her face. "Oh, I'm sorry. I thought you were someone else," she said. "I'm visiting my aunt up the road. Leona Troyer."

"Oh," he responded, letting a smile spread across his face, "she lives next to Mrs. Spencer, my aunt."

She nodded, not believing how stupid she had let herself sound to this strange boy from town. English too.

He grinned now. "I'm not this…what did you say? Atlee? But maybe I could be for a Friday night, unless he's your Amish boyfriend?"

"No," she said, shocked at his boldness.

"To the date, or to Atlee the boyfriend?" he asked, leaning out his window.

"Both," she said. "I'm engaged."

"But it's not Atlee?" he asked, chuckling.

Now her confusion was turning to irritation.

He grinned, reading her face. "Well, even the Amish have their troubles, I see. You want a ride up to Leona's?"

"No," she told him, "I'll walk."

"As you wish." He rolled the window halfway up and then stopped. "If you change your mind, let my aunt know. I'm good for a night at the movies."

She found herself glaring at him as he grinned, finished rolling up his window, and slowly accelerated the car until he disappeared behind the trees around the bend.

With him gone, the fear and the irritation left too, all in one big rush it seemed, leaving her weak and trembling. The urge to run from this place came upon her, but she didn't have the strength. Glancing around, afraid more cars might be coming, she was desperate to appear more normal. Walking up the road would appear normal, but it was out of the question at the moment.

Gone were any thoughts that Atlee might still be appearing. Pressing in on her was the certainty that all boys and men were surely defective. The thought must have been forming for some time, but now it bloomed with full strength and conviction. The brash young nephew of Mrs. Spencer had only confirmed the fact.

Atlee had promised and wasn't coming. How utterly stupid of her to even have thought it possible. She had made an absolute fool out of herself, waiting by this bridge like a schoolgirl dreamer. No doubt Atlee was already married to a beautiful woman and had children—having completely forgotten about her.

Rebecca would have left right then and there and marched up the road, but her legs still felt like they wouldn't carry her. She would have to wait a while to go back to Leona's. She just couldn't go back now. Her face would surely give away her foolishness. Instead, she found the rock where she used to sit while waiting for Atlee to finish checking his traps.

It was there, looking out over the rushing waters of the Flatrock

River, that the memories came again. How could they not? She saw him, as if it had been yesterday, bending over the edge of the bank, his black hair falling into his eyes, his look triumphant as he pulled a muskrat out of his trap.

He would look at the prize, then at her. First to glory in his catch but then to glory in her, his eyes shining with delight. He had loved her then, and she him. That it was a young love did not diminish the memory. She wept for herself and for the past with its hopes now dashed at her feet. *It was all a little too much to bear. No one should be asked to continue hoping when the object was just pulled away. What signs were there to say things would change?* None that she could see.

The thoughts came as thick as the tears, as she let them both flow. Another car, and then another, passed over the bridge, but she failed to notice them. Images of her life ahead of her rose in her mind. She saw herself going back to Wheat Ridge, marrying John, growing old with him, but could she ever love again?

Of course, she reminded herself, this decision still had its options open. *I don't* have *to marry John. Or anyone for that matter. Emma was single, so why couldn't I be single? Why not just go through life like that? Emma seemed to be perfectly happy and content. Yes, that is something I could do. I could be a schoolteacher, of which there is always a pressing need in the parochial schools. I could teach all my life, just as Emma had done.*

The tears stopped. She thought for a moment more, and then with resolution in her step, she walked to the water's edge and pulled the ring from her apron pocket. She took one last glance at it and threw it into the rushing water. It landed with a soft *plunk* and was gone.

Behind her an automobile drew to a stop, the slowing sound drawing her attention, pulling the air out of her lungs. When she heard the car door open, she dared not look.

Chapter Thirty-three

Rebecca's heart was pounding in her chest. *What if it is Atlee?*

"Dear," a voice came from the car, strangely familiar and distinctly female. "Are you okay?"

Rebecca felt embarrassment flooding through her again. *How can I be so stupid again? My feelings are like the wind that blows around the tree branches. Now some woman has stopped by to check on me.* Making no attempt to wipe her tear stains, feeling it was useless anyway, she walked toward the road.

"Is something wrong? I'm Mrs. Spencer," the lady said. "I don't mean to bother you, but my nephew Derrick stopped by." She shook her head. "I'm so sorry for what he said to you. He told me about meeting an Amish girl down here by the bridge. He told me you were kin to Leona. I thought right away it must be Leona's maid. Dear, Derrick shouldn't have said what he did. He doesn't understand Amish people very well. I hope you understand."

"It's okay," Rebecca said. "Yes, I'm fine."

"Why, you've been crying," Mrs. Spencer said. "You weren't running away or something?"

Rebecca shook her head. "No, it's a long story. I'll be okay. I really should get back to Leona's."

"Of course," Mrs. Spencer agreed. "Sorry about Derrick though. He should have known better. He meant no harm. He's always been a nice boy. Just likes to tease. Can I offer you a ride to your aunt's?"

"It would be nice to go back without walking. Yes, thank you."

When she had settled in the passenger seat, Rebecca asked, "Would he actually have taken me out on a date?"

Mrs. Spencer chuckled at the question. "Maybe you should have called his bluff."

"Maybe I should have," Rebecca said, still not certain it was just a bluff.

"That would have been something! An Amish girl with Derrick at the movies." Mrs. Spencer found the thought amusing.

Rebecca, on the other hand, found the image impossible. The thought of Atlee and her going Mennonite was hard enough to imagine, but an English boy was a chasm no bridge could ever cross.

"Does he have a girlfriend?" she asked to take the conversation away from her thoughts.

"Oh, he's had several—two at the same time, I thought once—although he denied it," Mrs. Spencer said and frowned, confirming Rebecca's opinion of Derrick. "He's a good boy though. No trouble that I know of. But nowadays...well, one never really knows."

"I've never been to the movies," Rebecca said, not knowing what else to say.

"Really?" Mrs. Spencer didn't sound too surprised. "Seems a little impossible...but I know that's the Amish way. How do you do it?"

"Parents. Teaching." Rebecca shrugged. They were passing Mrs. Spencer's place now, the big Christmas wreath hanging on the front door, Leona's driveway just up ahead. "You just don't."

"Sounds good to me. Just never worked for us." She chuckled again. "Children are hard to raise these days."

"I suppose so." Rebecca was thinking of her own sisters and their squabbles. "Mom has to spank a lot. Says it takes the Lord's help."

"That it does," Mrs. Spencer agreed, pulling into Leona's driveway. "There we are. Hope Leona has that baby soon."

"Thanks then—for the ride," Rebecca said, as she got out.

"Oh, you're sure welcome. I might see you later," Mrs. Spencer said, as she drove slowly away.

Rebecca stood in the driveway, struck by the stillness in the air. *Why is it so quiet?* she wondered.

The desire for human conversation returned—she wanted to talk to someone about Atlee. And it was then that the thought occurred to her that she must go and see Emma if she could find the time.

She hoped with all her heart she could. If the baby came today or early tomorrow, there would not be time, but if he came later, there might be. If she went in right now, prepared supper, cleaned what needed to be cleaned, and made some of the breakfast for tomorrow, Leona would surely let her go even today.

She could take the horse and buggy by herself because it wasn't used during the day. Leona could remind her of where Emma lived, and she would go and have a nice talk with her. Maybe Emma would know how to help her. She always knew best. If nothing else, Emma would simply tell her that there was an answer in God's answer book, and though she might never understand something in this life, it would be revealed on the other side.

Entering the house, she found Leroy and James standing around the recliner, looking at their white-faced mother who was clutching at the arms of the chair, her fingernails digging into the cloth.

"The baby's coming," she whispered before Rebecca had even closed the front door. Leroy and James were close to tears.

Rebecca's heart skipped a beat. *I have been gone too long! I should have come back sooner.* And there was also the realization she would not be going to Emma's. Yet, collecting her thoughts, she shoved aside her own plans and gave herself to the urgency of the moment.

"What shall I do first?"

Leona was breathing deeply, the contraction having passed for now. "Take the bag over there." Leona pointed to the hallway. "I got the children's clothes ready as soon as I knew it was coming. There's underwear, some shirts, and pants for the boys. Work clothes for the girls. They can wear the same dresses tomorrow for school. They'll figure all that out themselves. Go down to Mrs. Spencer's. Tell her it's time. She'll know what to do. If she doesn't remember, tell her to go to Fannie's first with James and Leroy. She can pick them up on the way back. Fannie will then pick up the rest of the children at school with her buggy—and then the midwife. I think there's time for the midwife to bring her own buggy. That way she can leave when it's over. The midwife likes it better that way—she won't have to bother a taxi for a way back."

"I'll be right back then," Rebecca said. "I just saw Mrs. Spencer's place. It won't take long."

Leona nodded, another contraction beginning, and whispered, as her fingers dug back into the armchair, "The baby won't come that quickly. It takes awhile."

Even with that assurance, Rebecca found herself hurrying, the brown bag of clothing held tightly against her.

She quickly arrived at Mrs. Spencer's and knocked loudly.

The woman opened the door and said, "The baby is coming?"

"Yes. Leona said you would know what to do. Here is the clothing to leave at Fannie's for the children."

"How's she doing?" Mrs. Spencer asked. "Here, step inside while I get my coat."

She held open the door, as Rebecca stepped inside and stood in the foyer. "I wasn't there when it started. She was already in labor when I walked in the door."

Mrs. Spencer bustled about finding her keys on the kitchen table and then took her coat out of the closet. "You might as well ride with me," she told Rebecca.

"Oh! I can walk!" Rebecca said.

"I'm going there anyway, dear. You might as well ride."

"Okay."

As they pulled out of the driveway, Rebecca asked, "What do I do if the baby comes while I'm alone with her?"

Mrs. Spencer smiled. "They normally don't come *that* quickly. But just in case, why don't I stop by after I let the midwife know. I'll stay with you until she comes. Would that make you feel better?"

"I wouldn't expect that."

"I understand. But, really, it's not a problem. You never know about these things. Leona's an expert at this, but they seem to come faster the more you have."

"Well, it would be nice if you would come. It would be better than being alone," Rebecca said. Mrs. Spencer then pulled to a stop in Leona's driveway. "I'll get Leroy and James and be right back."

Mrs. Spencer waited as Rebecca bustled the two boys out.

"*Vo sinn miah un gay?*" James asked.

"To Fannie's," Rebecca told him.

It seemed to satisfy him. Leroy followed his brother to the car, and they climbed in, James in the front.

"I'll be back," Mrs. Spencer said as Rebecca closed the car door. She pulled away, and Rebecca watched until she turned right on the state road.

Walking into the house, Leona was still in the recliner. "I'll take a glass of water," she said, apparently between the contractions at the moment. "Did everything go okay?"

Rebecca nodded. "Mrs. Spencer has left with the boys. She said she would stop back by and wait with us until the midwife comes."

"That's nice of her," Leona whispered, as the pain began again.

True to her word, Mrs. Spencer walked in without knocking twenty minutes later. She hurried about, doing things that Rebecca would never have thought to do, said all kinds of comforting words to Leona, and told her to keep breathing when the pain was intense.

The midwife arrived thirty minutes later. Rebecca went outside to put her horse up in the barn. By the time she came back, Leona was being walked up and down the hall. After a few trips, Leona asked to be taken to the bedroom. After the midwife settled her in and cleared space around the bed, the real work began.

Mrs. Spencer had to leave at four thirty and made one last effort to encourage Leona, assuring her that she would be fine.

Stephen came home a little after five, took in the situation, and offered to help wherever the midwife needed him. Rebecca figured food would be something she could do, so she retreated to the kitchen to make and set sandwiches out on the table.

The baby finally came a little after midnight—a boy with black hair already wrapped around his forehead, a red bundle of rage at being awakened to such a rude world. Laying the child, all wrapped up in a white blanket, on Leona's stomach, the midwife stood back to give them time together.

Rebecca noticed the pain leave Leona's face. It was replaced with joy as her hands closed around the baby. "You're Jonathon," she whispered to him. "Welcome to our world."

Things then began to settle down. Stephen hitched up the midwife's horse and buggy, and Rebecca, after a final check on Leona, went to her room and dropped off to sleep just as soon as she got under the covers.

The ringing of the alarm clock awoke her at six. Half stumbling into the kitchen, she got the breakfast ready for Stephen and packed his lunch pail. After he had eaten and left, she checked on Leona. Little Jonathon was fast asleep, his hands curled around his face, his cheeks still red. Leona too was sleeping peacefully, and Rebecca left them that way.

Next came baby laundry, baby feedings, baby cries, and the rest of the responsibilities of the family. Rebecca did not go to church on Sunday, but stayed home with Leona. Stephen brought back the news of the sermon and the visitors who had been there, relaying it to Leona, who sat in her recliner in the living room.

He also said a load was going to Wheat Ridge the following Friday. Did Rebecca want to go along then or sooner?

In the ensuing discussion between Rebecca and Leona, it was decided that next week was too long to wait, that the Greyhound option would be looked into in the morning.

Rebecca didn't voice the desire but hoped that before she left, a visit to Emma might still be worked in.

Chapter Thirty-four

The following morning—just after the children had left for school—the midwife stopped by to check on Leona. It seemed only seconds after she arrived that Rebecca heard her footsteps hurrying back down the hall.

As she entered the kitchen, she said, "Go get Mrs. Spencer right away. We need a doctor. I think she may have the signs of blood clots in her leg."

Rebecca quickly walked down to Mrs. Spencer's and explained the situation. Mrs. Spencer willingly dropped what she was doing, drove the two of them back to the house, and carefully helped Leona, Jonathon, and the midwife into the car to take them to the doctor.

Rebecca stood in the silence of the driveway with Leroy and James beside her, struck once again by the stillness in the air. They watched Mrs. Spencer's car speed up once it was on the blacktop, the sound fading as it moved farther down the road.

"Where is the doctor's office?" James asked. "Is it someplace bad?"

"No," Rebecca answered, assuring him, "it's a good place. Your mom just needs to see him soon."

"Is she coming back? And baby Jonathon?" he asked, wanting to know.

"Of course," Rebecca told him, hoping she was right. *Surely there is nothing life threatening involved. The midwife had seemed worried, but not quite that worried.*

"Let's go play," Leroy suggested, looking at his bigger brother, then pulling on his arm with both hands when he got no response.

"Yes, you can play," Rebecca told him, thinking he might need to hear her say that. Apparently she was right. James then assented to leaving and followed Leroy across the yard.

Rebecca returned to the kitchen to wash the breakfast dishes and then started gathering the laundry. Leaving Jonathon's diapers to soak in a bucket of water, she finished the other loads first, hanging them out on the line.

On the third trip back to the house, with her hamper now empty of the heaping wash, she heard the crunch of tires on gravel. Quickening her step, she came around the corner of the house to find Leona climbing out of Mrs. Spencer's car. There was no sign of the midwife. Apparently she had already been dropped off at her own place.

Mrs. Spencer waved as she left. It was a cheerful enough wave, Rebecca thought, so surely things must be under control.

"What was it?" she asked, coming up to Leona, who was still standing in the driveway and holding the sleeping Jonathon in her arms.

"It's my leg," Leona said, looking rather gloomily and reaching down to press the spot in question with her hand. "I'm on medication for a blood clot. Good thing the midwife sent me in. She's good, I must say. Starts out with just a little swelling, but she caught it. The doctor said that the clot is above the knee and that it can be serious, of course, if it breaks loose."

"Should you be resting?" Rebecca asked, the hamper still hanging in one hand.

"He said just the opposite. It's not good for me to be lying around all the time. I'm supposed to stay active—as much as I can."

"What's the problem called?" Rebecca glanced at Leona's leg.

"Deep vein thrombosis," Leona said wearily, letting the words flow off her tongue easily enough as if she had said it several times before. "We'll just call it *the blood clot.*"

"How long before you're better?" Rebecca asked.

"Doctor wasn't sure. He'll check on me next week again."

"Well, then I'm not going home yet," Rebecca announced without reservation. "I'll stay a while longer."

"Yes, you are going home," Leona said with equal conviction. "I can get Sarah if I need her. And, as the doctor said, I need to stay active anyway."

"Mom would want me to stay, and I'm staying," Rebecca said, thinking that might end the discussion.

"Sometimes your mom doesn't have much sense," Leona declared.

"She happens to think her sister is important," Rebecca said. "And so do I."

"I wonder sometimes just how important I am." Leona's face suddenly darkened. "Seems like all I do lately is inconvenience other people. Even the children wish their mother would be back for them."

"But you *are*." Rebecca looked at her with concern. "You're here."

"Not really. It's hard to bounce back after a baby's born. And now this time—I have to have this leg problem. And Stephen—poor fellow. He has to deal with a sick wife."

"But he understands," Rebecca insisted. "You've been working way too hard too soon."

"No, I need to be there for them—all of them—not just the baby. Sometimes it's just so hard," Leona said weakly, her hand going to her leg, tears spilling down her cheeks.

Rebecca felt a wave of fear because of this unexpected change in her aunt. *Is Leona in worse condition than anyone knew? What if the blood clot is letting go?*

"Well, you're *not* doing anything more today," she said sternly. "And your leg—let's take a look at it."

"It's nothing really." Leona didn't sound convincing at all. "I just should be able to do more. I always could with the other children."

"You've had eight children," Rebecca said sharply now, surprised to hear herself speak to her aunt like this. "Let's see the leg," she repeated.

Rebecca gently took Leona's hand and lifted it away, revealing a red and swollen section just above Leona's knee. The sight caused Rebecca to catch her breath. Touching the area gently with her fingers, she could feel the heat. "No wonder the midwife took you in." Rebecca was horrified. "Has Stephen seen this?"

"Not this morning."

"Has it gotten worse today?" Rebecca asked.

"I don't think so. Not by much."

"You have to rest now," Rebecca insisted, wondering where she was finding the strength to order her aunt around. She expected at any moment the old Leona would return, strong, wise, and untouched by her own pain.

"But there's so much to do."

"The recliner." Rebecca took her arm, gently leading until Leona got going. She then took baby Jonathon from her aunt, leaving the hamper sitting on the porch.

"And the extra weight," Leona moaned, "it's not going anywhere. I know Stephen notices."

"You shouldn't be talking like that," Rebecca said, slightly embarrassed.

"Here I am embarrassing you," Leona said, as she settled into the recliner. "And now you think you need to stay longer." Leona moaned again. "And Jonathon's been crying all morning at the doctor's office..."

"Well, he's asleep now. And I'm going to make you something to eat," Rebecca said. She then took the sleeping Jonathon to the bedroom, easing him gently onto the mattress, her heart glad that she seemed to know just what to do. It was what her mother would do, she was sure.

"I'm so fat," Leona said, as Rebecca returned on her way to the kitchen. "I shouldn't eat anything at all."

"Vegetable soup." Rebecca ignored Leona's remark.

"I have to stay away from food."

Leona's voice wasn't too firm, Rebecca noticed. "You'd like that?" she asked, keeping her eyes on Leona's face.

Her answer was a slight nod, followed quickly by, "But not too much."

"You'll feel better after you eat something, I'm sure."

"I don't think I'll *ever* feel better," Leona said.

"I'll be right back." Rebecca felt the need to ignore the remark. Her nurturing instincts, honed from years of taking care of her younger siblings, had proven her mettle, but now she became acutely aware that this was Leona—her aunt—and not a sibling.

She went to the garage and retrieved the can of vegetable soup. Stepping back into the kitchen, she turned the gas burner on high.

A quick glance into the living room satisfied her that Leona was okay. She was leaning back, her feet elevated on the recliner.

With the soup warm, she transferred some to a bowl with a dipper, took a package of soda crackers from a lower cupboard along with her, and arrived at the recliner just as Leona noticed her.

"I almost fell asleep," she whispered.

"That's what you're supposed to do," Rebecca said.

Leona's eyes lighted up at the sight of the bowl of steaming soup and the package of crackers in Rebecca's hands. "I feel like such a baby," she whispered again.

"How many do you want?" Rebecca asked, tearing the top of the cracker package carefully.

"Four, I think." Leona brought the recliner forward and reached for the bowl of soup. Rebecca gave her the four crackers, quickly handing her two more when the crumbled pieces of the four proved—by the look on Leona's face—to be insufficient.

Returning the package of crackers to the kitchen, Rebecca glanced back into the living room and said, "I'm starting on the wash."

"Oh, the wash. There's so much to do around here, and we should be thinking of you packing for the trip home, not doing the wash."

"No, this is why I came," Rebecca told her firmly. "You stay right there while I tackle the job."

She began by filling the washing machine. While the water filled, she turned her attention to the piles of wash, particularly aware of Jonathon's dirty diapers in the bucket because those were of primary concern.

No wonder women are exhausted, Rebecca thought, as she pulled the first diaper from the bucket of water. The fumes assaulted her nose again, and she unexpectedly gagged. Having grown up with small children in the house, she should be used to the smell, but it had been a while since any of her siblings had been in diapers. She turned her face away to lessen the effect, washed the diaper off in the bucket, and then reached for another. By the time a dozen were done, she no longer had to hold her face at a distance.

Funny what you get used to, she thought. *Such a sweet baby and yet also responsible for such a mess. Sort of like big boys are.*

Lifting the rinsed diapers into the washer, she started the motor with a roar. She hoped its sound was a comfort to Leona instead of cause to wake up from a much-needed rest. Pulling out the plunger on the side, the agitator began rotating, first left then right, swishing the wash around in the water.

While the load was washing, she prepared another pile of diapers. She had to step into the house momentarily to empty the bucket in the bathroom, and on the way, she took a peek in on Leona. Leona seemed to be sleeping, her chest rising and falling in even motions. And from the back bedroom, Jonathon was quiet too.

Back in the garage, Rebecca ran the load of wash through the wringer. She hung it on the line after that. The bright white diapers flapped in the morning breeze and started to dry.

Rebecca was already weary, and it was not yet noon.

Is it worth it? she wondered. *Boyfriends, then husbands, followed by babies and buckets of messy diapers.* She wasn't sure, but with this coming so soon after her experience at the bridge, Emma's single life was looking better all the time.

Chapter Thirty-five

Rebecca watched the rows of wash flap in the breeze. The pieces blew sideways with the movement of the air. When one would fall back faster than the other, it created a break in the rhythm.

So much like the ebb and flow of life, she thought. *Like clothing in the wind, that's how we all are. Washed out some days, bright with hope on others, and then dirty again the next. Used and then clean; used and then clean. That's how it is.*

At least she felt like that now. The memory of her time at the bridge was still fresh in her mind. How could she have been so stupid, so carried away with her hopes from the past, thinking it even possible that Atlee would remember her after all these years. Still, *she* had remembered, so why hadn't he?

Her heart ached with the pain of it, yet she had done the right thing in going to the bridge. If she had not gone, she would never have known if he had come. But maybe men were different in that way. They said things they did not mean. Promises they would not keep. *Love,* she pondered the matter, *the love of a man, so alluring, so full of promise, and so empty when it came down to it. That's what it was. On the one hand, they forgot you when it suited their purposes, and on the other hand, they clutched you so hard you couldn't breathe.* It would be so much simpler to stay as she was.

She would make the same choice Emma had. She might even teach and, thus, influence other young lives...again as Emma had.

It would be a good life, she told herself, nearly saying it out loud. *A good life and a wise choice too.*

Walking back to the garage, the low sound of the humming washing machine grew louder. She stepped inside and turned the washing machine's wringer around to squeeze dry the next load.

What a wise woman Emma really was. I've always felt a special bond with Emma, and now I will be like her. The first pleasant feelings of the day ran though her, bringing with them a sort of comfort Rebecca hadn't known in a long time.

Her thoughts were interrupted by the wail of the baby from inside, heard faintly above the noise of the washing machine. *He's got healthy lungs,* she thought. *Already able to make his needs known. It's the male in him.*

She quickly reached over to slow the washing machine motor down, but didn't turn it off. Figuring she would be back before long, she left it running rather than restart the motor when she came back out.

She disengaged the wringer and swung the bar out of the way of any danger. The motion was out of pure habit because there was no one around at the moment to get their hands caught while she was gone.

Stepping inside, she noticed that Jonathon's wails were louder now. Leona was already awake and getting to her feet.

"I'll get him," Rebecca said quickly, rushing past the protesting Leona. "You need to stay off your feet."

"I have to do something around the house. You'll have me feeling completely worthless."

"With eight children you have plenty to do," Rebecca said over her shoulder, as she hurried down the hall.

The back bedroom door was open, baby Jonathon's voice filling the hall. His cries quieted abruptly as she came into the bedroom, as if he heard her footsteps cross the invisible line of the door's threshold.

He was waving his little arms and legs vigorously and trying to fix his eyes on Rebecca. She drew close and said, "Hungry, are you?" He seemed to be trying to fly as she lifted him into the air.

"Are we ready for Mama?" she asked him. "Little Jonathon want to eat?"

He moved his feet in his excitement, one soft punt landing to the side of her nose.

"Now, now," she said, her heart melting. All the bad things she had thought about him while washing diapers left her in an instant. *This* was what she would be missing if she followed in Emma's footsteps.

I'll just enjoy my cousins, she told herself, yet the words left an emptiness in her heart. She pushed the thought away as baby Jonathon puckered up, ready to cry again.

"To Mommy we go," she said, taking quick steps down the hall before his wailing began again.

Leona's face lighted up as Rebecca approached with Jonathon. Immediately she set to nursing him. And Jonathon, on his part, calmly forgot about everyone around him and got busy filling his stomach.

"Hungry as a man," Leona chuckled. "How's the wash going?"

"About half done," Rebecca said, quickly calculating the remaining wash loads in her mind.

"Is it too cold to dry them outside?"

"Not yet."

"I'm so sorry you have to work this hard today, and with me sick yet. I feel so useless."

"Your family really needs you."

"I know." Leona's mood seemed to worsen with that statement.

"I didn't mean it that way," Rebecca said quickly. "They need you to get better."

"I know what you meant," Leona was clearly trying to rally her sagging feelings. "It's just this darkness that hangs over me. It comes down heavy when I'm least expecting it. I shouldn't let it bother me. I'm so sorry."

"You have to rest," Rebecca declared, stating the tried and true—and the only thing that seemed to make sense. Then something from her childhood came to mind. "Do you remember what you said about a sunrise when I was a little girl? It meant a lot to me."

"No, I don't remember," Leona said.

"It was a long time ago," Rebecca said. "I had stayed overnight at your place. You took me out to help chore. You were just newly married then—none of your children had been born. There was a beautiful sunrise that morning." Rebecca paused, remembering. "The sky was bright with reds and blues, a low bank of clouds hanging right on the edge, orange all over the top in streaks of light."

Leona was listening.

"You said that mornings were when God liked to show off."

"What an awful thing to say," Leona almost gasped.

"No, it wasn't," Rebecca said. "It made me think of what a big God He was."

"It was still awful," Leona protested, but Rebecca saw the hint of a smile on her face.

"He's *still* a big God," Rebecca said, knowing as she said it that she meant it for herself, not just for Leona.

"Even when He doesn't make sense," Leona said, her mind grasping at the hope offered. Rebecca thought then that Leona might best be left alone. Some thoughts were best unuttered except to the One who knows those thoughts before they're said.

"I'll be going back to the wash," she said softly.

Leona simply nodded and said, "I'll put Jonathon down when he's ready."

Chapter Thirty-six

With one more load of wash left to finish, Rebecca stepped back into the house to peek in on Leona. She seemed to be sleeping peacefully in the recliner, with little Jonathon resting awake on a blanket at her feet. His hands were by his side, his face calm, his eyes open, appearing to be lost in his babyhood experience.

Not having eaten lunch, Rebecca was hungry and suspected Leona was too. But sleep was the mother's more pressing need. Rebecca tiptoed into the living room, and the baby turned her way. She half expected him to cry out, but he didn't. It was all she could do to keep from picking him up, but Leona seemed to be sleeping yet. She satisfied herself with making a puckered up face in his direction, which she supposed he couldn't see anyway.

"You can pick him up—I'm not sleeping," Leona said suddenly, startling her. "Just can't seem to keep my eyes open."

"I'm sorry I woke you," Rebecca said quickly. "I tried to come in quietly."

"I've been awake awhile already. It wasn't you. Just thinking of all the things that need to be done. How's the wash coming?"

"Looks like one more load to go."

"Weather holding up?"

"Still warm enough. Things are drying well. Are you hungry?"

A smile played on Leona's face. "I must say I am. Maybe some more of that soup will do."

"I'm going to make sandwiches for us," Rebecca said firmly, heading into the kitchen. "You can decide then whether or not to eat it."

"Didn't your mother teach you not to spoil people?"

"You need taking care of," Rebecca said, firmness still in her voice.

"Sounding like your mother, are we?" Leona had only tenderness in hers.

"You miss your sister?"

"If you mean do I miss your mother's bossiness, the answer is *no,*" Leona said in a complaint Rebecca had heard before.

"Oldest children are that way sometimes." Rebecca came to her mother's defense. "I get complaints all the time—being the oldest one still at home."

"I was just thinking," Leona said with a weak smile, "how thoughtful your mother is, sending you to help me. But then, bossiness aside, she always was like that."

Rebecca began the sandwiches. She found some slices of cold beef in the refrigerator, paired it with some cheese, and put it all between slices of homemade bread.

Leona's voice continued from the living room. "I suppose that's what I miss about growing up. I thought being in a family of ten was a little suffocating at the time, but now it feels...safe, I guess. You look so forward to being away from it and on your own, with your own family and your own house. Then suddenly—you feel alone."

"You have children," Rebecca said, trying to be helpful.

"It's not the same. Even in the midst of ten, you were responsible pretty much for yourself. Now it's me—and Stephen, of course—but still, just the two of us with so much to do."

"That's how Mom feels sometimes," Rebecca said. "I try to help, but I imagine it's not the same."

"No...it isn't," Leona agreed. "You'll see when your time comes."

"*If* my time comes," Rebecca said. And since the subject had come up, she decided to ask, "Do you think Emma's life is lonely?"

"But Emma's single," Leona said. "By choice, I suppose. She had chances though."

Rebecca's silence must have aroused Leona's suspicions.

"Rebecca, you're not thinking of remaining single, are you?"

Rebecca didn't answer, but because the sandwiches were done, there was nothing left to do but go into the living room.

Leona's eyes searched Rebecca's face. "But what about John?"

Rebecca shrugged, smiling at Jonathon. He seemed on the verge of bawling for some reason.

"But you've been serious about him for some time. You can't just change like that."

"He's asked me to marry him," Rebecca said, figuring her aunt might as well know.

"Well, then that settles it." Leona's face relaxed. "You scared me for a minute."

"What's wrong with Emma's life?" Rebecca asked.

"Nothing. It's just not for you."

"But I'm not married to John yet."

"You're promised."

Rebecca thought for a second and then said, "Promised? Does everyone keep their promises? What if things change after a promise is made? What if I find that I prefer Emma's life—teaching school and keeping to myself?"

"It's not like having your own family...and your own man." Leona was looking worried again. "You're not thinking about going back on John?"

Rebecca's silence was all the answer Leona needed.

"Oh, Rebecca! What brought this on? Not being here with us, I hope!"

"No. Something else."

"You've met someone else?"

"No, I haven't met someone else." Rebecca couldn't keep the bitterness out of her voice, and Leona noticed.

Reaching out for one of the sandwiches, Leona motioned to the couch, saying, "Sit down. Eat. Tell me about it."

"There's the wash yet to do," Rebecca protested.

"Then talk fast."

"I can't."

"Just tell me." Leona glanced at Jonathon, who was puckering up his face to cry. "Just wait, little man. You can't be hungry yet." Leona reached down and turned him over onto his stomach. "That better?"

It must have been because Jonathon made no more efforts at crying, his head turned to the side, as he weakly tried to lift it up.

"John can be a little jealous at times," Rebecca said, remembering John repeatedly questioning her. "And men don't seem to want to keep their promises," she added, thinking of Atlee. "It might be better to just stay single."

"You really want that?" Leona was already halfway through her sandwich.

"That's just it. I don't know," Rebecca said, grinning a little. She bit into her sandwich, chewed, swallowed, and then said, "How *do* I know I shouldn't stay single?"

"You must leave that to God," Leona said firmly. "He knows the future. If He wanted you to be single, He wouldn't have sent you John."

"Maybe," Rebecca managed.

"You should be happy," Leona said. "I've never met John, but I'm sure he's good for you. Your mother would have said something if he wasn't."

Rebecca glanced at the clock, and it reminded her of her unfinished duties. "I have to get back to the wash."

"Finish your sandwich before you go. I'll just rest again till Jonathon wants his feeding."

Rebecca nodded, rising quickly. "I'll eat it on the way."

"Wake me to help with the folding then, when the laundry is dry."

Rebecca looked skeptically at her aunt.

"Yes," Leona replied, nodding firmly, "the girls can help when they come home from school. I'll do what I can too."

Knowing that protests were useless, Rebecca left with quick steps. She knew that the afternoon would be over before she wanted it to be.

Chapter Thirty-seven

The wind had picked up vigorously an hour earlier, and the wash was drying rapidly. Rebecca already had piles of diapers dumped out on the living room floor in front of Leona's recliner. At least three more hampers full of wash were still on the line.

Verna, who was busy folding the wash, asked, "What is there for supper? Not soup again, I hope. We've just been having too much soup lately."

Leona sighed, her face tightening up. "I'll make something special tonight," she announced. "What will it be? Who wants something special?"

"You really shouldn't," Rebecca protested. "It's too soon for that. Tell you what...we'll make it together. But I must do the hard work."

"A good supper," Leona proclaimed. "A good supper would taste so good. Stephen—poor man—would certainly appreciate it."

"What will it be then?" Rebecca looked at the two girls.

"Oh, I wouldn't let them pick," Leona said. "They might want pancakes for supper."

"Yes," Verna agreed, exactly on that point. "Let's have that."

"See what I mean?" Leona groaned. "What have I been doing wrong?"

"Nothing," Rebecca said firmly. "They're just children."

"Mother wasn't serious," Lois informed her sister, trying to help out. "I think a meat loaf would be the thing. Maybe a salad and canned corn, with a cake for dessert. I can stir up the cake."

"That's not bad." Leona looked impressed with her daughter, her mood lighter now. "I think that's what we'll do. It can be a frosted meat loaf. Lois can make a chocolate cake."

"Let's do it then," Rebecca said quickly. "Supper will be ready before we know it."

"I'll keep working on the wash for now," Leona said, a little more cheerful. "The girls can start helping you."

"Let's have Verna stay and help you," Rebecca said. "Lois and I will be fine in the kitchen."

"Works for me," Leona sighed, getting up off her chair. "I really have to be moving around some, though."

"I'll help you," Verna offered. "Then you can stay sitting."

"I need to walk, dear," Leona said. "My leg needs it. Let me take the boys' folded laundry to their room."

Verna bent over to reach for the clothing when Leona stopped her. "No, I need to bend over too. It's good for me."

"I'll take this pile then," Verna offered, going out of her way to be cooperative.

"I'll be better soon," Leona groaned to no one in particular. "Thanks for being a help, Verna," she added.

"I think you'll be better soon too," Verna agreed.

At the sound of buggy wheels, Verna ran to the window. "It's Fannie."

Leona reached for her sweater and went outside to greet her sister-in-law.

"I hear you're having a rough time of it," Fannie said sympathetically, still seated in the buggy. "I heard you were to the doctor today. Will you have Rebecca much longer?"

Leona nodded. "Thankfully, yes."

"How long till the blood clot clears up?"

"Don't know."

"Doctors give you any estimate?"

"You know what they always say. A few days...a week...we'll have to see."

"We'll hope for the best then. Are you coming Sunday?"

"Don't think so. Sitting that long probably wouldn't be good."

"We'll catch up later then—I have to be going," Fannie said, wrinkling her forehead. "Haven't made supper yet."

"Same here," Leona said. "Rebecca and Lois are getting it started."

"Let us know if you need more help." Fannie shook the reins, alerting her horse that it was time to go.

"Thanks," Leona said and stepped aside as the buggy took off. She watched as Fannie pulled out to the blacktop and turned right.

The late winter daylight was fading, the sun hanging low in the sky. Feeling a chill run though her, Leona pulled the sweater tighter around her shoulders, willing the darkness in her mind to go away, but the task felt as impossible as holding back the falling dusk.

It will go away, she told herself. *It will. I just need to hold on till it does.* She would just have to try to get through this the best she could. At least Rebecca was here. For some reason that brought more comfort than even the thought of Stephen being home.

He will be home soon, and I have to get the house in order before he arrives. The thought of the wash still lying around the living room made her move quickly back into the house.

As she entered, Verna was just disappearing down the hall, her arms full of folded clothing. The noises coming from the kitchen told Leona supper was well underway. She almost bent over to work on the wash piles, but couldn't resist. *I have to see what they're doing,* she told herself.

"Supper coming along?" she asked, glancing around the kitchen.

"Of course," Lois said, not looking up, her arms flecked with cheese from the block of Swiss she was shredding.

"It's coming," Rebecca told her, draining white potatoes from boiling water.

"Maybe you shouldn't have tried such a big task," Leona said. "The meat loaf will take an hour to bake."

"That's all right," Rebecca said. "The potatoes were my biggest concern."

"They look fine from here," Leona said. "Mattie did train you well. But I should leave you alone."

"Never hurts to check," Rebecca said. "Mom says that too."

"Rebecca's a good cook," Lois assured her mother. "Daddy will like the meat loaf. I'm sure of that."

"Mom," Verna's voice hollered from the boys' bedroom. "Where do these socks go? Their drawer is full."

Leona set off to help, while Rebecca finished mixing the hamburger for the meat loaf.

"Rebecca, I'm glad you're still here," Lois said.

"Just because I make meat loaf?" Rebecca asked with a laugh.

"No...but I suppose it helps," Lois said sheepishly.

When Rebecca said nothing, Lois asked, "Will Mom be better soon?"

"Sure," Rebecca said quickly, "the doctors are taking good care of her. Why?"

Lois shrugged. "I heard her crying this morning."

"I should have noticed too," Rebecca said. "I didn't know."

"It's not your fault," Lois said. "We're just so glad to have you. You are the one making it better." Lois stopped to wipe a tear.

Rebecca gave her cousin a hug from the side, then said, "We'd better get this meat loaf ready for the oven, don't you think?" She smiled, showing her appreciation of the younger girl's efforts at making her feel better. "You can start making the bread crumbs. We need three cups for the double batch."

"Mom will get better though?" Lois asked, her concern returning.

"I'm sure she will," Rebecca said, then added, "but it is up to *Da Hah,* of course."

"Why is everything up to Him?" Lois asked.

"Because He is God," Rebecca said simply.

"Who made Him then?"

"No one."

"Did He just make Himself?"

"I don't think so." Rebecca reached over to help Lois break the bread crumbs. "He just always was."

"That's an awful long time, then," Lois said more than she asked.

Rebecca nodded. "Yes, I suppose so."

"He's pretty big too. Isn't He?"

Rebecca nodded again.

"Why can't He run His world right, then?" Lois asked, bread crumbs falling into the bowl, her fingers reaching for another slice.

"Maybe He is," Rebecca said uncertainly.

"But there's so many things going wrong all the time." Lois sounded unconvinced.

"I think He must have trouble figured into His plans somehow," Rebecca ventured.

"I guess that would take a big God."

"Pretty big," Rebecca agreed.

"A little one couldn't work with trouble, right?"

"I suppose so," Rebecca allowed, mixing the ingredients of the meat loaf together in a larger bowl. "From what I've heard, the false gods only promise health and wealth or use trouble to scare people."

"I hope He knows what He's doing, then." Lois wrinkled up her face. "If I were God, I wouldn't work with trouble."

"I guess that's why you're not." Rebecca had to chuckle at her own statement. "Let's get this meat loaf into the oven—then we'll help your mom with the wash."

"Rebecca, now that you're twenty-one…are you going to marry soon?" Lois asked, abruptly changing the conversation.

"Well, I don't know." Rebecca was caught completely off guard.

"You wouldn't tell me anyway, would you?" Lois asked knowingly.

"Let's just say that when I marry, I'll be sure to invite you," Rebecca answered quickly with a smile.

Chapter Thirty-eight

Darkness fell as those around the kitchen table bowed their heads in prayer. *"Unser Geliebter Gott, der Schöpfer des Himmels und der Erde, darauf die Einstellung des Tages, machen wir Pause, um Ihnen Dank zu geben..."*

When Stephen finished, they lifted their heads but waited, the reverence from his words constraining their movements as if they had not yet made the transition from hearing spiritual nourishment to partaking of the physical.

"Well," Stephen pronounced, to no one in particular, "the meat loaf is getting no warmer. And such a meat loaf. We have good eating tonight." His smile stretched across his face as his eyes once more took in the prepared supper.

Out of the corner of her eye, Rebecca watched Leona's face darken. She wished Stephen were a little less excited about the food, but then she decided he was not to be blamed. Men did like to eat.

"I'm sorry I haven't done better with the meals," Leona said quietly, doing her best to keep her voice steady. "Even tonight, if it weren't for Rebecca..."

"It's not your fault," Stephen said, glancing at her, a healthy serving of the meat loaf already on his plate. "You're a good cook. You're just a little under the weather right now."

"It's good Rebecca came," Leona said. "At least you're getting some decent food."

"Now, now," he said, turning sideways, his chair scraping on the hardwood floor, "you have no reason to feel bad. There's no one better than you in the kitchen."

Leona offered no response, the meat loaf bowl in front of her.

"You have to eat," he said. "You're still recovering."

"I'm too fat. I'm not losing the extra weight," she said so quietly Rebecca could barely hear it.

"Look," he said, noticing that the children were beginning to squirm, "you have nothing to worry about. Really." Reaching over, he put two spoonfuls of meat loaf on her plate and passed it on. He then started the corn and salad, taking plenty for himself and then some for Leona's plate before passing them on. "Eat," he said quietly in Leona's direction.

Leona glanced up at him, her face still dark, but meeting his eyes now. Uncomfortable, Rebecca looked away, took a helping of meat loaf, and passed it on. When she turned back, Leona was eating. Her face still held a trace of melancholy but was more peaceful than Rebecca had seen all day.

"So what's the news from school?" Stephen asked, the comforting sound of the gas lantern hissing on the ceiling above them.

"I got a 97 on spelling," Lois announced.

"I did too," Stephen Jr., the first grader, proclaimed.

"You sure about that?" Stephen was skeptical of his son's recollection of things. He glanced at Lois for confirmation.

"I did," Stephen Jr. insisted. "It was a good grade."

Lois shrugged her shoulders. "I didn't see his grade. First-grade spelling is a little easier than the hard words we have to do."

"Teacher almost broke her arm at lunch playing ball," Thomas announced, injecting fresh news into the conversation.

"She just fell," Elmo corrected him. "It wasn't broken."

"I heard her say it hurt like it was broken. I heard her say so." Thomas made a valiant effort to convince the family of his version of the events.

"That's not the same as broken," Stephen corrected him.

He gave in to the force of his father's eyes on him and turned back to his plate.

"You'd better be careful about such things," Stephen said, not willing to drop the topic yet. "We have to tell the truth. Always. Even when it might sound better to tell more than what really happened."

"I wasn't lying," Thomas protested, his pleasure in the meat loaf on his plate temporarily suspended.

"Maybe not," Stephen allowed. He watched Thomas sigh in relief and resume eating. And then he continued, "Stretching a story or adding to it can be just as bad."

Thomas rapidly nodded, wanting to demonstrate his absorption of the lesson. He stopped long enough to add corn to his mouth full of meat loaf. Picking up the buttered bun beside his plate, he bit into it.

"We are having a math contest next week," Elmo said, not too much delight in his voice. "Each grade against itself."

"You don't sound too excited," Leona said. "You're usually pretty good at that."

"He's studying hard," Lois said to the others. "I see him with his nose in his math book. I think he wants to win this time."

"Really." Leona smiled at her oldest. "What's the prize?"

"We don't know yet," Verna announced. "Teacher isn't telling."

"Last year it was a real nice tablet with drawing pencils. The first grade got little bags of candy," Thomas volunteered. "It's usually different each year."

"So what's your weak point?" Leona asked Elmo. "Still long addition?"

Elmo nodded despairingly. "That and the story problems. We just have two minutes to solve each one."

"That's all you get," Thomas added. "When the time is up, you have to stop even if you're not done."

"That's Martha's idea," Lois said. "Last year we had three minutes."

"She's from Daviess County," Elmo muttered. "There's strange ideas coming from down there."

"Now, now," Stephen spoke up, "they're no different from us."

"Sometimes they are," Elmo insisted. Then glancing at his father's face, he added, "She just has different ideas, I guess."

"That's good sometimes," Stephen told him. "We can learn from each other."

"I suppose so." Elmo must have thought it better to agree but couldn't help himself. "Two minutes is mighty short. Especially when you're trying to think fast."

"Maybe if you'd just relax, your mind would work better," Leona suggested.

"Then it stops completely," Elmo declared, sounding horrified. "I have to push it."

"You should try that." Stephen seconded Leona's suggestion. "Might surprise you."

"Is that true, Rebecca?" Elmo turned in her direction, his face skeptical.

"It does work," Rebecca said, thankful she didn't disagree with Stephen and Leona. "You don't *stop* thinking. You just relax a little beforehand and then let your mind work on the problem."

"Did you ever win any math quizzes?" Elmo still wasn't convinced.

"I'm afraid not," Rebecca lamented. "Wasn't too good at math. Emma tried to teach me, but…well, I guess I did okay."

"I *like* math," Elmo stated firmly. "Maybe if this relaxing thing works, I might win. You think it works on long addition too?"

"I suppose so," Rebecca allowed. "Being tense doesn't work well on anything."

"Worry doesn't either," Leona said for everyone's benefit. After a few moments of eating, she added, "If we're just about done, it's time for the cake."

Rebecca wasn't paying attention. Instead, she was thinking about what she had said about being tense, wondering if it could have anything to do with her problems. She had sure been tense about Atlee. John too. She shoved the thoughts away, turning to listen to Leona.

Instead, it was Stephen who was speaking, "I have a surprise," he said. "I didn't know about the cake in the oven. I just took the chance." A happy grin spread all over his face. "Even your mother doesn't know about it."

There was silence as they waited, but he seemed to be teasing them.

"Okay," Leona said, after a few moments had passed, "let's hear it."

"Ice cream!" he said, his grin getting even bigger. "Schwan's. The truck stopped nearby where we were working...and just at quitting time."

A chorus of smiles around the table greeted his announcement.

"But," Leona replied, not joining in the fun, "where is it? It must be melting."

"Safe in my cooler," Stephen said, "on ice."

"But that won't keep it forever," she insisted. "You have to bring it inside."

"Who wants to go out and get it?" Stephen asked, to which Lois answered by getting up.

"It's in the backseat of the buggy," he told her. "Colder outside too."

Leona looked at Stephen and said, "I guess I didn't notice you didn't bring your lunch things in. You are a sneaker."

"Not always," he said, as their eyes met again. Something wonderful seemed to pass between them, causing Rebecca to turned away lest she be embarrassed.

Stephen was doing Leona a lot of good tonight, that was for sure. Perhaps men were good for something besides trouble. Trouble and broken promises. Emma might not have a man to cheer her up, but neither did she have a man to bring her down.

With that conclusion, she got up to get bowls for the ice cream.

"The spoon is in the third drawer," Leona said. "There's also a small scoop there."

When Lois returned with the cooler, the content was carefully removed and transferred to the bowls. Once all were served, the household fell silent except for the sound of softly clicking spoons.

"It's good," Leona said for all of them.

"Butter pecan—the best," Elmo said. "Better even than homemade."

"Not better than Fannie's ice cream," Verna protested. The comment set the two boys thinking.

When they didn't answer, Verna prodded them, "You agree, don't you?"

Neither boy said anything, both taking another sample of ice cream, making a show of tasting it slowly, and sliding their spoons back out of their mouths.

"Nope," they said in unison. "This tastes better."

"Than Fannie's?" Verna looked incredulously at her brothers.

"Well," Elmo answered, "Fannie's—and Mom's too—is good. Maybe not quite...but almost. Mom makes a good strawberry, but this is..." he searched for the right words and then added, "so store-bought and rich and creamy."

"They're *both* good," Stephen declared. "Schwan's is different than homemade. You'd get tired of this too, if you had it as much as you have homemade ice cream."

"I like it because you don't have to turn it with a crank," Stephen Jr. said.

"You never do anyway," Thomas reminded him. "I do most of the turning."

"He does help." Leona came to the six-year-old's defense. "He makes a few turns every now and then."

"I'll do more when I get bigger," Stephen Jr. volunteered. "I'll turn all of it."

"All in good time. You are growing fast enough already," Leona said.

"Will Jonathon grow up fast?" Stephen Jr. wanted to know, as the newest member of the family made himself known with a wail from the living room.

"He will too," Leona assured him, getting up to tend to the baby.

"Let's pray first," Stephen said, stopping her.

"But the baby," she was already half out of her chair.

"Okay," he said, "get him. Then he can pray with us."

Rising and moving quickly, Leona was back in moments with Jonathon. He peeked out over his mother's arms, his eyes unblinking and staring at their faces as Stephen led out in prayer again.

Chapter Thirty-nine

The next several days passed in a blur of meals, wash, and children going to and returning from school. Rebecca was too busy to leave the house. Leona, after another visit to the doctor, was assured that she was recovering quickly enough. By Wednesday morning, she appeared in the kitchen and was determined to help.

"I'm doing okay," Rebecca assured her, flipping the eggs in the pan on the gas range.

"But you're leaving the day after tomorrow. I have to get going somehow."

"Just don't overdo it."

"I won't. Jonathon isn't too fussy during the night. I'm getting my sleep. I'm so thankful for that."

Rebecca took the plate of eggs and set them on the kitchen table. Stephen was coming down the hall, the sound of his footsteps getting louder. This morning she had biscuits and gravy ready for him—her first time preparing them without her mother around.

Leona noticed. "So you tried biscuits and gravy?"

"Yes. I hope they're good."

"I'm sure they are. I think I'll sit down and have breakfast with Stephen. Why don't you join us?"

"The children are getting up in a few minutes. I don't have their eggs made."

"They can wait. It won't take that long. Sit down and eat."

Wearily, Rebecca took the chair beside Leona, after making sure all the food was within reach.

After they had prayed, Leona brought up the subject Rebecca had thought would never come up on its own. "Is there anything you'd like to do before you leave? You've been cooped up here for days."

Seeing her chance, Rebecca said, "I'd love to stop by and see Emma. I saw her in church the first Sunday I was here, but that's not like talking to her alone."

Leona fully agreed and quickly replied, "Certainly. You should do that. There's really no reason not to. I'm coming along just fine. How about tomorrow? You can take the horse and buggy over by yourself."

"Really?" Rebecca said, trying not to sound too eager.

"Absolutely. Plan on that for tomorrow."

"You'll have to tell me where she lives now. I can't remember exactly."

"It's easy enough," Leona assured her. "It's just on the other side of Milroy."

So it was that, on Thursday as soon as she could get away, Rebecca was on her way to Emma's house. The day, which dawned with a few snow clouds, was now breaking into sunshine, and Rebecca was thankful.

Pulling on the reins of the unfamiliar horse, she brought it to a stop at Highway 3. Nervously, she hoped it would stand still long enough for the road to clear. It hadn't seemed too skittish when she hitched it to the buggy, but one never knew what quirks each individual horse had.

Keeping the reins taut, she waited for the cars coming from each direction. Their approaching sounds seemed not to affect the horse—calmly it kept its head pointed toward the town of Milroy and raised no objections to the stop. Once the highway was clear, she let the lines out slowly, relieved.

Following Leona's directions, she drove through Milroy, with its full blaze of Christmas decorations, and then south on Base Road. Once she was past the next junction, she started looking for the house. It wasn't hard to find. The house was on her left, the driveway circling past the white two-story house to the red barn.

A buggy was already parked in front of the barn. It was unhitched and cross corners to the barnyard. That could be Emma's buggy, but Rebecca doubted it. Emma would likely keep her buggy inside or at least under the barn overhang. It must belong to Luke, who Leona had told her worked for Emma.

As she pulled up, she caught sight of a figure out beside the third barn, working with the cattle. His black hat hid his face, but he had Luke's shape and height. He showed no interest in her arrival or made any attempt to come in her direction and offer to unhitch the buggy for her.

Pulling up to the hitching rail and avoiding the parked buggy, Rebecca got out. She leaned back into the buggy and retrieved the tie rope from under the seat, where she had placed it for easier retrieval. The horse made no objections as she tied it securely to the rail.

Following the sidewalk, she arrived at the front door and timidly knocked. When it opened, Emma's face instantly broke into a broad smile. "Oh, Rebecca. I wondered who drove in. I figured it was probably business and Luke would take care of it. By all means, come in."

Rebecca, her schoolgirl shyness coming over her, stepped inside. Emma was as imposing as ever. Tall for an Amish woman, her now nearly white hair was neatly tucked under her hair covering, but it was her demeanor that made the most impact. At church on Sunday, it wasn't as apparent, but here in her own house during the week, the effect was unmistakable. Emma was used to giving the orders.

"I thought I'd stop by," Rebecca said. Then feeling that more of an explanation was in order, she added, "There's something I'd like to ask you."

"Don't tell me you've come all the way over here with some confession about cheating during your school days. Seems like I have heard enough of those already," Emma exclaimed, motioning toward the living room. "Can't say I ever expected it of you, as hard as you had to work."

"No, no." Rebecca was thoroughly flustered. "That's not it at all!"

"Well! *Dank Da Hah,*" Emma exclaimed. "It would have disappointed me quite a lot. Let me get you a glass of water or orange juice."

"Water's fine," Rebecca told her.

Emma wrinkled her brow. "Well, I wanted orange juice. So let me get you both. Then if you don't drink it, nothing's lost."

Without waiting for approval from Rebecca, Emma went to the kitchen, her stride firm and brisk. Returning, she set two glasses beside Rebecca and went back to the kitchen for her own glass.

"So you live in Wheat Ridge now?"

"Yes."

"For what? Three, four years?"

"Something like that."

"Do you like it?"

Rebecca's face lit up. "Yes. Wheat Ridge is a wonderful place to live. We've really made ourselves at home there. Mom likes it, I think. Dad is doing well with the farm. A lot of businesses are along that road. Amish ones. I suppose Dad could get work with one of them, but he likes the farm."

"You still milk?"

"Yes. And Matthew is just learning how to chore," Rebecca said. "Poor fellow. He had to learn fast when Mom decided to send me out to help Leona."

"Oh, ya. You're here for the baby. On Sunday they said it was a boy."

Rebecca smiled. "Jonathon. He's already growing fat. Sleeps well at night too. That is helping Leona get better faster."

"Wouldn't know much about babies myself. I'm just a schoolteacher."

"And a good one," Rebecca said with affection.

"I always liked you too." Emma allowed similar feelings to creep into her voice. "So what was it that you wanted to ask me?"

Now that the time had come, Rebecca hesitated, thinking about the consequences, then plunged ahead. "It's about Atlee."

Emma raised her eyebrows. "You two get in trouble together? That's a whole lot worse than cheating. How did I miss that? I remember I was just about to the point where I was going to tell your mother that she needed to keep you two apart. Then his parents went Mennonite."

"Oh, no," Rebecca shook her head and replied, "it's not that at all. We didn't do anything inappropriate."

Emma looked relieved. "I'm glad to hear that. What is it then?"

"Well," Rebecca took a deep breath and continued, "one of the reasons I was glad Mom let me come out to help Leona is that I needed to find out something."

"Yes?" Emma was waiting.

"I needed to know. To understand. About Atlee and me. Something that was scaring me."

"And?" Emma was looking at her.

"I realized it the day Leona had Jonathon. I loved Atlee. I loved him more than I have ever loved anyone. And..." she said hesitantly. *Should I really tell Emma about the promise?* "Well, Atlee asked me to promise to wait for him. That is, that when we were adults, we'd come back together..."

Emma was silent as Rebecca collected herself.

"We had promised to meet each other on my twenty-first birthday. And that was last week. And so I came to the bridge where we were supposed to meet." She ended with a gasp and tears. "I had to tell someone."

"Of course you did," Emma said quietly. "He didn't show, did he?"

"What am I going to do?" Rebecca asked, her eyes large. "He didn't come. I...I've even thought about not marrying...about staying single. Like you. You've always seemed so happy."

Emma let out a breath. "Well, first off, Rebecca, I don't think you ought to hold it against Atlee for not coming. You were both so young then. Things change as we get older. We forget what once seemed so important."

Rebecca was crying softly, but didn't speak.

Emma sat back in her chair. "Tell me, Rebecca. Has there been anyone else since Atlee?"

"Yes. John Miller in Wheat Ridge. He asked me to marry him just before I came out here."

"And you said what?"

"Yes."

"Tell me more about you and Atlee."

Rebecca looked over toward the fireplace. Its smooth stones stood out from each other, each a different shade of earth tone, held together by gray mortar. She took a deep breath and then began, "It was on one of the last days he was in school. He gave me a ring that he had found. Asked me if I would keep it until I turned twenty-one. That he would come back for me then. He said that I should wait for him. I told him I would, Emma. I even promised."

"What did this ring look like?"

"Oh, it was pretty. But that's not what's causing me trouble."

"I know. It's your heart that's causing you trouble."

Rebecca nodded.

"Do you still have the ring?"

"No. I threw it away when he didn't show up. Do you think he's going to come back?"

Emma didn't think long before replying, "No, dear, they never do."

"But I loved him with all my heart."

"Yes. I know you did. That was because you were young. Young hearts fill up easily," Emma said, taking Rebecca's hand. "You can learn to give all that love to John now."

"You think so?"

Emma nodded, squeezing her hand. "He's an Amish boy? This John?"

"Of course!" Rebecca said in horror. "I wouldn't date anyone else."

"That's what I thought." Emma's lips stretched into a thin smile. "Does he love you?"

"Yes, he says he does."

"Well, now, that's something wonderful. An Amish man who loves you. Rebecca, the very best thing you can do is to love this John right back."

Rebecca nodded, still unsure.

"What time do you have to be back at Leona's?" Emma asked.

"Soon. I'm leaving tomorrow with a load going to Wheat Ridge for Christmas visits. I need to pack."

"So why don't I show you the house, and let's continue our visit. Let's get you cheered up. Okay?"

That was fine with Rebecca. She followed Emma through the house, taking in the details and the history. It was clearly built by the English because it had a fireplace.

"My brother, M-Jay—did you know him, Rebecca?"

"I think I may have met him when I was little, but I don't really remember," she said.

"He left me this farm—and two others. Good farms too."

Thirty minutes later, Rebecca was back on the road, her heart much lighter. She would go home, she decided, and learn to love John as she had loved Atlee. Emma had come to her rescue as always. Her heart was now bigger, and she would give it all away again. She would let John's love fill all of her heart.

She was a quarter mile or so short of the stop sign where she would turn onto the state road toward Milroy. That's where Rebecca noticed the blue car following her. When she guided the buggy to the side of the road to give the car room to pass, it made no great effort to do so. It moved over slightly and drove up even with the buggy.

She glimpsed a male face inside the car, intently scrutinizing the interior of the buggy as it inched by. *This could be any one of many things,* she thought, *a curious tourist, some local who thought he knew her, or worse, perhaps a total stranger with evil on his mind.*

Whoever it was pulled to a slow stop ahead of her and opened the car door to get out. She saw clearly that it was a young man, clean-cut and wearing a T-shirt and denim pants. Thinking fast, she thought about giving Leona's horse full rein and making a run for the main road where she might get help.

Instead, she waited as he approached the buggy, his step confident. There was no use in avoiding his presence, so she slid open the buggy door, keeping the reins firmly in her left hand.

"Rebecca?" he asked, stopping just short of the buggy steps, a half question in his voice, a smile playing on his lips.

"Yes," she said because he already seemed to know her name.

"I thought so," he said. "You just came from Emma's place. I passed you coming down."

When she kept a stony look on her face, he asked, "You don't recognize me, do you?"

"Should I?" she asked, finally looking full into his face. And then at once the years shed themselves in front of her eyes. The freckles were gone, the face was etched with lines—as if he had somehow suffered in life, but his hair was still brown and his eyes as blue as ever.

"Atlee," she said with what breath she could muster.

"Yes, Atlee," he said, his head slightly deferring to her, his eyes lowering momentarily.

"But—" she managed, "you—I thought you didn't come."

"You went to the bridge, then?" he asked, his smile gone now.

"Yes, and you weren't there. So why are you here now?" she asked.

"To do what I hope is the right thing, Rebecca."

"So why weren't you at the bridge?"

"Did you want me to be there?"

The question caught her off guard, her thoughts racing. Should she tell him the truth? Would she hurt him if he knew she had not wanted him to show up after all?

"See I forgot," Atlee said, letting his eyes fall to the ground again, saving her from answering. "Yet, somehow, even if I had remembered, it wouldn't have seemed right. That place was for us to fulfill a promise. But what we promised can never happen. I think you know that."

Rebecca found nothing to say.

"Rebecca, the truth is we've both changed. And I know you're getting married to someone else. John."

"How could you know that?" Rebecca asked.

"Mary told me."

"Mary? How do you know Mary?"

"She's Mennonite...and so am I. She and I have known each other for a few years. When she mentioned your name and described you," Atlee said, smiling sheepishly, "in detail, I was sure it was you. She told me about John. And it was then that I remembered you might be at the bridge. Rebecca, to be honest, I had forgotten. It was so long ago."

"Yes," Rebecca said, "a long time ago."

"But Rebecca, I've not forgotten you," Atlee continued. "I felt something very strong toward you when we were young. And you felt the same. I treasure that memory."

"I kept the ring all these years," Rebecca said.

"Did you? I remember that ring. I remember giving it to you that day."

"Yes, it was..." Then Rebecca faltered. "I threw the ring away at the bridge."

Atlee shrugged his shoulders. "That's okay. I couldn't let you leave thinking *you* were forgotten. You weren't. It's just that we've both changed...and, Rebecca, I'm getting married too. The wedding's in the spring. A missionary girl from Peru where my uncle works."

"Oh." She felt her interest peak. "You're a missionary too?"

"Served for two years with my uncle. I'm back in the States now to stay." Another car approached them from behind, slowed down before passing, but caused Atlee to steady himself against the side of the buggy.

"I'll be going then, Rebecca. I'm glad we had this chance. May God bless you and John."

"Thank you. And you too."

Atlee took her hand and gave it a slight squeeze, to which Rebecca didn't draw back. And then he turned and walked back to the car. She sat there while he pulled out in front of her.

"My..." she said, startling herself with speaking out loud. Surprised at her emotions, but because it felt so good, she did it again. "Well, who would have thought?"

She felt a great gladness rise in her heart. She was free now in more ways than one. She was free to trust again, without feeling in the back of her mind that Atlee had forgotten everything. Atlee had not forgotten her, and not only had he not forgotten, he had cared enough to explain. This was really for the best. The past was the past. Atlee was right. They should not try to bring their feelings back.

Rebecca snapped the reins and guided the buggy onto the road again. Thinking about this chance encounter on the rest of the drive home, she decided to tell no one about it. Everything—the ring, the promise, their love—had been Atlee's and her secret from the start and could remain so till the end.

She turned right at the schoolhouse and then south toward Leona's place, thankfulness still in her heart.

Chapter Forty

Standing at the front window, Emma had watched Rebecca leave. She then sat for a few minutes in her rocker, deep in thought. Finally she walked over to her desk, pulled out her legal notebook, and composed a letter.

She signed the finished document and placed it in an envelope. As she sealed the envelope, she made plans to take the letter to the mailbox later.

When Luke arrived that morning, he went straight to work. He figured that Emma would come out and find him if he needed any special instructions. He couldn't get it out of his mind that Rebecca, whatever her last name was, had visited yesterday. What did she want anyway? She was pretty, he'd give her that. Prettier than Susie, that was for sure. That girl Rebecca represented all the things that Susie wasn't. Beauty, class, and most of all, *unobtainability*.

Last Sunday night with Susie had turned out so lovely. He had savored the thoughts of his time with her all the way home, throughout the past few days, and up until Rebecca came by yesterday. She had reminded him again of what he was missing out on—and about the money.

Confounded money. A lot of good it did anyone, as troublesome as it was proving to be. Yet his mother had started in all over again about it last night. Luke's father had still been out in the barn when

Luke arrived home, which was when he had taken the chance to tell his mom that Rebecca had stopped by Emma's. He knew his mother well enough not to discuss news about Emma, however innocent, around his father.

Not that he understood what Rebecca had to do with the money, but it was the mention of her that set his mother off. Maybe Rebecca was a reminder of her desire to move to Wheat Ridge or of wealthy relatives when they had so little.

Whatever the cause, Rachel wanted to know every detail about Rebecca's visit. He told her that he had been out back working with the cattle during her visit and could remember very little.

"Why didn't you go up and help her unhitch or something?" his mother demanded. "Maybe she would have told you why she was there."

"I'm not going to do something like that," he told her. "It's too embarrassing."

"You could have, at least, gone inside the house while she was there and asked Emma something made up."

He shook his head, feeling like the dirt from Emma's barnyard. No, more than that, like a lowly worm digging beneath that dirt.

"You really need to do a better job watching Emma," she said. "You let that one letter get away, all while mailing it yourself. You likely had the answer right there with you. You let it get away. You're going to have to do better, Luke. How do you expect Susie to ever be happy with you if you're as poor as a barn mouse?"

"I don't know," he answered. "Her family doesn't have much either."

"That's all the more reason for you to do better. Luke, you really need to wake up. You could get a better girl if we were better off."

That was what tormented him, both then and now. The vision of Ann Stuzman rose before him, blond hair creeping out from under her head covering, her slim neck turning with the ease and grace of a summer's flower bent over with the morning dew. If not her, then her sister, a year younger and even better looking. Somewhere, somehow, he—Luke Byler—was supposed to have more than what he did.

He brought the New Holland around in the field, catching the sight of Emma walking to her mailbox, hands full of letters. He could see that none of them was brown and thick, at least from what he could see from there. He had just gotten started with his duties when the urgency hit him. Something would have to be done. If he went home again and told his mother that Emma had been to the mailbox and that he didn't know what it was about, things would not go well.

How, though, was he supposed to get to the mailbox before the mailman came and without Emma seeing him? The solution came to him as he watched Emma reach the box, open the lid, deposit her handful of letters, shut the lid, pull up the flag, and start the walk back toward the house.

He would pretend to smooth out the driveway with his New Holland. It needed it anyway. He would smooth it out even while Emma was walking back. That would look completely innocent and in order.

Revving up the engine, he pulled up to the gate leading to the front red barn. Hopping out, he opened it, drove through, then hopped out to close the gate again. Barely able to latch it in his haste, he lost several precious seconds. *Letting cattle out is no way of endearing myself to Emma, who,* he told himself, *still pays me well.*

Driving behind the barn, he exchanged the forks on the New Holland for the flat bucket. With that done, he was on his way out the driveway. Emma was almost to the walks when he passed her.

Slowing down the engine enough to tell her, "I'm smoothing out the driveway," he went on by.

She nodded her approval and continued to walk. When he arrived at the end of the driveway, he parked, leaving the engine running at full speed. Perhaps it would sound natural enough, certainly not the attention it might attract if he slowed the motor. There might even be some explanation in Emma's mind for why he was climbing out, if she should turn around to look.

Sticking his head out, he saw that Emma was still walking toward the house, her back turned. He took a leap toward the mailbox, opened the lid, pulled the letters out, and flipped through them with trembling hands.

The third one, as white and normal looking as the others, was addressed to Bridgeway & Broadmount, Attorneys at Law, in Anderson, Indiana, the same address and the same handwriting as the big brown envelope he had mailed in Milroy.

Slipping the white envelope out, he slid it into his pants pocket. The rest went back into the mailbox. He quickly jumped back across the ditch to his New Holland. A glance up the driveway revealed that Emma was almost at the door, her back still turned. With a smile, he set the bucket down and dragged it up the driveway.

Back at his buggy, he dared to take the envelope out and gently opened it. If the letter needed to be mailed later, he told himself his mother would be able to fix the tears. Letting the page drop open in his hand, his eyes skimmed over the words until he found what he was looking for.

> *Due to my continued serious illness, I wish to deal with the money appropriations to my family, and the three farms given out according to my wishes.*

Nervously, Luke stopped reading there and glanced around quickly. He had read enough, he figured. Emma was giving the farms back to their rightful owners. His mother would be very happy with him tonight.

Chapter Forty-One

As Rebecca opened the barn door, James and Leroy stuck their heads down from the opening in the small haymow. Leroy, making as if to climb down the ladder, changed his mind when he saw it was Rebecca.

"You boys misbehaving? she asked them. *Likely not,* she thought, *but they are boys after all.*

"Nope," they said in unison, their faces cherubim-like.

"What are you doing then?"

"Watching Missy eat a mouse," James said. "She's chasing it around in circles."

"I wonder why she does that," Leroy pondered aloud.

"She's just a cat," Rebecca told them. "That's just the way cats are. She'll eat it soon."

"She just did," James said loudly. "It crunched. Missy looks scared."

"Probably feels guilty," Rebecca remarked, with a little vengeance in her voice. She led the horse to its stall, gave it a scoop of oats, and then opened the stall door to the outside barnyard.

Leroy and James had disappeared from the haymow opening, apparently to watch the last of the mouse disappear. Rebecca smiled and walked toward the house. *Nothing like life as an education.*

"You see anything of Leroy and James?" Leona asked when Rebecca walked into the living room. Hampers of freshly collected wash sat in front of Leona, as she sat folding them.

"They're watching Missy eat a mouse."

Leona laughed. "Real boys. You're back from Emma's early."

"I thought I took too long," Rebecca said apologetically, glancing at the clock on the living room wall. "I guess it's not as late as I thought."

"I told you to take all the time you needed."

Rebecca shrugged. "I'm just so glad I got to go. Emma is so wise."

"I suppose so," Leona said dryly.

Rebecca caught the tone in her voice. "Oh, nothing against you. It's just different, I guess. I always liked Emma when I was in school."

"Teachers often have a special place," Leona agreed. "Aunts too. But don't worry. I wasn't serious—just tired I guess."

Rebecca gave Leona a long, hard look. "Should I be going home already? Mom will let me stay longer, if you need me. I'm sure of that."

"No," Leona said firmly, "you should catch a ride while you can. It's much more pleasant than taking the Greyhound."

"But that makes no difference. Really—it doesn't," Rebecca protested.

"It's been long enough." Leona was firm in her decision. "I can't remember the other seven recoveries being quite this long—the tiredness. But then, I'm getting old and forgetful already. People will start talking soon enough, if I keep my *maut* forever."

"I wouldn't worry about that," Rebecca said.

"You might not be, but I am," Leona assured her. "And what about your John? I never saw you write to him. Did you? Or call? You should at least have done that. The furniture store has a phone. I'm sure he's worried."

Rebecca wondered how much she should confide in her aunt. "Well, to tell you the truth, I was working through some things about John and me while I've been here. And now everything's fine. I'll see him very soon." Wanting that conversation to end, Rebecca turned to her duties. "What should I do now to help you? Wash diapers? I see Jonathon has been busy as usual."

Deep down she was a little surprised at how very glad she was to be going home tomorrow. Not that she would admit this in front of Leona, but she was really looking forward to seeing John again.

"Yeah, diapers..." Leona was saying, "I'm beginning to see them in my sleep."

"Hopefully washed and hanging on the line." Rebecca made a face.

"The other option is not a vision one wishes to dwell on," groaned Leona. "Start the wash though, and I'll help."

"You sure you can?" Rebecca asked.

"I helped on Tuesday, didn't I?"

"Yes, but—"

"You're being too soft on me—really." Leona gave Rebecca a firm look. "Start the first load."

"And we need to make bread today, don't we?" Rebecca remembered seeing the low supply yesterday.

"We still have enough for today," Leona said. "I'll bake some tomorrow. Your last day here shouldn't be completely full. You'll have nothing but unpleasant memories."

"No I won't." Now Rebecca was being firm. "I'll bake bread today. I couldn't leave with that on my conscience. No good *maut* would do that."

"You're a good *maut*," Leona assured her. "I wouldn't know what I would have done without you."

"Then I'd better get busy," Rebecca said, gathering up a full load from the closest hamper of diapers.

"Did Emma say anything about her health?"

"No, she looked okay. Why? Is she having problems?"

Leona nodded. "She saw a doctor about her heart. They put in stents, but the doctors don't know exactly what's wrong."

"Surely not?" Rebecca's face registered her sadness at this news.

"Our time comes when the Lord wills it," Leona told her, noticing. "We just have to be ready."

As Rebecca headed to the garage, Leona said, "Let me know when the wash is ready to hang on the line. I need some fresh air."

"Okay," Rebecca called back, as she made her way to the garage.

As she pulled the starter rope, the motor sputtered for a moment and then finally caught. Against the background of its noise, she let her thoughts go to Emma and her sickness. Surely Emma was not passing soon? Yet that was possible. Finding comfort in the fact that she had been able to pay a visit, Rebecca was grateful for the opportunity.

When she went back inside, Leona was already working on the bread.

"I've decided on two batches," Leona said, "so it will last us awhile."

"Let's make three batches then—because it's my last day," Rebecca volunteered.

"I thought of that." Leona looked sheepish again. "Mean of me, I know. Trying to get all the help out of the *maut* I can—I know. Sorry."

"Quit complaining," Rebecca said. Then, thinking that some fresh air might be just what her aunt needed, she said, "The wash is ready for the line. It's a nice day. Might be good for you."

"I do need something," Leona agreed with a sigh, her eyes on the bowls spread on the kitchen table. "Okay, I've started the yeast. The liquid mixture is ready as soon as it cools down. You can then start adding the flour. The bread pans are in the second drawer over there." Leona motioned, then added, "Here I am prattling on with instructions as if your mother never trained you at all."

"Bread making is still a little scary," Rebecca said, "even after all the many times I've made it. Does it get any easier as you get older?" she asked.

"Yes, it does." Leona's eyes glanced around the kitchen as she prepared to leave and hang the wash on the line. "Took time for me too. But everything done often enough eventually becomes familiar—I guess. Getting married helped too," she added. "That adds plenty of responsibilities."

"I'm looking forward to it," Rebecca said quickly because—still somewhat to her own surprise—she was.

"I'm going to have to go over to see Emma myself sometime," Leona said with a smile. "She was good for you. She told you the right thing."

"How do you know what she told me?" Rebecca asked a little skeptically.

"I can see it on your face," Leona said, the smile still playing on her own face. "I would say you have found your answer—and it is good."

"Yes, I think I have," Rebecca admitted.

When the door of the garage shut, Rebecca allowed her thoughts to go where she didn't dare with Leona in the kitchen, for fear her face would turn red. She allowed the memory of John's eyes to come back, the longing she had seen in them. She remembered the gentle trickling of the running water under the bridge that Sunday, the wind blowing in the bare branches above them, the slight winter sunshine reaching them, the feelings she had felt when he asked whether she would always be his.

I said yes, she told herself, almost saying it out loud again because it brought her such pleasure. She was thrilled to discover that this pleasure was back, that she had found the answer to God's will for her. *Atlee had been a wonderful boy,* she told herself, *but we were young then, and our love was a young love—a first love—but now I am an adult with an adult love to fill my heart.*

She bowed her head right then and there, tears of joy forming in her eyes, and thanked God for the gift of John's love. Her experience with Atlee had been what it was, and she would never call it wrong, but it was now part of her past. John was her future.

Thankfulness for Emma and her wisdom also filled her heart. Also for her mother and Leona, for all the help they were willing and able to give her. She was surrounded with so many wise counselors, who wouldn't let her down as she and John started their new life together. God was more than good to them.

She looked down at the liquid mix in front of her, finding it to be the temperature she wanted. Dumping the contents into a larger bowl, she gradually stirred in the flour till the consistency was just right.

This was the art—her mother had told her many times—to find the right texture of the dough. This art couldn't be taught from books. It had to be experienced, to be felt with one's fingertips, to be watched and observed until the knowledge came full and certain. Only then could one make excellent bread. Bread that came out of the pan fluffy and light, that sliced well under the knife, that fully delighted those who ate it.

She gently stirred in the flour and then divided the dough into the right sizes for the pans. After shaping each loaf, she left them to rise on the kitchen table. No noise came from the bedroom where Jonathon was sleeping, even when Leona came in from hanging her load of diapers on the line.

"Whee!" Leona exclaimed. "That did me good. Jonathon's not awake yet?"

"Nope," Rebecca said, placing the last of the bread dough in a pan, glad to see that Leona's mood had improved.

They took turns baking and doing the laundry—as one went to the washing machine, the other went to the kitchen. They kept this up until lunch. Leona was in the kitchen when the time came to make the sandwiches. As Rebecca came in from the garage, Leona hollered out the door for Leroy and James, bringing the two boys on the run

"We were getting real hungry," they said, panting.

"Your mom has sandwiches ready," Rebecca said. "Sit down at the table."

They were more than willing and seemed to finish their sandwiches before Leona and Rebecca could barely get started.

"Children," Leona warned, "haste with food goes away with maturity."

"I must be maturing then," Rebecca said, knowing it was true, but not sure if she quite liked the adult feeling it gave her.

Leona only nodded, distracted by the bawling of baby Jonathon in the bedroom. "There you go," she said dryly, getting up and leaving her half-finished sandwich. "That brings maturity too."

After their final bite, Rebecca said, "It's time for your naps." They both looked like they were ready to bolt outdoors again. Rebecca's words elicited groans, but they obediently complied, shuffling toward their bedrooms.

With them gone and Leona with baby Jonathon, Rebecca went through her list of things to do. She came to the conclusion that there would be little time left in the day to accomplish it all. Leona would certainly see to it that she had plenty of time to pack, but from the looks of things, there wouldn't be time to prepare a large supper. She wished she could have because it was her last night here.

Soon I'll be home, she mused. Thinking of John again, glad that things were right between them, that her promise to marry him had been the right thing to do, that Atlee was an appropriate thing of the past.

She was looking forward to tomorrow, the ride home in the van, and above all glad that she was glad.

Hearing footsteps behind her, Rebecca turned to see Leona.

"You'll be gone tomorrow," Leona stated simply. "Home to John, right?" A smile played on her face.

Caught up in the emotion, Rebecca said, "To tell John I love him." Blushing deeply at the sound of her own words, she wished she hadn't said them in Leona's hearing.

"It is good," Leona replied, not seeming to mind. Her face now solemn, she declared, "*Da Hah* has no doubt willed it."

About Jerry Eicher...

As a boy, **Jerry Eicher** spent eight years in Honduras where his grandfather helped found an Amish community outreach. As an adult, Jerry has taught in Amish and Mennonite schools in Ohio and Illinois, has been involved in church renewal, and has conducted in-depth Bible study workshops. Jerry lives with his wife, Tina, and their four children in Virginia.

To learn more about books by Jerry Eicher
or to read sample chapters, log on to our website:

www.harvesthousepublishers.com

If you enjoyed *Rebecca's Promise*, you'll enjoy the sequel, *Rebecca's Return*.

Rebecca Keim returns to Wheat Ridge full of resolve to make her relationship with John Miller work. But in her absence, John has become suspicious of the woman he loves. Before their conflict can be resolved, John is badly injured.

Will his serious and possibly permanent injuries change Rebecca's mind about their future together? And will Rachel Byler's plans to finally get the wealth she deserves succeed?

Available at your favorite bookseller now.